Chelsea would never forget the moment when she hung in midair on Mount Everest,

nothing between her and death as she anxiously searched for Kurt against the icy cliff.

When she'd heard him yell her name, she'd been sure he'd fallen. Immediately, she had been stung by pain and guilt. If Kurt died, it would be her fault. She was the one who had hounded him to bring her back to the place where her sister had plunged to her death.

Her heart had rolled over. A useless lump of lead in her chest that refused to beat without knowing Kurt was safe. The moment her eyes had latched on to his red anorak against the gray-blue sky above her, it went into overdrive.

From now on, no matter what Kurt said, or how much he protested that he was no good for her, she knew in her heart she could never love anyone else as much as him.

The difficult task would be convincing him.

Dear Reader,

Make way for spring—and room on your shelf for six must-reads from Silhouette Intimate Moments! Justine Davis bursts onto the scene with another page-turner from her miniseries REDSTONE, INCORPORATED. In *Second-Chance Hero*, a struggling single mother finds herself in danger, having to confront past demons and the man who haunts her waking dreams. Gifted storyteller Ingrid Weaver delights us with *The Angel and the Outlaw*, which begins her miniseries PAYBACK. Here, a rifle-wielding heroine does more than seek revenge—she dazzles a hot-blooded hero into joining her on her mission. Don't miss it!

Can the enemy's daughter seduce a sexy and hardened soldier? Find out in Cindy Dees's latest CHARLIE SQUAD romance, *Her Secret Agent Man*. In Frances Housden's *Stranded with a Stranger*, part of her INTERNATIONAL AFFAIRS miniseries, a determined heroine investigates her sister's murder by tackling Mount Everest and its brutal challenges. Will her charismatic guide be the key to solving this gripping mystery?

You'll get swept away by Margaret Carter's *Embracing Darkness*, about a heart-stopping vampire whose torment is falling for a woman he can't have. Will these two forbidden lovers overcome the limits of mortality—not to mention a cold-blooded killer's treachery—to be together? Newcomer Dianna Love Snell pulls no punches in *Worth Every Risk*, which features a DEA agent who discovers a beautiful stowaway on his plane. She could be trouble…or the woman he's been waiting for.

I'm thrilled to bring you six suspenseful and soul-stirring romances from these talented authors. After you enjoy this month's lineup, be sure to return for another month of unforgettable characters that face life's extraordinary odds. Only in Silhouette Intimate Moments!

Happy reading,

Patience Smith
Associate Senior Editor

Please address questions and book requests to:
Silhouette Reader Service
U.S.: 3010 Walden Ave., P.O. Box 1325, Buffalo, NY 14269
Canadian: P.O. Box 609, Fort Erie, Ont. L2A 5X3

Stranded with a Stranger

FRANCES HOUSDEN

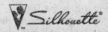

Silhouette®

INTIMATE MOMENTS™

Published by Silhouette Books

America's Publisher of Contemporary Romance

I'd like to dedicate this book to my original editor
at Silhouette, Leslie Wainger, with thanks.
And also to Sir Edmund Hillary, my inspiration
for this book, who proved that although Kiwis can't fly,
they can still reach the top of the world.

 SILHOUETTE BOOKS

ISBN 0-373-27424-6

STRANDED WITH A STRANGER

Copyright © 2005 by Frances Housden

This edition published by arrangement with Harlequin Books S.A.

Visit Silhouette Books at www.eHarlequin.com

Printed in U.S.A.

Books by Frances Housden

Silhouette Intimate Moments

The Man for Maggie #1056
Love Under Fire #1168
Heartbreak Hero #1241
Shadows of the Past #1289
Stranded with a Stranger #1354

*International Affairs

FRANCES HOUSDEN

has always been a voracious reader, but she never thought of being a writer until a teacher gave her the encouragement she needed to put pen to paper. As a result, Frances was a finalist in the 1998 Clendon Award and won the award in 1999, which led to the sale of her first book for Silhouette, *The Man for Maggie.*

Frances's marriage to a navy man took her from her birthplace in Scotland all the way to the ends of the earth in New Zealand. Now that he's a landlubber, they try to do most of their traveling together. They live on a ten-acre bush block in the heart of Auckland's Wine District. She has two large sons, two small grandsons and a tiny granddaughter who can twist her around her finger, as well as a wheaten terrier who thinks she's boss. Thanks to one teacher's dedication, Frances now gets to write about the kind of heroes a woman would travel to the ends of the earth for. Frances loves to hear from readers. Get in touch with Frances through her Web site at www.franceshousden.com.

Prologue

Dear Chelsea,

I can imagine your astonishment as you open this. I can almost hear you gasp, "A letter from Atlanta!"

How many years has it been? I move around so much I've lost count. Far, far too many, though. My fault. As eldest, I shouldn't have let a childish rift go on for so long. I just hope I haven't left it too late to set matters right.

What's it all about?

Well, for a start, I'm worried.

Oh, not over making the climb of Everest I'll be doing soon. I lost all fear of heights years ago, when I swapped my ballet slippers for climbing boots. It was only to be expected *marrying an adventurous man like Bill Chaplin. And when you love someone the way I love Bill, wherever he goes, you follow.*

That's right, I used the L word. No matter what you thought of the arrangement back then, our father never forced me into this marriage. I've had fifteen blissful years. Not many people can claim that. You were far too young to understand back then, barely thirteen. I hope time has achieved what I couldn't, and that you understand at last what it is to truly love another person heart and soul.

But I'm getting off track. It's not myself I'm worried for— it's you. Though chances are we might both be in danger, not many people can reach me up here, so I reckon I'm pretty safe. It takes a special kind of man to climb Everest, and I'm certain Arlon Rowles isn't one of them.

Yes, I'm talking about our cousin Arlon. It seems making him CEO of the business father left us, in order for us to avoid facing each other across a boardroom table, was a huge mistake.

I received a letter yesterday from Madeline Coulter. You remember Maddie? She worked for Father. According to her, Arlon has been siphoning money out of the business for the past five years and salting it away in a Swiss bank account.

Five years. My God, he must have started soon after Father's death. She says that she has the proof locked away in a safety deposit box. This is the number: 44578—Bank of America, Jamestown. Don't lose it. It's in both our names.

Along with the letter, she sent me a key. I've decided it will be safer on my person for now. I'm wearing it on a chain around my neck.

But this is where it gets down and dirty. I called Maddie by satellite phone and her sister answered. I couldn't have been more shocked. Dear old Maddie was shot and killed, in an apparent mugging. It happened not long after she mailed the letter. Coincidence? I don't think so. She was found in an alley, and the shopping she'd done on her way home from work was scattered all around her, yet they don't live in a dangerous neighborhood. And if someone was desperate enough to kill her for money, why leave her purse and the shopping behind?

I don't want to scare you, but I've had a dreadful feeling ever since her letter arrived that this situation is going to get a lot worse before it gets better. So watch your back, sister dearest. I mean it. Watch your back and don't go out alone at night.

I expect you're wondering why I'm not coming straight home to help you deal with this. Bill would insist on it. That's why I haven't told him. For years he's wanted to climb Everest. We've trained for this moment in Switzerland and in South America, where we met our guide Kurt Jellic, then in New Zealand, where Kurt comes from. Besides, by the time this reaches you, I'll probably be back from the summit and on my way to the States. It took Maddie's letter three weeks to reach me. Why should this one be any different?

You're probably wondering how I found your address. I've always made sure I knew where you were. And yes, maybe I should have phoned you, as well. But after all these years of silence I couldn't be certain you would take my call. Please accept this olive branch and try to forgive me for deserting you. I know you always found Father hard to deal with—and with me gone? Well, enough said for now. Maybe once this is over we can meet up in Paris, now that you've made your home there.

Darn, reading back over this I know it sounds slightly paranoid. All I can say is, you'll probably feel as I do after reading it.

Speaking of paranoid, ever since we climbed back down to Base Camp, even before Maddie's letter arrived, I've felt that someone is watching me. Stupid, huh? I couldn't be farther from cousin Arlon's idea of civilization if I tried, but I can't shake the sensation of being watched.

Tomorrow we go back up. The weather looks good to reach the summit, and we've spent a lot of time climbing back and forth between Camps One, Two and Three, acclimatizing to the thin atmosphere. Yet, in a way, I'll be glad to get back up there.

Everest has a way of making our human troubles appear puny, insignificant. And I really need that right now.

I know I'm thrusting a heck of a lot of responsibility on you, but if we can't stop Arlon and the company goes belly-up, thousands of people will lose their jobs.

Father must be turning in his grave. Not that you'll give a damn about that. But if there was one thing that mattered to him, it was the business he built up from nothing. What he really wanted was sons, not daughters.

I'll call as soon as I make the descent. We can go fetch the papers together and make sure they get to the proper authorities. Or maybe we ought to contact them first and get some protection before we open the safety deposit box.

Take care, and I really do mean watch your back. Maddie was shot from behind.

Your loving sister,
Atlanta

Chapter 1

Chelsea watched the guide's pale blue gaze shift away as if he couldn't meet her eyes. "Sorry, Ms. Tedman, I can't help you. Kurt Jellic from Aoraki Expeditions is the one you want to ask. He is the only one who knows exactly where the bodies are hidden…in a manner of speaking."

Basie Serfontien's smirk faltered as if the big South African's harsh-voiced faux pas had just dawned on him.

"Thanks for your help."

Chelsea began turning away, wanting out of there before Serfontien, the last guide on her list, could get a full view of her trembling lips. Failure. Again.

She wouldn't cry in front of these hulking great men—not

if she could help it—but now she was down to her last and also her best hope, Kurt Jellic. Her mouth twisted in a wry semblance of a smile as she forced herself to turn back. Trust her to forget the most important question. "I don't suppose any of you know where Jellic is? No one I've asked has seen him for days."

The guide and his team all shook their heads.

It was the fifth time she'd asked someone to guide her up Everest. She had heard rumors about Jellic, and some of the suggestions to look for the man had an if-you-dare quality about them, as if they knew something she didn't. Too bad. The man could be Frankenstein's long-lost brother for all she cared, as long as he took her to where the last member of her immediate family—her sister, Atlanta Chaplin—had been killed.

The accident had happened just a few days after she'd received Atlanta's letter. They had not reached the top as planned. And though that did not seem to matter now, she wished Atlanta and Bill could at least have had their wish before they died.

Atlanta's letter was tucked in Chelsea's breast pocket, as if somehow keeping it close to her heart would change the past.

The night when she had caught the news on CNN of another two climbers being lost to Everest had turned her life upside down. She had looked at the screen, taken in the names, but refused to believe. Atlanta and Bill Chaplin?

No, it had to be a mistake. The bodies hadn't been recovered. She'd held her breath, waiting for better news, even as she had made her arrangements to travel to Namche Bazaar.

Then she'd arrived in Nepal, walked from Lukla to Namche Bazaar, and hope was no longer an option. She touched the letter through her anorak. Its paper had lost its crispness and stopped crackling.

She was sick of getting the same answer to her question. "I'm sorry about Bill and Atlanta. They were a nice couple. But we can't take our other clients off the beaten track to help you look for their bodies. You want to talk to Kurt Jellic."

The invisible man. She had begun feeling she was being given the runaround. Chelsea swiveled on her heel, disappointment weighing on her shoulders. Before she could stride off in the direction of her hotel, a hand touched her elbow. "Excuse please, lady." She turned and the hand dropped away. Its owner, embarrassed and blushing, lowered her dark eyes. The young woman was almost breathtakingly beautiful, the skin of her round face smooth and lustrous. Such a pity that life in the mountains and the wear and tear of this harsh landscape would show on those perfect features before too many years had passed.

"Namaste," the girl lisped in her delightful accent.

"Namaste." Chelsea repeated the greeting she had already learned meant "I salute all the divine qualities in you."

The Sherpa girl fitted the mountain village scene much better than Chelsea did in her pseudomountaineering gear bought in Paris. She'd never been up a mountain in her life.

No matter—she was determined to climb the biggest of them all, or part of it, at least. Leave the summit for those who needed that sort of buzz. She just wanted to find her sister.

"I am Kora. I know where Kurt S'ab is. I saw him yesterday."

"You did?" Chelsea gasped. *Hope at last.*

The girl nodded a couple of times from the waist up, her many layers of clothing swaying with her in a rainbow of rusts, browns and blues. "My brother, Sherpa Rei, works for him."

Chelsea couldn't restrain her smile. "Good. What is he like? What kind of man is he?"

"Kurt Sa'b is very big man, very big." Kora drew in the air

with her hands, but Chelsea wasn't sure what to take from that. Was it his stature or large ego that impressed Kora the most?

Yet her heart beat with excitement as she asked, "And where does Kurt Sa'b live? Is it far? Can you take me to him?"

"He lives now in a tavern over in the old town."

The old town? Chelsea looked around her. Although they were standing on the outskirts of a street market dangerously close to the edge of the terrace, none of the buildings built into the other side looked terribly old. She supposed Namche Bazaar had once been a small, quiet mountain terrace village hanging on the side of a hill. Then hordes of foreigners had disrupted its peace, determined to pit their skills against Everest. Once Sir Edmund Hillary had "knocked the bastard off," as he had put it, nearly every man and his dog had declared open season on the mountain as if it was some sort of macho ritual. Why else had Bill Chaplin dragged Atlanta up there? Not to get himself and Atlanta killed, that's for sure.

The girl nodded. "Kora can show you the way."

"Great, wonderful. Can we go now?"

"Sure ting." Laughter tinkled out as Kora's smooth golden face creased into dimples. "Follow me, lady. This way."

Marketplaces like the one they were walking through were always a good indicator of the culture of a country, the food in particular. The scents here were so different from Paris, where the aroma of freshly baked bread frequently led her by the nose.

They passed a stall, and for all her urgency, Chelsea's taste buds were stirred by the spicy tang of barbecued meat. Her mouth watered. How long since she'd eaten? Breakfast, at least. She'd been far too busy chasing after mountain guides.

On any day but this she would have let the sounds of the market and unfamiliar accents soak into her mind. She always did this in a new place. Sounds and smells were her way of storing the memory so she wouldn't lose it.

But the little Nepalese girl was swift on her feet, weaving with ease through the multinational crowd, a mix of locals and tourists, and Chelsea needed to keep up with her. She let the murmur of voices slip past her, although the wind chimes ringing on every stall to keep evil spirits away were a different proposition, as were the birds that sang their hearts out in cages. The sound was lovely. It reminded her of a canary Atlanta had bought her for her fifth birthday.

Oh, God, why couldn't she have waited for me?

All her life her sister had taken off to places where Chelsea couldn't possibly follow.

The street opened out onto a small square dominated by a Buddhist temple. Prayer flags flapped overhead in a breeze perfumed with food and incense, and brown hands turned prayer wheels as they passed by. Did those wheels and flags work, or were they just another pretty superstition to ward away evil?

Chelsea wouldn't have been surprised to discover they were as redundant as her own prayers. She'd said some for Maddie after her sister's letter arrived. Maddie had been a friend since childhood, a woman who would never have intentionally hurt a soul. She hadn't deserved to die. Chelsea had called the detective in charge of the case, but had gained no helpful information. Didn't a woman's death matter anymore?

Spinning a prayer wheel was probably as useless as the entreaties she had sent upward that Atlanta was really safe. All her hopes of them coming together again, her chance to correct past mistakes, had died on the mountain.

But no prayers would be as profound if she couldn't find her sister and that *key.* Too many huge American firms had toppled recently, brought down by creative accounting, and this could be another instance. If only she could be sure what was in the safety deposit box.

Last quarter's financials had been down again, but if Maddie *was* correct, she needed to find the proof.

That was the only way to stop cousin Arlon.

Kurt squinted at the figures written in his small accounts book. Not that he thought scrunching his eyes would change the fact that if he didn't score some work soon, his business would be in the red. It had cost him $65,000 to use the fixed lines and aluminum bridges put out by the Sherpas' association at the beginning of the season. If he didn't get more work soon…

The up-front payment he'd received from the Chaplins had been eaten up and then some. And he wasn't such a boor that he would claim from the estate of a couple of friends who'd been killed on his watch.

"Aargh." He cleared his throat as if that would get rid of the rumors that had been circulating since he'd come back down the mountain without Bill and Atlanta.

The local magistrate had more or less cleared him. That is to say, nothing could be proved one way or another. All they had was his word. But in a close-knit society, once a rumor took hold it was hard to contradict it.

Bad news always traveled faster than good.

If he could get his hands on the bastard who had started them, he'd kick him to hell and gone. His family knew only too well how rumor and innuendo could ruin a life. But when his father had died it had been Kurt and his brothers and sister who'd been left to deal with the mess. Were still dealing with it.

He looked up from the lined page and realized he should

blame the poor light for the problem with his eyes. At five-thirty in the evening his attic room always flooded with gray watery light as the sun dropped behind the Himalayas. He shut the book with a snap. The sound was like a thunderclap in the quiet room.

Though he had taken lodgings on the top floor of a tavern, the old stone walls were two feet thick and swallowed up the noise from the barroom, keeping it to a low murmur he barely noticed.

Kurt scrubbed his hands over his face and combed his untidy hair with his fingers. He needed a shave. His stubble was four days old and as black as his hair. What was the point? He had no one to impress. Clients were staying away in droves.

He pushed up from his cross-legged position on the floor. The wooden boards were ten times more comfortable than any flat spot on Everest. He stretched, his fingers brushing a large beam. The slope of the roof made it necessary to stoop at the far side of the room by his bed, and he had to take care not to knock his head for the first couple of steps after he emerged from the attic.

Running his hands over his pockets, he felt for his matches. Time to light the lamps before he started falling over the furniture and his bags.

A wooden stair cracked outside. The sound of it ricocheted through the silence like a bullet bouncing off the walls. He recognized the sound. That particular step was five from the top.

His hand slid to the knife on his belt. He unsheathed it as he crossed to the door in his sock-cushioned feet and listened for the creak of the step one down from the landing outside his door.

He'd been robbed twice in the short time he'd lived here.

The door didn't have a lock, but then anything of true value he carried on him.

Whoever was climbing the stairs must have been taking them two at a time. The next noise he'd been waiting for didn't arrive before a gentle tap on the door started it swinging open. Not only did the heavy wooden slab not have a lock, its catch didn't work worth a damn, losing its grip at the slightest pressure.

There was no announcement. No "Hello, is anyone there?" Only the door moving closer to his shoulder as it was pushed wide. The footsteps were light, as was to be expected in a country where most of the inhabitants were head and shoulders shorter than him.

He let the intruder take no more than two steps into the room, then, knife poised in one hand ready to strike, he wrapped his other arm around the thief from behind. "Don't move. I have a knife and it's pointed at your throat."

The intruder let out a squawk that nearly deafened him. He almost dropped the knife as a padded elbow dug into his ribs. If the aim of the elbow hadn't warned him his target was taller than he'd imagined, the handful of fluid feminine breast told him he was definitely below the mark by eight inches or more.

It had been so long since he'd touched a woman, touched anything that filled his hand with such soft fullness, that his palm burned through the contact, even through several layers of clothing. Stunned by the unexpected rush to his groin, he grabbed a breath and smelled a floral perfume that clouded his reason and made him squeeze, just once.

As the heel of her boot stomped down painfully on the bony arch of his foot hard enough to make him wince, a second mistake leaped to mind. Her struggles had brought her dangerously close to the blade of his knife. Kurt flung it from him before its sharp edge could slice something a lot more fragile than nylon rope. Before the clatter of metal on wood reached his ears he'd bundled the squirming mass of female body tightly in both arms. "Take it easy, easy. I'm not going to hurt you."

"All right for you to say now I've knocked your knife out of your hand," she boasted.

Well, at least he now knew she was an American.

She wriggled some more, her butt rubbing against his groin. It reacted accordingly.

"I threw it away," he growled, unable to stifle his indignation that the woman had laid claim to his act of chivalry.

"So you say now."

He felt the muscles in her butt tighten against him as she lifted a knee, but he was too busy spreading his legs to avoid her heel to enjoy the sensation. As her foot jarred against the floor its echo went straight from her to him. It was about then she appeared to recognize what was happening behind her, and she squawked once more. "Let me go, you…you lecher."

The bands of his arms tightened, quelling her renewed struggles. This was getting out of hand. Didn't she realize this situation was as painful to his ego as it was to her sensibilities? Only one thing for it, he decided.

Letting his arms slip lower without losing their hold, he picked her up. The softest landing place in the room was the bed. No sooner thought than done—he hefted her up and released her onto the mattress.

He could hear her pushing herself backward to the head of the bed, her heels catching on the covers. "Keep away from me. I know karate. No way I'm going to let you rape me."

"Pity you never got past lesson one, where they taught you to stamp on your opponent's feet. And while we're on the subject, who snuck into whose room? Believe me, you couldn't be safe. I've no urge to have sex with a shrew."

"You should be so lucky."

"Hold it! Hold it right there. Not another word. If I'm going to be accused of sexual assault, and believe me, I've been accused of a lot worse recently, then for a change I want to look my accuser in the eye." This time the matches sprang to his hold in the first pocket he searched. He lit one, but it didn't pierce far into the gloom, and the shape on the bed could have been man or woman. But having touched her, he knew better.

"Actually, no one mentioned sexual assault, only..."

He froze, still as a statue, the match flaring in his fingers, as faint and tiny as the light at the end of the tunnel called his future. "Only what?"

"Whatever they say about men like you."

"Men like *me* don't go in for rape either."

He could tell she'd heard the rumors, but he hadn't expected her to back down. That made her either a coward or a woman who desperately wanted something he had. And she'd already let him know it wasn't his body. He blew out the match, then took his ire out on the full backpack he'd left on the floor, kicking it in front of the door to make her escape harder.

The annoyance didn't go away. Striking another match, he murmured under his breath, "The woman wriggles around against a guy as if she's giving him a lap dance and she wonders why he gets a hard-on."

Kurt had done a lot of talking to himself lately. Especially since people he'd once counted as friends had appeared to be avoiding his company. As if they would become guilty by association.

So she'd been asking around, had heard the stories that got worse as they went from mouth to mouth. He could have told her about rumors—that if they won't go away, you have to learn to live with them.

Without turning his back to her, he lit the first couple of yak-butter oil lamps. Their glow was enough to illuminate long jean-clad legs. The third brought out the curve of her hips. He knew, to his cost, they were softly rounded where his were lean. The lilac anorak was a fashion statement no mountaineer worth his or her salt would wear. Its quilted folds hid the full breasts his palm had lighted on by mistake. He smiled softly as he picked up the next tiny copper bowl filled with oil.

Her hair was black, short, spiky, a match for the dark clumps of eyelashes framing her huge gray eyes. Eyes wide and staring at him as if he were the devil incarnate. As if she too thought him responsible for Bill's and Atlanta's deaths.

Sometimes he wondered if maybe he was.

While her expression nagged at his conscience, something in him acknowledged that contempt wasn't the emotion he wanted to draw from the woman sprawled across his bed. But he wasn't willing to go deeper into his motives.

With the final lamp lit, a gas cartridge one, the last of the gloom receded to the edges of the attic. Kurt walked up to the bed and looked down at his unexpected guest. Her eyes flashed a warning and her hands bunched up fists of the top cover as if it were the only thing preventing her from leaping at his throat.

"Hi, I'm Kurt Jellic. And you'd be…?"

"One moment you're threatening to slice my neck, and the next you're making an introduction as if we'd just met at a garden party," Chelsea sniped, taking advantage of what seemed to be a truce to push herself into a more dignified sitting position.

"Sorry," he said. "I'm all out of cucumber sandwiches and Earl Grey tea, but I can offer you a whiskey. They do say it's good for shock. Perhaps it would make you remember your name."

Taking a good look at him in the lamplight, she was left in no doubt that this guy could have killed her if necessary. She'd watched him move from lamp to lamp with lethal grace. Gradually each small increment of light had revealed the man Atlanta and Bill had trusted to get them safely to the summit of Everest and back again.

Why hadn't that happened?

Oh, yeah, they had fallen. And she'd heard the word *accident* flung around with abandon. Kurt Jellic had been with them, and like a few other people she wondered how *he* had survived.

He threw her a grin, quirking his eyebrows as if to say, "Well?" His teeth were a slash of white in a face brushed with the kind of dark stubble film stars affected, as if it made them unrecognizable. His slightly gaunt features were dominated by dark unreadable eyes under black eyebrows, both sitting above an uncompromising straight slide of a nose.

"I've no trouble recalling my name. It's Chelsea Tedman."

She waited for a reaction, but wasn't overwhelmed with surprise when she didn't get one. Why would Atlanta have mentioned an estranged sister she hadn't seen since before Chelsea entered high school?

He stepped around a heap of red and yellow ropes on the floor in front of a huge old-fashioned chest, then lifted a bottle. The reflection from a butter-oil lamp glimmered through the amber liquid sloshing near the bottom. The bottle had been well and truly broached. Hell, she hoped he wasn't an alcoholic.

That was all she needed.

"Okay, now the formalities have been taken care of, how do you take your whiskey—straight or straight?"

"I take it in a glass."

The bottle made a hollow clunk as he set it back down and picked up the glass sitting next to it. He peered into its depths and didn't look particularly happy with what he saw.

Chelsea almost choked on a breath as he pulled out the tail of his tan-and-brown-checked shirt and proceeded to wipe the glass with it. His glance caught Chelsea's horrified expression. Kurt's embarrassed smile was almost boyish, if anyone with bristles could be likened to a boy. "What did you expect? This isn't the Ritz. No room service. It's either use what you have to hand or put up with a layer of dust floating on your whiskey."

Apparently satisfied with his efforts, he poured some liquid into the glass, then opened the top drawer of the chest. He withdrew a blue plastic mug and emptied the rest of the bottle's contents into it.

Chelsea's innate fastidiousness made her hesitate to take the tumbler, even considering that alcohol was an antiseptic.

"Will it help if I tell you I put this shirt on clean not more than two hours ago?" He lifted the blue mug as if toasting her. "And you were the one who insisted on a glass."

She took the tumbler, lifting it by the rim, wary of touching any part of this man whose sexual heat had burned through her as if he hadn't held a knife against the tender skin of her throat.

He hadn't actually said she was acting like a wimp, but she certainly felt like one. How had it come to this? Atlanta had been the delicate flowerlike child, while she had been the tomboy. Her sister had gone the ballet-and-piano-lessons route, while she had ridden horses and played basketball. Even at thirteen she'd been two inches taller than her elder sister and had made an ungainly, sulky bridesmaid at Atlanta's wedding, letting everyone know she was doing it under protest.

When had their roles reversed? Atlanta roughing it on a mountain in boots and anorak, while Chelsea swanned off to watch the ballet in Paris dressed in the latest fashion as if she were a changeling.

And she was. She fluttered around Paris like a dilettante, playing at being a translator at the American embassy. Well, she was a translator for real. Though in truth, she worked in a basement office of the embassy, translating secrets that terrorists would give their lives to get their hands on. That's if they even knew IBIS, the Intelligence Bureau for International Security, existed. Jason Hart, the bureau chief and initiator of the bureau, had taken extreme measures to insure its anonymity.

Kurt knocked his mug against her glass. *"Sláinte."*

"Cheers." The sip she took burned all the way down, and her face flamed as Kurt Jellic settled his massive frame on the edge of the bed, making the mattress dip. She was honest enough not to blame the blush on the whiskey. It had been a long time since she'd let down her guard enough to get this close to a man on a bed, even fully clothed.

"So what brings you to this neck of the woods, Chelsea Tedman?"

"I want to go up Mount Everest."

A spark lightened his eyes, but not the intensity of his gaze on her. "And?"

"I was told you were the one to take me."

He frowned, his black eyebrows coming together, shading his eyes as well as hardening his expression. "So no one but Aoraki Expeditions could fit you into their group?"

"Not where I wanted to go. But they all said *you* were definitely available."

He took a slug of whiskey out of the incongruous plastic mug, but if he'd done it to hide his reactions it hadn't worked. There was nothing enigmatic about the twist of his mouth, or the way his nose flared as he breathed in hard. "Did they tell you why?"

"They didn't have to. I'm Atlanta Chaplin's sister. And I already knew you were the one who took her and Bill up Everest."

Something between a growl and a moan ripped from Kurt's lips as he sprang to his feet, turning his shoulder to her for a second. She would almost have preferred he'd stayed that way. She wasn't prepared for his ominous glance.

It was a relief when he tipped back his head and drained the whiskey from the blue mug, a relief to no longer feel like a slug he'd almost stepped on. Finished, he wiped his mouth with the back of his hand. "You took your damn good time before mentioning that. So what's it to be—pistols at dawn, pushing me down a crevasse when I'm not looking, or are you going to get your lawyer to sue me? I warn you, you won't get much. Everything I own is tied up in a half-built lodge in Aoraki, New Zealand. And as it stands it's not worth much."

"I've no intention of suing you. Do you think I'm so stupid I didn't check out the circumstances of the accident with the local magistrate? I'm not as green as a cabbage."

"Huh, looks like I passed, or you wouldn't be here. But anyone less like a cabbage I've yet to meet."

"I'll take that as a compliment, but at the moment I couldn't give a hoot if you thought I had buck teeth and a squint. All I want from you is your help in recovering my sister's body."

"I'm not sure that it can be done. Even if we could reach

them and get their bodies out of there, transporting them down the mountain is almost impossible. Anything of any size is transported either up or down on the backs of Sherpas. Climbing takes two hands. Apart from that, a lot of Sherpas believe the bodies of fallen climbers should remain with the mountain goddess."

Chelsea felt safe to scoot to the edge of the bed. Holding the glass made her efforts awkward but didn't deter her, not now that she thought her goal was in sight.

"Here, give me that." Kurt took the tumbler from her and she rose from the bed.

She stood in front of him and found she had to look up. "You don't look like a superstitious guy."

"I'm not, but I am cautious. You don't succeed at mountain climbing by rushing into stuff hell-for-leather."

"Good. I haven't got a superstitious bone in my body." Kurt ran his glance over her as if checking out her bones—or rather what covered them, she decided, as the flame in his eyes took her straight back to that moment when his hand had covered her breast. Fear for her life hadn't been enough to stifle the arousing quality of his touch, or the discovery that her breast had fit perfectly into his palm.

He took a sip from her glass, but she felt no inclination to mention it, nor do anything to stifle the persuasive power of the whiskey. For all his faults, her father hadn't raised a fool.

"It won't be cheap. If we can recover the bodies, we'll need a large team of Sherpas on the way down to carry them in relays."

"Money is no object. Getting my sister home is all that matters." Her statement suddenly felt like a boast, a clunker dropped into this attic where money was obviously scarce.

She kept her eye on Kurt in case he appeared to see it that

way, too. He ran his tongue around his teeth as if pondering the situation. Then, as if realizing he was still holding her glass, he thrust it toward her.

"No, you keep it," she said coolly. "I prefer mine with soda."

He took her at her word, taking a smaller mouthful than the one that had made his throat work as he swallowed the last of the whiskey in the mug. "Okay. Prepare yourself for it taking a week or more to get everything organized. Where are you staying?"

"At the Peaks Hotel."

A raised eyebrow was his only acknowledgment that the hotel was the most expensive accommodation in Namche Bazaar.

"Have you done any climbs with Bill and Atlanta? Better tell me what experience you've had." He waited expectantly

This was the crunch moment that would make or break her chance of recovering her sister and the key. "No, I've never climbed with my sister and her husband. We didn't see each other that often. I live in Paris and…well, you know where they lived."

"So what's it been—the French Alps, Mont Blanc?"

"None of those. I stayed in Paris mainly, but I belong to this gym with a huge climbing wall and my speeds on that are considered expert level."

He let out a whoop that ran around the attic, bouncing off the walls and coming back to her more times than she appreciated. What did he know? She *was* expert level.

He stopped chortling long enough to spit out, "A climbing wall? Lady, you crack me up." Then he sobered. "No way am I taking a rookie climber up Everest. My reputation is shot as it is. It would be dead in the water if I took up an inexperienced climber. It was hell losing your sister and brother-in-law. If I lost a third one I might as well shoot myself. I couldn't live with that on my conscience."

"But—"

"No. Don't try to persuade me, or bat those eyelashes my way. If you think *that* would work, then you *are* greener than a cabbage."

Chapter 2

She let Kurt lead the way out of the attic, quite content to follow him into the darkness of the stairs instead of tackling them first.

He'd thrust his arms into a red anorak on the way out, a color that would be glaringly obvious against ice and snow. Chelsea had noticed how he automatically angled himself to exit without brushing his shoulders against the doorjambs on each side.

As Kora had said, he was a very big man.

Every few steps Kurt stopped and lit one of the small lamps set into shallow alcoves in the wall.

The creaky steps hadn't seemed so steeply pitched when she'd climbed up them, and losing her balance on the way down was the last thing she needed. She would never be able to persuade him to take her up Mount Everest if he thought she couldn't manage a flight of stairs.

No use pretending a few drinks would loosen this guy up. He'd drunk his whiskey, then hers, and it hadn't affected him one iota.

She might have to use her feminine wiles.

Oh, God! She might be reduced to begging.

Chelsea squared her shoulders before once more measuring the width of Kurt's, which were so wide, so reassuringly strong and masculine.

Kurt reached the green door leading into the barroom that she had come through earlier. Kora had inquired of the barman as to Kurt's whereabouts, then hurried away smiling, her fingers curled around the tip Chelsea had slipped her. It was a small price for finding the one man in Namche Bazaar who could help her. As he reached for the handle, Kurt turned and gestured for her to go in front of him. "After you."

His cheekbones cut two curved slashes of shadow in the hollows of his cheeks, yet the leanness of his face didn't fool her into thinking that this was anything but a strong man.

A man, a tiny voice told her, who sounded as if he saw things in black and white, right and wrong. Not one to put her in danger no matter how much she pleaded her case.

She should be extremely careful never to get on his wrong side. Thanks to the experience of their first meeting, she knew the man carried a knife and wasn't afraid to use it. All of that aside, she would do whatever it took to succeed. Beg, cajole, seduce.

Come up with a plan.

More was at stake now than at any other time in her life.

Inside, the tavern walls were lime washed, same as the outside, though around the fireplace, white had given way to smoky gray. Someone had lit the fire since she had stood there with Kora, and now more than ever the place reminded her of an Indiana Jones movie set. More tiny pots of yak-butter oil burned on a ledge that ran around three sides of the room, throwing pockets of light into the gloom. Overhead, the same pots tipped the branches of the wooden chandelier that swung in the breeze they'd brought in with them. Chelsea held her breath waiting for the main door to slam open. Out of the wild and windy landscape Indy would stride into the barroom in all his whip-cracking, world-saving majesty.

She suddenly saw the humor of it. That's what she'd come to Nepal looking for, hoping for—a man to help her save her world. But was Kurt Jellic that man?

The door shut and Kurt crowded behind her, so close she could feel his deep voice rumble where his chest touched her shoulder. "Live up to your expectations?"

"I don't know if I had any, but it's certainly something else. I'm just letting my eyes become accustomed to the light, or lack of it, so I won't fall over anything."

"All right by me."

His breath on her neck caused her to shiver.

Of course he noticed. "If you're cold we can sit near the fire."

"No, thank you. Let's find a happy medium. I would soon get overheated next to the fire and have to start shedding."

His eyes narrowed as he studied the men sitting around the tables. "I don't think there are many here who would object, but to be on the safe side we can take that table in the corner."

As they reached the table he'd pointed out, a gust of wind blew down the chimney, adding to the smoky atmosphere, well aided by two of the older citizenry puffing on their pipes at a table between them and the fireplace. "I take it that this end of town doesn't have electricity."

"Scared of the dark?"

She twisted around to answer him. His eyes stared into

hers, and there was a question in them she didn't know how to answer. Not yet. She blinked, hiding her awareness of his gender. He was all predatory male, and it would take a brave woman or a fool to march into his territory and expect to get away scot-free.

She hoped it would be worth her effort.

Her gaze fell and focused on his mouth. She bit her lip and stifled a laugh. Damn, she'd outed herself, but what was she? A fool, or just a woman doing the best she could with what she had?

His hand touched her shoulder as he smiled wryly. "You sit nearest the wall so you can take in the sights." She did as he suggested, and now she took a good look around the tavern. The sights were on the rough side, and not all the men were Sherpas or Nepalese. One huge man wore a fur hat that screamed of the Russian steppes, an impression colored by the way he was scowling into his glass.

Kurt waited until she was seated. "What can I get you to drink, and how hungry are you?"

"Whiskey, with water this time since I don't suppose they have soda, and whatever you're having. I could eat a horse."

"Be careful what you wish for. I'll see if they have any lamb or goat kebabs."

Kurt towered over the bar. The tough-looking guy serving behind it wasn't nearly as tall, just bulkier, with a neck that overflowed his shirt. As she got her bearings she noticed blue smoke issuing from a door behind the bar. It curled up high and twisted around Kurt's dark hair like a halo.

A dark angel? No, there was nothing angelic about this guy. He was too big, too tough, too much of everything—overwhelming.

When he'd turned and looked at her on the stairs she could

have sworn he could see right through her, see past the front she always wore to the woman underneath. Could she trust him enough to tell him the truth about her quest? That she not only wanted her sister back, but also had to find the key Atlanta had worn around her neck.

Bad idea. Atlanta hadn't even told Bill, but what if someone had found out? Her sister hadn't believed in coincidence when Maddie died, and one death plus two others amounted to one huge coincidence that beggared belief. Thank God she'd used IBIS's facilities to have Jellic checked out before she left Paris. He had come up clean as a whistle, but there had been some blot on his father's record. She didn't believe in all that sins-of-the-father rubbish, though.

Her own father, Charles Tedman, had a lot to answer for.

Chelsea sucked in a breath and took in all the flavors of the room right with it. Apart from the butter oil and tobacco there was a definite hint of barbecued meat. The smell made her mouth water. Would it spoil her chances of getting what she wanted out of Jellic when they diluted the effects of the whiskey with food?

On his way back from the bar, Kurt juggled a whiskey bottle, two shot glasses and a jug of water. Although he'd been the one to ask her downstairs for a drink and some food, her ready agreement somehow raised his suspicions that there was more to Chelsea than met the eye. It wasn't what he'd expected after laughing at her climbing experience. But the moment he'd suggested it and she'd said, "I'm starving—aren't you?" his stomach had felt as if it was sticking to his ribs.

He began filling their glasses. Chelsea had reassured him that the tavern wasn't below her standards. But compared to the hotel she'd booked into, this place was in a class of its own.

That's why he'd picked it; no one he knew frequented this type of dump.

"Here's looking at you." He lifted his glass and tossed half of it back. The name on the label should have been Rotgut, but he didn't care. He'd needed the burn lately to prove that, unlike Bill and Atlanta, he was still alive.

"Cheers," she said, and followed suit. The woman had guts, because once he'd poured her drink the only room for water had been a meniscus on top of the whiskey.

He pulled out the chair kitty-corner to hers and sat letting his long legs sprawl under the table. She pulled hers back out of the way as he invaded her space, again. Chelsea had taken off her lilac anorak and hung it over the back of her chair, and the black sweater she wore under it, though thick wool, assured him that he hadn't imagined the fullness of the breast he'd cupped. Their greeting hadn't been as politically correct as a handshake, but it had been a hell of a lot more fun.

He leaned forward while she was busy taking a more wary sip of her drink. "You don't look anything like Atlanta. I'd never have taken you two for sisters."

He ruffled the hair above her ears. It was soft, straight and slippery, sliding through his fingers like water. "Where'd you get all this black hair from? Atlanta's curls were as blond as they come."

She almost choked on her words as the whiskey went down. "Same father, different mothers. Atlanta's mother died in a car accident, and mine didn't fare much better. She fell off a horse and broke her neck."

"With that kind of history I wonder your father didn't keep the pair of you wrapped in cotton wool."

If Chelsea was his, he wouldn't let her loose around mountains.

Hell, where had that come from? The whiskey must be talking back at him.

"Not so much wrap us in cotton wool, but he made a good show of running our lives. It had to be the best schools, the best clothes. Nothing was too good for us as long as we did everything his way." Her chin rose and there was a trace of a pout on her lips as she murmured, "I was the rebel of the two, the one who wouldn't conform, unlike Atlanta."

He noted the belligerence in her eyes. Kurt gathered she was harboring some held-over resentment from the past. He recognized it easily. Didn't the same type of emotions emanate from his twin, Kel, the moment their father's name was mentioned? The trouble with the powerful bond between identical twins was that no words were necessary to know what the other was feeling.

Kel had been the first to call him via satellite phone. Kurt had been back at Camp Three less than half an hour after the tragedy. Dazed with shock, he'd had to force himself to speak to Rei, his head Sherpa, and Paul Nichols, the only other paying customer on their team. He'd never discovered how Kel had found him, but his brother was the twin with connections, working as he did with the Global Drug Enforcement Agency.

"It must have come as a great shock when you heard of your sister's death." He said the words gently, for Chelsea's sake, though part of him still raged inside because of what had happened and the way it had happened. He hadn't had an accident on any of his climbs until this one. He still could hardly believe it himself, though he had only to shut his eyes at night for the tragedy to start playing over and over in his mind.

Every night, as he lay there in the dark, his own doubt assailed him. Was there anything more he could have done?

What a waste of two good lives.

"I caught it on CNN. I always watch it in the evening to catch up on news from home." He watched her sigh and wondered if the deep sigh had been dragged up from the same kind of place he kept his regrets.

"I'd received a letter from my sister two or three days before I heard of the tragedy. Her death brought a lot of emotions bubbling to the surface—besides grief, that is. We'd planned a reunion…in Paris." Chelsea dipped her head, but he could see a sparkle of tears on her lashes. It gutted him that he had to turn her down, but it would be suicide—hers—to take her up a mountain that showed no mercy. Rookie climber or old hand, one wrong move and they fell off the top of the world to their deaths.

Everest took no prisoners.

"If there was any way I could help you, I would do it— you know that, don't you? I'll be honest. I need the work. There have been a lot of rumors doing the rounds of Namche Bazaar. Not one of them is true." Her hand lay on the table, and he reached for it.

To comfort her or himself, he had no answer.

Though she wasn't a small woman her hand felt tiny, fine boned compared to his. The temptation to cling tightened his grip, a reflex based on the same instincts that had made his palm measure her fullness when she came tiptoeing into his life.

"There's one way you can help—give me a chance to take my sister home."

Without preamble he changed the subject. "You still hungry? I've ordered a whole swag of food."

Tears ceased to sparkle on her lashes. He hoped this meant he'd turned her thoughts away from climbing Everest. It had been ages since he'd had a chance to talk to any woman but Atlanta. In the three years since he'd met her and Bill, she'd become like a sister to him, closer than his own sister, Jo, whom he hadn't seen for years.

One difference—in his exchange with Atlanta he hadn't gotten the sexual buzz he felt now. Part of him wished he were able to grant Chelsea her wish and take her with him—and not just because of the amount of money involved. Sure, he was practically broke, but he had broad shoulders and knew how to work. He'd be all right someday.

She pulled her hand from his, lifted her glass to her lips and spoke over the rim. "What kind of food?"

"Strips of barbecued lamb and some flat bread to wrap it up in. I thought that would be more filling than kebabs."

"Great. I seem to have been hungry ever since I arrived in Nepal." She sipped some more whiskey. He'd bet the shudder went right down to her toes. "Must be all the clean air."

He found another smile and gave it to her with genuine pleasure as he looked around the smoky room. "You're easily satisfied."

"That's where you're wrong. I'm not one bit satisfied. I won't be until I get up that mountain and recover my sister's body."

He heard undertones of poor-little-rich-girl in the ringing echoes of her empty glass as she slapped it down on the wood.

Bill had been a good friend to Kurt. A rich man in his own right without the added advantage of his wife's money, he had never made himself out to be better than anyone else. And listening to Chelsea, he didn't like the fact that she almost never used his name. "I notice it's always your sister you mention when you talk about retrieving the bodies. What about her husband? Where does Bill's body figure in your scheme?"

Was she that obvious? Had Kurt looked into her psyche and seen the grudge she'd carried for fifteen years? "All right, you got me. I never liked Bill."

Kurt drew back and sat up in his chair, as if to get away from her. "What's not to like? He was a great guy, never harmed anyone."

"It's not that I want to leave him up there. It's just that Bill's the reason for the gulf between Atlanta and me. Aided and abetted by my father, of course."

Although Kurt had distanced himself, no longer stretching his legs out under the table at ease, she felt relieved when he propped his elbows on the table and nursed his glass between his hands. "You've lost me. Start at the beginning, for we seem to be talking about two different guys. Bill was one of the kindest people I ever met."

Just as she opened her mouth to begin, Chelsea had a light-bulb moment. She licked her lips, but the words refused to come. In a blinding flash Chelsea had seen how she must appear to Kurt, and the picture wasn't pretty. She pointed at the bottle. "Can I have another shot?"

"You don't think you ought to wait until the food arrives?"

"No. I need it now." She held out her glass.

As he poured, he lifted his eyes so they clashed with hers, and it was as if he could read her mind and knew all her secrets, but all he said was, "Dutch courage?"

"Something like that." She took a mouthful and threw it back, the burn mellowing the more she drank. Or maybe the first few sips had cauterized her nerve endings. Whatever it was, the whiskey slid down easily.

She'd heard you could tell a stranger things you wouldn't dare tell a friend. In another moment of revelation, she realized she didn't have a lot of friends who wouldn't make some use of her confession if it were told to them. Which didn't say much for her taste in friends. A pity Kurt didn't look like a priest. It would make this a whole lot easier.

"You've got to remember I was only thirteen—"

She broke off to regroup her thoughts. Had that sounded like an excuse or what? She needed to tell it straight and start at the beginning. "Atlanta would have been four when my mother married Charles Tedman. They had a very short courtship, and I guess she was already pregnant and that hurried things along, because I was a seven-pound premature baby—though who gives a damn about how close the wedding is to the birth these days. Except maybe if you are Argentine, and come from a proud family like my mother did.

"I think I fell in love with Atlanta from the moment I opened my eyes and was able to see her. Even then I recognized our differences. She was so pink, white and gold like a china doll."

"You're not without top-notch qualities yourself."

Chelsea smiled as the memory brought up an image from her childhood. "She was like my little mom, always there when I woke up. My mother was a horsewoman who traveled the world riding in the top events. She was better at schooling horses than children."

"So, who brought you up? Did you have a nanny?" He reached out and tucked back the strands of black hair that were blocking her view of him, and vice versa, and she wished he hadn't. Bad enough spilling her guts without catching his expressions of sympathy or otherwise.

Suck it up, Chelsea, she told herself, but as he ran the tip of his index finger around the curve of one ear, his touch made her quiver.

She felt her color deepen, and lowered her eyelids as if that would hide her reaction to him. "No, just a housekeeper and Atlanta. By the time I started kindergarten she was ten and used to boss me around, but at the same time she always made sure no one picked on me. I was the black moth in a field of butterflies, too exotic for most of the cool New England blondes I went to school with. Atlanta had no problem. Her mother had been one of them and Father had loads of money, even if he was a self-made man."

She flashed a smile meant to say *But look at me now—I got by,* but sensed that Kurt saw through her bravado.

"How many did you beat up?" he asked.

"Not too many. Remember I had Atlanta."

"I have a twin. That made fighting our battles easy. Besides which we're identical and it was difficult to know which of us to blame. Of course, if the crime was too bad, Grandma Glamuzina punished us both."

"Poor you," she teased.

"Don't get me wrong—the punishment rarely fit the crime. But this is your story. What happened when you were thirteen?"

"Atlanta married Bill. She was only eighteen and Bill was almost thirty. God, I'll be thirty myself soon, but to me he looked like an old man and I couldn't see how she could love someone that old. I blamed it on my father. He'd made two profitable matches himself, and I knew that if Bill had been poor my father wouldn't have let him through the door."

Chelsea laughed as she remembered something else. Another swig of whiskey eased her throat. She couldn't remember the last time she'd talked so much straight up. "You should have seen Father when he discovered Bill had decided to give up making money and live on what he had. He went apoplectic. I don't think my father took a day off work in his life, except to get married. Though I guess you could say that was all part of business. Thank God neither of us took after him. Cousin Arlon is the nearest thing he had to a son."

Her stomach curdled as she remembered what had brought

her to Namche Bazaar, and this tavern, and this man. "It didn't make any difference, though. Father didn't believe in leaving money out of the immediate family, not even to a cousin."

And there of course was the problem. A good-paying appointment wasn't enough for Arlon. He wanted it all.

Her gray eyes went opaque, making the dark rim around the irises stand out. Kurt wondered if maybe he shouldn't have poured her that last drink. But she brightened up as their food appeared on a large wooden platter for them to share. "Last one in is a rotten egg," she said as she grabbed a piece of flat bread before starting in on the barbecued meat. "Ooh, this is hot. Watch your fingers."

"The tips of my fingers are like asbestos. That's what years of climbing mountains does for you." He still felt the heat, though, as he grabbed a few strips from the huge pile of meat, and for a few minutes all they did was chew and moan about how good it tasted.

"Mmm, I think I've died and gone to heaven. I can't remember the last time food tasted so great. I must take some of these spices home with me. Think I can buy them in the market?"

"I should imagine so. They sell almost everything else there." As he spoke he watched her reach for another round of bread and begin filling it with more lamb. The way she ate was very sensual, without a hint of prissiness. She'd chomp down with her white teeth, laughing with sheer enjoyment as the sauce hit her chin. He was amazed how disappointed he felt when she pulled a handkerchief out of the reaches of some pocket to clean her face and hands. She'd only to say the word and he would have licked them clean.

Just the thought of it made him grow hard, and he was glad the table sheltered his problem. Bad enough her knowing that wiggling her butt against him turned him on, without letting her in on the secret of the effect watching her eat had on him.

Time to change the subject and save his hide. "You didn't finish your story. Tell me what Bill did to create a gulf between you and Atlanta besides being an old man. I mean, you're what, twenty-eight, twenty-nine, and I'm past thirty-four. So far this conversation hasn't done wonders for my ego."

"Okay." She put her roll of bread and meat on the edge of the half-empty wooden platter. "Short and sweet this time. Bill took her away clear across the country and I never spoke to her again."

Chelsea rolled her eyes at him. "Maybe I shouldn't have gulped down all that food. This seems to be turning into a guilt trip. I was a little witch back then, stubborn as they come. After that, everything I did was the opposite of Atlanta. No ballet lessons for me—I rode horses, played basketball. In short, I became a tomboy. My father went ballistic. I didn't care. He wasn't turning me into the perfect little daughter so he could marry me off to a rich old man."

Chelsea sniffed, looked at her small stained handkerchief and rubbed the tip of her nose with the back of her hand. "I needn't have worried. No way did I fit the criteria for a good upper-crust wife…but that's another story."

Kurt searched his pocket, then handed her a handkerchief. "Here, take this—it's clean." He eyed her warm black sweater. It might be a slightly chunky knit, but that didn't exclude elegant from its description. "And don't worry, the tomboy image didn't take."

"But it did. I still spend a lot of time at the gym. I'm strong. Want to feel my muscles?" She held out her arm.

Nuh-uh—hands off, boy. "I'll pass, thanks."

He wanted to feel a lot more than her muscles, and if he started there he might not stop. From his memory of her pulled against his length there was absolutely nothing hard about her, just soft warmth that fitted against him perfectly.

No point in heading in that direction, though. Even if the unheard-of happened and the attraction did turn out to be mutual, the accident would always come between them. The memory of a tragedy whose edges were as sharp and jagged as the mountain it happened on would be equally difficult terrain to get over. From what he could tell, both of them were carrying a heap of guilt. Not a good thing to have in common.

"Well, for your information, I'm quite the basketball star. We make up a couple of teams from the embassy and play at least once a month—clinging to our roots, don't you know."

"The embassy?" Why was he just hearing this?

"Yes." She looked quite proud. "I'm a translator at the American embassy in Paris. I like to keep busy."

If ever he needed another reason not to take her up Everest, this was it. She might act as if she were alone in the world now that Atlanta had gone, but he'd met a few of those embassy types and he was certain she'd have more people watching her back than she realized.

Time to bail out. He made a show of looking at his watch, surprised to see that in Chelsea's company time had actually spun away from him much faster than he'd guessed. "It's getting late. I ought to walk you back to your hotel."

Her eyebrows rose and her accent became snotty. "There's no need. I can take care of myself. You don't have to."

"Yes, I do. You might have noticed this isn't the most salubrious neighborhood. Why do you think I greeted you with a knife? I've been robbed twice, and foiled another attempt before it got started."

"In that case I accept your company." Chelsea proceeded to shrug into her lilac anorak, sliding the zip up to her neck. It didn't make any difference that her curves were covered by a jacket cut in a similar fashion to his; he still couldn't see her as a tomboy. No, Chelsea was all red-blooded woman. And the pity of it was, after tonight he would never see her again.

In this quarter of town the street lighting was practically nonexistent, but he wasn't taking her back up to his room to fetch a flashlight. It was too dangerous. Just the thought of being alone in his eagle's nest with Chelsea gave him a testosterone high.

His luck was in. A three-quarter moon rode in a cloudless sky and was enough to light their way back to her hotel.

"Here, better take my arm. These cobblestones are rough underfoot," he said, discovering—by letting her come close—masochistic tendencies that had never surfaced before. But then, he'd never claimed to be all wise. If he had been, he would have sent her packing before he decided to feed her. However, after he dropped her at the hotel he never had to see her again.

"Kurt, I'm not ready to give up on this yet. I'm certain that given the chance I can persuade you I'm not a liability. When can I see you again?"

No one was more surprised than Kurt when he heard himself say, "How about lunch tomorrow?"

Chapter 3

Shank's mare was the main mode of transport in Namche Bazaar, and for once Kurt was glad of it. Walking gave him time to phrase the exact wording of the refusal he meant to hand Chelsea once he reached her hotel. He would hang tough. She wasn't about to catch him oversexed or underprepared, not this time.

The trouble was he liked her. More than liked—wanted.

Chelsea was something beyond his experience. He couldn't remember meeting another woman quite so…damn it…intriguing.

Only look at the way they'd met. Their rude introduction hadn't sent her into screaming fits of hysteria.

He felt a stirring in his groin as he indulged in a wry, one-sided twist of a smile at the memory of those few minutes.

"Hell." He shook his head. If ever a dame was ballsy.

All kidding aside, he had no intention of taking her anywhere near Everest. *Not damn likely.* Nothing Chelsea Tedman could come up with would change his stance on that. The bones of his guiding career had been picked clean since the accident. He had nothing left to offer as far as that was concerned.

Besides, turning up at Base Camp with Atlanta's sister in tow would only add grist to the rumor mill.

He turned a corner and headed up the slope that would take him from one terrace to another. The Peaks Hotel was on the highest terrace looking down on Namche Bazaar, but then that's what five-star accommodation was all about.

"Hey, Kurt…Kurt Jellic."

Kurt spun around. He recognized Basie Serfontien and stopped to let him catch up.

"Where have you been hiding, man? There is this woman, a bit of all right. She wants to recover the Chaplins' bodies for burial, God help her. I told her you were the only mountain guide who wouldn't be booked solid."

And I bet you told her why.

"'S okay, mate. She found me."

Smiling, Basie slapped him on the shoulder. "Good news, man. You need to get back on the horse."

Kurt shook his head. "Not if it's likely to take me for a ride. I'm still thinking about it."

"Ach, you'll be mad if you don't, man. She's easy on the eye, that one. And money is no object for the Tedman woman."

Kurt shook his head. He couldn't be like Basie. If a client had money but no experience, the man would just add a couple of extra Sherpas into the equation to drag the wanna-be climber up to the summit. "I'll probably see you up at Base Camp, either way. Someone has to do more than just leave the Chaplins lying there."

He waved Serfontien off and carried on his way. The South African's easy-on-the-eye comment sent his thoughts wandering back to the restless night he'd spent. Hours of half-remembered dreams where Chelsea fitted over or under him, skin to skin, pounding heart to pounding heart in earth-shattering sex.

Kurt let rip a heartfelt groan. It earned him a surprised look from a guy he was about to pass. "What's up, mate?"

Tourist. Australian. One look was enough to distinguish the climbers from the wanna-bes. Some of them actually climbed as far as Base Camp, using up much-needed space on the rocky lower reaches of Everest, including adding to the horrendous pollution when they left their rubbish behind.

Kurt shook his head. "'S all right, mate. No worries." He saluted him and walked on. The sight of these pseudoclimbers was so common that the Aussie's presence evaporated from Kurt's mind before he'd taken another two strides.

Back to Chelsea.

If only she hadn't mentioned that one of her pleasures was horseback riding. The vision that had conjured up had played in some of the more erotic fantasies he'd had in the night. Yet he wasn't so blinded by lust that he couldn't recognize his dreams were just visions distorted by a bad case of desire. And all of it brought about by wishful thinking.

In other words, it wouldn't happen in a million years.

For one thing, he *dared* not let it.

If he felt the rumors about his part in the accident were bad now, no matter what Basie Serfontien thought, getting involved with Chelsea would be like throwing gasoline on a fire to put it out.

At first sight Chelsea had christened her hotel the Raffles of Nepal. The all-white interior, combined with punkah fans that adorned the ceilings of the first-floor rooms as well as the bedrooms, reminded her of a trip she had once taken to Singapore. Everyone ought to experience Raffles Hotel at least once.

But unless the weather improved, she wouldn't be switching on the fan in her bedroom. She imagined July and August really heated up, but early May was still reliving the crisp spring days of April.

Even so, she'd heard that on Everest it was easy to get sunburned by the reflected rays piercing the thin air. At least, she'd read it in one of the Everest books she'd brought to read on the plane.

"And you're still a long way from there, *bébé*," she mused.

Paris felt like a lifetime ago. Maybe it was? Sooner or later everything was bound to change. Her job at IBIS looked likely to be the first casualty now that her responsibilities to Tedman Foods and its employees had increased ten thousandfold.

A server dressed in a short white jacket appeared in her peripheral vision. "Can I bring you something, lady? A cocktail? Some tea?"

She looked up at the steward. He was very young and no doubt glad of work that didn't entail carting seventy-five pounds or more up a mountain, strapped to his back with a strip of webbing across his forehead to balance the weight.

"No, thank you. I'm going inside for lunch as soon as my friend arrives."

The chairs of the veranda weren't the high-backed cane found at the Raffles Hotel in Singapore, but the seating did provide Chelsea with a comfortable spot to formulate her plan of attack while she watched for Kurt to arrive.

What had she just called him? Her friend? She wasn't certain they could ever be friends. Lovers or enemies? Only time would tell. Her brain said be wary, but her body had a mind of its own.

She rested her head on the back of her chair and let the peace soak into her. The veranda was fairly deserted. Tourists didn't pay the fortune it cost to get here to waste their time watching Everest from afar. An idea about that had occurred to her that morning over breakfast, but would Kurt go along with it?

Kurt Jellic. Now, there was a man of contrasts. He looked rough, hard-bitten with his unshaven face and dark, almost black Gypsy eyes. Not what she had expected when Atlanta had said in her letter that he was a New Zealander. She tried to picture Kurt, with sun-bleached hair and light blue irises, sliding down a wave on a surfboard, her former stereotypical idea of a New Zealander.

It didn't take, but she couldn't discard the impressions that came from being held against his long, lean-limbed body, while her life trembled on the edge of the knife blade in his hand.

Color and heat rushed to her face and scorched her insides with a sudden rush of arousal. He'd certainly proved he was human…and the attraction was mutual.

Would it be an underhanded trick to use that attraction against him? Despite his initially forbidding appearance, Kurt had turned out to be a nice guy. Hadn't he listened to her without complaining while she provided him with proof positive she had been the kind of spoiled teenage witch he probably hated?

A teenage witch who had fought against losing the closest thing to a mom she had ever known.

Her eyes welled with unshed tears. Damn, Atlanta's death had made Chelsea's intentions of saying, "I'm sorry, sis—I didn't mean it" an impossibility. There was only one thing she could do for her now. One *last* thing.

Her tear ducts overflowed before she could prevent it.

They had been doing a lot of that lately. Chelsea opened her eyes wide to halt the hot slide of teardrops onto her cheeks, and then changed her mind. Scrunching her eyelids together to form narrow slits, she let her full weight sag against the cushions in an attempt to relax.

The rustle of prayer flags accompanied the sighs that whispered over her lips until a few minutes later she hovered on the edge of sleep and the world around her became a jumble of light and dark shapes.

Bam! She was wide-awake. One of the shapes lost its hazy edges and turned into a living, breathing Kurt Jellic.

"Am I disturbing your beauty sleep?" His voice had the husky edge it had lost when she had imagined him into a nice guy who would jump to do her bidding and give in to her every whim.

But Kurt was more than that. More than she had remembered. He was, first and foremost, disturbingly and attractively, all male.

She pushed against the cushioned seat of her chair to stand up, eager to reach a height where his size wasn't such a disadvantage. It wasn't easy.

Her hands sank deep into the pillowy softness that had almost seduced her into sleep. However, the angle of the seat—knees higher than her bottom—made it impossible to stand with any semblance of elegance.

"Here, let me." Kurt held out his hand and, fool that she was, Chelsea took it in hers. The world blurred at his touch. He pulled her to her feet and released his hold. And with its loss she felt nothing would ever be the same again.

He was dressed in the same casual outdoorsy style as most of the guides she'd met in Namche Bazaar—sun-faded khakis topped by a checked shirt under a black anorak. On him it had a style she hadn't perceived last night. The long stretch of muscled legs moved with a singularity that made him stand out in a crowd. She took a drawn-out look, knowing something was different.

Sure, he'd shaved, she'd give him that. But it wasn't simply that the razor had highlighted the dimple on his chin that made her stomach flip over, or the fact that the touch of his hand had sent an icy shiver down her spine.

No, it was in his eyes and the way he held himself. He reminded her of someone, but for the life of her she couldn't say whom. She returned his gaze and recognized awareness in his eyes, a knowing that hadn't been there before, as if in a past life they might have been lovers.

Flustered, she bent to flick the creases out of her skirt till it swung lightly from her hips, skimming the tops of her calves. When she had picked out the light cream cashmere top and natural linen skirt, she hadn't considered its subtle sexiness as part of her plan to get her own way. Now she realized that like everything she had done since their first meeting, it had been part of her strategy, part of her seduction.

Too bad she hadn't reached a definite conclusion on how to go about this master plan.

Just when it counted most, she was going to have to wing it.

Chelsea was used to controlling her own life, and it showed as soon as they entered the restaurant.

On the other hand, weighing in at 220 and standing at least three inches above most other men, as well as running the kind of enterprise he did, Kurt had become used to commanding attention, not being superseded. He didn't remember Atlanta being so bossy. She and Bill had always consulted each other, but then they had been a couple, two halves of one whole.

Kurt turned his attention to Chelsea, who had already picked her selection from the menu, told him he would enjoy it and informed their server they'd have two of everything.

The sibilant lisp of the sommelier did nothing to smooth Kurt's ruffled feathers. "Your meals will be here directly. Meanwhile if I can suggest a good wine to accompany them…" The wine list was fluttered at Kurt's face like a fan.

He scowled his annoyance at the undeserving sommelier, then asked Chelsea, "You want some wine?"

"Yes, I'd like that." She smiled at the sommelier and held out her hand for the wine list. "Do you have a—"

"I think a Pinot Gris will go best with what we've ordered," Kurt said before Chelsea had a chance to pipe up. He took the list, glanced over it, then pointed. "This one."

It paid to have a brother who was a Master of Wine and made his living tasting and writing books about the fermented juice of the grape. Drago was the eldest of the Jellic boys—men. He'd been out on his own a lot longer than the rest of them.

Circumstances of late had wrought a change in their slightly dysfunctional family, starting with the marriage of Jo, his younger sister. Since then, Franc, his genius kid brother, had found a great job, with loads of responsibility, in one of his new brother-in-law's firms. The family ties were now less fractured than they had been since the day his father, Milo Jellic, committed suicide.

His sister had married a man with money to burn, probably with the same kind of class Chelsea had. Not that he had aspirations in that direction—not even as a solution to his problems. Didn't matter that one glance at her sexy body had his insides turning every which way.

No, he was sure his twin brother, Kel, would agree with him that one millionaire per family was enough.

Kurt glanced around the almost empty dining room as the sommelier left. They'd been the center of attention as waiters vied to pass them menus and then take their orders.

"So where did you learn so much about wine?" Chelsea leaned across the table, one hand toying with her empty glass.

The movement emphasized the lush curve of her breasts where her cashmere sweater clung to them. He had to admit she had style. It didn't matter that her hair looked as if she'd cut it by herself without the aid of a mirror. He guessed it was the latest trend, but all it did was make her look younger, more vulnerable. He hardened his heart and refused to fall for it.

"I don't spend all my life on top of a mountain. New Zealand may be a small country, but it's big on wine."

That said, he tried to shrug off the feeling he'd made a mistake coming here. The contrasting digs they'd chosen—the tavern he'd shacked up in and this upmarket hotel where the cheapest room cost five hundred dollars a night—escalated his estimation of the class barrier he'd sensed looming between them.

It wasn't anything that had required much thought with Atlanta. She had been a friend; he hadn't been attracted to her. But with Chelsea, the attraction presented itself like a minefield in no-man's-land.

The quickest and easiest way out was to say no.

Chelsea's eyes lit up as she smiled at him. "Alone at last."

Kurt had an unwelcome impression that her eager eyes saw him as a parcel, tied with a big blue bow that she couldn't wait to hack into with her scissors.

He glanced over his shoulder, totaling the number of stares

from hovering waiters focused in their direction. "I've felt more alone in Grand Central Station."

"They do pride themselves on exemplary service here. At least, that's what it said on the hotel Web site. But it isn't quite so overpowering at dinnertime when the restaurant is busier."

"I'll have to take your word for that. This isn't the style I look for when I'm thinking of climbing a mountain. Although a certain amount of comfort between climbs is attractive to people with money. At least, that's what I had in mind when I started converting an old farmhouse near Aoraki National Park into a lodge."

He could see Chelsea was dying to question him about the place that had been a huge drain on his purse for the past year, but the sommelier beat her to the draw.

He held out a bottle so Kurt could read the label. *French.* This far from New Zealand he'd known he couldn't expect everything. Meaning a bottle marked *Marlborough,* one of New Zealand's top wine districts. He nodded his acceptance and an opener materialized from the guy's pocket.

"Aoraki? Where is that?" Chelsea asked.

He briefly lifted a hand to signal her to hold a moment.

"Let me taste this, then I'll tell all." Kurt swirled the wine in his glass the way Drago had shown him, took a sniff and then tasted the wine. It had the pearlike aroma but not the rich, ripe fruitiness he'd expect if it had been a New Zealand wine. Still, it would pass muster. He glanced up at the patient sommelier. "Excellent. Thank you."

It was apparent that Chelsea agreed. Her gray eyes seemed to lift at the corners smiling at him over the rim of the glass as she took her first taste. "I'm pleased to know your taste in wine exceeds your choice in whiskey."

"I'm versatile. I use what's on hand. Sometimes a compromise is necessary." But there would be no compromising where Chelsea's safety was concerned.

"You wanted to know about Aoraki. It's the Maori name for Mount Cook. It translates as *cloud piercer.*"

"I like that. Much more romantic than Mount Cook."

Trust a woman to find the romance in a hunk of rock. After last month's accident he was having trouble finding anything vaguely quixotic in his chosen field. It had become a means to an end—that end being his lodge. "I'd be telling a lie if I said there was any fairy-tale romance connected to my lodge. It used to be a sheep station, but it's years since anyone lived there. Most of the land was ceded to the state in lieu of back taxes. The land itself is pretty barren, a flat valley scooped out at the foot of the Southern Alps by glaciers during the ice age. My interest in it is its accessibility to the Alps and Aoraki. It's close enough to the township of Lake Tekapo not to be completely isolated. Lots of tourists pass by on the way to Queenstown."

"But it must be exciting making a project like that come to life."

"Exciting would be good, but when I think about the lodge, all I see ahead of me is hard work and lots of it."

"Why aren't you there now working on your property instead of climbing Mount Everest?"

"I need the money. Besides, it's winter in New Zealand, lots of snow and rain—better for skiing than climbing, though there are plenty of fools who still want to risk it. My aim is to build up a training establishment attached to the lodge where I can teach guests to climb safely."

Kurt cleared his throat in an attempt to dislodge the lump that had settled in his craw. "You might not believe it, but I had one of the best safety records going until last month. Hell, they do say pride comes before a fall, but I'd rather have died myself than lose anyone on my watch, especially Bill and Atlanta."

"I know that feeling well. It's called guilt. No wonder we're together. They say misery loves company."

Kurt's mind latched on to only one portion of her last sentence. "But we're not together. After we've eaten I'll go my way and you'll go yours. Tell me something. When you were trying to hire a guide, did you give them all your name and your reasons for going up Everest?"

Chelsea leaned back in her chair as if distancing herself from him. Hardly worth the effort, given they were already sitting at opposite ends of a table for two. "Yes. Why not?"

"No reason." He gave her the lie, knowing after today he wouldn't see her again.

He watched her lift her glass and pour some wine into her mouth as if she were drinking straight courage.

He tried some of his own, just a sip, and waited. He wasn't lacking in courage, but something told him if he didn't keep his wits about him, Chelsea would try to tie him in knots.

His stomach had already taken a few twists and turns since he'd arrived. Sexual attraction could steal a man's soul. Look at Adam. Even *he* wasn't immune to the allure of a good-looking woman. But then, he'd had only one to choose from. Why, out of all the women Kurt had met, was Chelsea the one to stir feelings that had lain dormant since he'd given his love to the mountains?

He wasn't the type to court danger and leave a family at home. No, there was nothing of his old man in him, except maybe going for the thrill. He couldn't see why, as a cop, his late father had taken to dealing drugs. It couldn't have been for the money. None of it ever appeared on their table. They'd been a big family, and after his mother died, Grandma

Glamuzina had managed the way she had in the old country, working on a shoestring budget.

After his father drove his car off a cliff, the fat hit the pan and the truth came out—or what had passed as the truth. He'd come to think that his need to climb stemmed from being able to get above everything else, up high where the stench of corruption couldn't taint him.

His sister and her husband, Rowan McQuaid Stanhope, were now in the process of trying to unravel the mystery of who'd done what. It was after he heard about their efforts that he'd decided to start work on the lodge. Even to himself he hadn't admitted that maybe this had been the catalyst for thinking he could settle down at last, maybe find himself a wife.

Yeah. That explained this sudden rush of testosterone to the brain; he'd given his instincts permission to find some woman attractive. But why Chelsea?

She was the last person he could have a relationship with.

"I could fix your money problems."

"Whoa, back up there. That wasn't why I mentioned them. If I was into borrowing money I would have asked Bill—I'd known him a lot longer than I've known you." This woman's mind worked faster than a black cat disappearing at night.

She was hard to keep up with and knew exactly which buttons to push. He'd have to learn to keep his mouth shut and not give her another opening. He polished off the rest of his wine in one gulp.

Chelsea signaled the sommelier to refill Kurt's glass, but kept her smile tucked inside her mind as she did it. She'd learned negotiating on her daddy's knee and knew not to blow the deal by letting the other side recognize you could see the winning post streaking toward you. "I'm not talking about a loan. You have something I want and I have something you need. Fair exchange is no robbery. Let's *parler*."

Her mind clicked to possibilities that hadn't entered her plans when she sat outside on the veranda. Now it took shape, a plan she hadn't considered before. "I think the least you can do is give me a trial. I deserve at least that. I believe I can cope. You don't. Take me up there and give me a chance to prove what I can do."

She saw Kurt's lips quirk, pulling his mouth up at one side. The action emphasized the depth of the dimple in his chin and distracted her attention from his words for a moment, but only a moment.

"You really think you can take the leap from a climbing wall to the highest mountain in the world in one go?" He gave the question a facetious quality with the lift of one eyebrow.

Chelsea wasn't used to being talked down to, even by men who were six inches taller. But she now knew she had an edge. Seduction and feminine wiles didn't have to come into her proposition. This was business. Her territory. "I'll never know unless I'm given the chance to try. Look at it this way—you're here, you're available and you need the money. I have money, I want to find my sister's body and you have the opportunity to make sure I'll be safe before you take me on. Or rather take me up the mountain."

"Why don't you just pay me to go up and recover the bodies and bring them down to Namche Bazaar?"

"No… Definitely not. That isn't the way it's going to go down. I have to be there." She couldn't take the chance on someone else finding the key before her.

His dark eyes glinted as if he sensed she wasn't telling him the whole truth. She was right. "What's so important about you being there?"

She rolled her eyes at him and thought fast. "If this is the moment when you expect me to spill all my guilty little secrets about my relationship with Atlanta, forget about it. I don't remember what I told you last night, but that was whiskey-on-an-empty-stomach talking. All I've had today is a few sips of wine and a big breakfast."

The mention of food appeared to trigger the arrival of their first course—corn and feta fritters, layered with bacon strips and vegetables. It had sounded good on the menu, but at the moment it had lost its appeal by slowing the momentum of their conversation. Kurt had already made it clear that he didn't care to have a discussion in front of any of the dining-room staff.

It didn't matter to her who knew she wanted to go up Mount Everest after her sister's body. There was only one secret she needed to keep, apart from her connection to IBIS, and that was the whereabouts of the key. This was the first time in her twenty-eight years that she had felt the lives of thousands of employees lay in the palm of her hand.

She didn't look on it as a burden. All she knew was there was no way she wanted to let them down. She hadn't even stopped long enough to check out wills or anything. Maybe someone from Bill's family owned part of Tedman Foods. She didn't give a hoot. As a Tedman, Chelsea was the last of that name, Arlon Rowles being her father's first cousin only because their mothers had been sisters.

The server left and Chelsea picked up her knife and fork, but didn't use them. She wasn't able to start eating. Getting her own way was more important than food, even if she had been starving.

She watched Kurt cut into a fritter and layer it with bacon and tomato on his fork. Once his mouth was full and he had no choice but to listen, she made her move.

"If you're worried about my safety, don't be. It won't make any difference. I will go up there, either with you or someone else, even if I have to fly an experienced guide in from the States. They can't all be in Namche Bazaar right now.

"What you have is a chance to make sure I can make it. I'm fit. I have some experience with ropes, knots, carabiners and ascenders. Teach me enough to get me up to where Atlanta and Bill are lying. I know you trust yourself. Well, forget about the accident. I trust you enough to get me up there and back again in one piece. So what do you say? Have we got a deal?"

She gripped her eating utensils hard.

Not that that would stop her hands shaking, or dissipate the sense of urgency coursing through her veins as if her life was at stake. She thought of Maddie and knew that it could be, if knowledge of the key Atlanta had been carrying got out.

The sooner they did this the better.

Chelsea meant what she'd said. She trusted Kurt Jellic with her life, only she couldn't tell him that her life was more likely to be in danger from an external force, not the mountain that had taken her sister.

Kurt's face was grim. Did he consider that what she asked amounted to blackmail? But like it or not, fate had linked them in this endeavor. And like it or not, there was no going against fate. The monks in the temples of this high mountain stronghold would be the first to agree with the supposition that it was already written in the sands of time.

"Since you put it like that, you leave me no choice."

He took a sip of wine while Chelsea held her breath.

"I know someone who owns a place we can use. It's not on Everest, but it's within four days' walk from here, maybe three depending on your stamina. The mountain it's close to isn't anything like as high as Everest, so we won't have to worry about oxygen. We won't need tanks where you want to go, in any case. We don't have to climb to the top.

"What Ama Dablam does have is a glacier, an icefall that's easier to reach than any of the others. And if you can't make it on this one, you'll never be able to reach the couloir where their bodies fell."

She wanted to punch the air and shout *Yes!* Her next reaction was to tell him *I'm glad you see things my way,* but they were still in Namche Bazaar and neither reaction was what she would call politic. Also, Kurt's face looked carved out of the ice he'd told her about.

But she couldn't hide the excitement fizzing through her veins. She could make this happen. Hard work, danger—hah, she laughed in their faces. She *would* do this. "When do we start?"

"As soon as we've got you kitted out and I've instructed Sherpa Rei to rehire one of his cousins and some more Sherpa porters to carry our gear."

"Good. I can't wait."

The sooner the better.

She flashed him a smile that had nothing to do with getting her own way and everything to do with knowing she was going to spend some quality time with this guy. "Eat up, then let's get out of here. I don't know about you, but suddenly I'm filled with energy."

Chapter 4

They spent three nights on the trail to Ama Dablam, sleeping in tourist lodges on the way, their first stop at Tengboche within sight of the great Buddhist monastery.

The distance wasn't great, but the path rose and fell steeply, winding between tall, leafy, scented trees, some of them seemingly growing straight out of the rocks. But once their path branched away from Mount Everest and Base Camp, their height above sea level rose and the green shade was left behind.

At Ama Dablam, one look was enough to tell Chelsea that when Kurt said, *I know someone who owns a place we can use* he wasn't talking about the type of mountain lodge you might find at Aspen, or near the standard of the lodges dotting Sagarmatha National Park.

The almost squalid little shack was like nothing she'd ever experienced. Its owner, whom Kurt knew well enough to ask a favor from, was a Sherpa, another relative of Kora's brother.

Once inside, she sniffed the stale air, sure the tiny building had mice. She was certain she could smell them, and it made her shudder. And though the porters and Sherpas had supposedly readied the place for their arrival, she looked around for a broom.

Another sweeping couldn't hurt.

No one at IBIS would believe this was Chelsea Tedman sighing in pleasure at the sight of a broom without enough bristles to fly a witch. It was enough to make her giggle. What a pampered life she'd led, even though her training with IBIS had been rigorous.

Prior to moving to France, the only cleaning she had ever had to do was her room at the sorority house. In Paris Mme Guignard, the concierge of her apartment block, let the cleaner in three times a week. Chelsea hadn't considered it an indulgence. It was what she was used to, and she could afford the service.

At first glance she had thought the outside looked quaint, with its rough plastered stone walls put together like a kind of upright crazy paving. The gable roof was fashioned from rusting corrugated iron. It was hard to imagine it being transported this distance on the back of a yak without taking off in the wind.

The last settlement they had passed was called Syalkyo—less than half a dozen houses—and to get to where they were they'd had to cross a glacial river, colored by the run-off from the glacier. Kurt had mentioned it was similar to the Tekapo River near his half-built lodge in New Zealand. The wood-slat-and-rope bridge they had traversed had been an eye-opener for Chelsea. The solid tree trunks they had crossed before Tengboche had been Brooklyn Bridge in comparison.

With a pack on her back, and a blue-gray-and-white foaming river rushing over rocks underneath, she had felt less than steady matching her steps to Kurt's as the boards sprang and bounced under her feet on the fragile swaying suspension bridge.

Chelsea began her final sweep to make sure she hadn't missed anything. Crouching low, she reached the broom into the dark under the two trestle beds. Someone had unrolled a thin foam mattress on top of each bed for her and Kurt to sleep on.

"What on earth are you doing?" Kurt filled the low doorway, stealing most of the light and steeping the interior in a gloom the two small windows couldn't counteract.

"I'm making sure that it's clean. If we have to live here for almost a week, let's at least begin in a semicivilized fashion."

Chelsea stood and faced him as she spoke. Kurt was such a giant of a man, she should have felt intimidated, but she didn't. She had watched him interact with the porters and Sherpas, taking some weight off the load of a young boy who couldn't have been more than twelve years old. She had learned there was a kindness in the man that he seemed to take pains to hide from her.

He used his gruffness as a shield the way she used her bossiest sorority-princess manner to keep him at arm's length. She could see danger in getting too close to this man and was doing her best to avoid the inevitable clash if either of them lowered their guard. Sometimes she caught a glimpse of flame in his dark, almost black eyes when he glanced in her direction.

Heaven forgive her, she became more obnoxious with each sighting, hoping to douse the fire.

Kurt took the broom from her. "This isn't the Ritz. A few days of climbing over the icefall of the Ama Dablam glacier and you'll be delighted to come back to the luxury of this little abode."

"I'll take your word for it." Chelsea stepped to one side, the backs of her knees hard against the wood-frame bed as Kurt hoisted his backpack onto a hook on the wall.

"Which bed do you want?" he asked.

Her gaze traveled from Kurt to the bed six feet away on the other side of the room. She'd noticed when she swept underneath them that one looked better constructed than the other. "You'd better take the one under the window. It appears more likely to take your weight."

"'S that right?" His mouth tightened. His darkened jawline hadn't been shaved in the days since they'd had lunch at her hotel. And though she hated to admit it, stubble must have been invented for a strong face such as his. Most men in her tight little circle at the embassy wouldn't be seen dead with a five-o'clock shadow, much less stubble. *Unless he was working undercover.*

Maybe the contrast was why she found him so attractive.

"I wasn't implying that you were fat, just heavy…er, b-big boned," she stammered as he pinned her with an intense look from his deep-set eyes. Her heart kept racing after he went outside.

Who among her associates had raised her pulse rate? None that she could name offhand, and as for making her tremble—never.

While Kurt kept busy with tasks that had to be done before night fell—lantern wicks trimmed and sleeping bags unrolled—he noticed Chelsea staring into space. The death of her sister had hit her hard. Hell, it had hit him hard, and he wasn't related.

Atlanta had had a lot of guts for her size—not just a reckless foolhardiness, which he suspected was the case with

Chelsea. This week would tell, for it would separate the sheep from the lambs, so to speak.

He lifted her pack and chucked it on top of the bed she'd decided to use. It didn't make any difference to him which of the two he slept on—he was used to sleeping on a bed of rocks. But it had been a long time since a woman had slept a few feet away. A woman he was determined to keep his distance from. So what if he was partially aroused half the time he was in her vicinity? It took two to tango. He refused to get caught up in the dance.

He undid the Velcro straps on her backpack. The sound seemed to pull her back to the present. "Better sort out what you'll want for the morning. It will still be dark when we set out. I want to be near the foot of the glacier by dawn."

"You want us to get up before dawn?"

Was that panic he saw in her expression? He'd bet she was more used to arriving home as the sun rose, in the glamorous world she inhabited. "That's what I said—*dawn*—so be prepared to hit the sack early tonight."

"Excuse me if I appear uptight, but there is the question of privacy, with us sharing a room."

He did what he could to prevent a weary grimace showing, but it was almost impossible. "You weren't thinking of wearing a fancy silk nightie to bed by any chance?"

God, he'd love to see her dressed in a Parisian fantasy of lace and silk. Face it, Jellic, for all your protestations of dampening down the attraction, you know you'd rather see her wearing nothing but her skin. The less there was to remove, the sooner he'd discover if his imagination had done her justice.

It was too dim inside the little hut to see if she was blushing as she pronounced a drawn-out "No-o-o."

"Good. That wasn't one of the things on the list I gave you

to pack. You'll sleep in your long johns, of course, and if you ever make it up any higher, be prepared to sleep in your clothes. There are times when you'll be glad to pull on every stitch of clothing in your pack before going to bed." Kurt lifted his bulky backpack off the hook and began undoing the zipper.

Turning again, he caught Chelsea in the middle of an exaggerated shudder. "Isn't that unsanitary?"

"Didn't I warn you to enjoy your shower at the lodge before you left? That it would be the last one you had in a while?"

"Yes, but…"

"What did you think you would do—wash in a mountain stream? It's butt-freezing territory. You have to keep warm, keep your circulation flowing. I've seen the results of frostbite, and I wouldn't wish that on my worst enemy. If a *lady* like Atlanta could do it, then so can you." Digging deep into one of the side pockets of his pack, he drew out a box and tossed it to Chelsea. "Here, you'll need these and I brought extra."

"Baby wipes?"

"They're the closest you're going to get to a shower for a while. Use them sparingly."

She laid them on the end of the bed and, like him, began pulling out her sleeping bag. It was red, a color he had reckoned she should wear more after she'd held it up in front of her, asking for his opinion of it in the shop.

"I guess my inexperience is showing, but I can get past that. I'm a quick study." She bent her head over her pack and began removing some gear, but as he turned his attention to his, he could have sworn he heard her mutter, "I have to be."

He wished he knew what she wasn't telling him. With all

her grim determination it had to be something big, something more than just seeing her sister into a proper resting place.

Chelsea had said she trusted him with her life. What could she be hiding from him that was worth more than surviving Everest?

After long minutes when the only sound in the room was the noise of climbing boots hitting the floor and the rustle of down-lined jackets and pants being shaken and fluffed, the room grew too dark to see what was in the bottom of their packs.

"Time to put some light on," he said. "This kerosene lamp will throw out good light, but we don't want to waste the fuel. Like everything else that has to be transported this distance, it's a precious commodity. I suggest that as soon as we've eaten, we get into our respective sleeping bags. If you want to read, or get up in the night, use that light on the headband. Better put it someplace handy."

"Did you mention food? I could eat anything put before me."

"Thanks for the warning. I'll keep out of your way."

She yawned, covering her mouth with her hand, murmuring sleepily, "I don't think I'll need to read myself to sleep after the walk we did today. It was the longest trek yet."

He watched her stretch her facial muscles, finishing with a semblance of a grin. "It's not so much the distance is it? It's the walking uphill and then down again to get where you are going. It gets you in the back of the knees. As soon as my head hits the pillow, or rather the folded, down-lined jacket I'm going to stuff inside the matching pants, I expect to fall asleep."

Chelsea didn't sleep, though. She lay for an hour going over different types of knots, determined not to let herself fail when they reached the icefall and began seriously using ropes.

Then she reflected on the country they'd trekked through. They had passed a lot of porters returning to Namche Bazaar or Tengboche for a break or supplies, but away from the track, where the trees couldn't grow, lay an empty land where the mountains were king and their subjects few and far between. Yet the culture was fascinating. Wherever one looked there was a monastery where the sounds of chanting and prayer wheels were as common as radios and car horns in Paris.

One part of her, the part that wanted to avoid confrontation, almost wished she could stay in Nepal, where the life seemed so simple, but that was an idealistic view. Even Nepal had its problems. At Namche Bazaar and then Tengboche they'd had to go through military checkpoints because Maoist rebels were stirring up small pockets of trouble.

She'd heard that tourist numbers had dropped by 20 percent. Some people were willing to sacrifice anything, even their lives, for what they believed in, but it often led to terrorism. That's how she'd ended up as a translator with IBIS. Jason Hart had conceived the idea after his wife had died at ground zero on 9/11. Ex-naval intelligence, he'd had all the right connections.

Chelsea snorted and rolled over. She could include herself on that list of those willing to make sacrifices. Tedman Foods couldn't be compared with a whole country, but they employed thousands of people. Her sigh lingered in the air. What would happen if she didn't get her hands on that key?

Was she doing all this for nothing? If she had gone to her boss instead, would IBIS have had the power to open the safety deposit box? The bank-held key wouldn't undo the lock on its own.

Too late to worry about the unknown. Without the key she couldn't find the proof they needed to open it forcibly.

"What's wrong—can't you sleep?" Kurt's voice rumbled across the gap, as if her huffing and puffing had wakened him.

"I want to sleep. It just won't happen. My brain won't shut up." She knew she sounded sulky, but she was frustrated she couldn't face sleep.

"Want me to read you a bedtime story?" he teased.

Good idea. "Tell me about Atlanta and Bill. It's a dreadful admission, but the things I know about my sister's life over the last fifteen years could be counted on one hand. I've missed a great deal, and I can't get those years back."

Kurt waited a moment as she grew silent, then took over the conversation. "I met them first in western Argentina."

"Another coincidence. My mother was born in Argentina, but my grandparents died before I was born, so I've never had anyone to visit," Chelsea said—almost to herself, it seemed.

"The Chaplins were climbing with another outfit, but we were camped close together at the foot of Mount Aconcagua," Kurt continued. "We'd light a fire at night and sit around and talk. I suppose the first thing I noticed about them was how happy they were, how much of a team, as if they shared thoughts. You know, finishing each other's sentences, laughing at jokes no one else understood."

"I'm glad they were happy, but it makes me even sadder."

"Yeah, there are always regrets. Who hasn't wanted to change the past?" Him for one. How different would his life have been if his father had been content to be the good cop he'd seemed?

"Before we went our separate climbs, I gave Bill my address and phone number in New Zealand, said if they ever got down there to give me a call. Then we met again at the airport. Turned out we were taking the same plane. I was in cattle class and they were in business, but they invited me to come up to this place they had in Colorado to do some skiing."

"Sounds great." Chelsea's voice, though flat, floated softly to him in the darkness. He could tell the story was beginning to work.

"I had a great time. You should have been there," he teased her. "Wouldn't it have been funny if we'd met then instead of now?" Would the attraction he felt in his gut when he looked at her have burned as it did now, knowing she was only a few feet away and all he had to do was walk across the room to take her in his arms? "This trek would have been easier on you if we hadn't met as strangers."

He heard her sleeping bag slither silkily on the mattress as if she was turning on her side to face him. "Living so close, we won't be strangers by the time it's over, will we?"

"No, I guess not. But I would have liked to have met you without this whole business between us. Under normal circumstances, I think we could have been friends." More than friends.

Chelsea echoed his thoughts out loud. "I think we could have been more than friends. Isn't it a pity we'll never know now?"

Her voice was husky with regret, as if for all the great sex they would miss. It made his pulse race in an instant.

Knowing it would never happen calmed him down. It was a shame, all right. The rumors that had circulated around Namche Bazaar had cut him to the quick, but it was a small leap from there to worrying about the type of slant they would put on his getting cozy with Chelsea.

He was there to look after her, not make her the target of his lust. To do that he needed to keep his mind on the next day and ensuring Chelsea was as fit and as agile as she'd led him to believe. She'd certainly managed the four-day trek.

Before he could return to his story, she whispered, "Thanks for the story. Good night."

At least he was good for something, if only sending her to sleep. Now he was wide-awake, but not for long.

Dawn flowing in candy-pink over the glacier was something not to be missed. But Chelsea felt she should tell Kurt that if this was to be the routine every morning—rising at 4:30 a.m. and munching a protein bar as they tramped within reach of the icefall—the experience could grow old very quickly.

They had been traveling almost an hour when the man in question looked over his shoulder at her. "How you going, Chelsea? Not too much for you?"

She bit her tongue to hold back a *wouldn't you just love it if I chickened out before we'd even started* remark.

"Excellent. I'm really…enjoying myself. A new experience for me…but it's beautiful in a weird sort of way." She hated the fact that on top of the exertion, the thinner air was making her pant. She didn't want to give Kurt an excuse to say she wouldn't make it.

Kurt stayed put, and with another few noisy paces across rock and ice she came level with him. "Actually, it's not as cold as I thought it would be."

"Yeah, we've got us a clear sky and no wind." He ran an eye over her outfit—matching Gore-Tex shell trousers and pants in a shade of pumpkin that would make her look like a huge chunk of squash from a distance. But hey, beggars couldn't be choosers—it was all they'd had in her size.

"Toward the middle of the day as we climb higher and the sun reflects off the ice, you'll be tying that jacket around your waist and stripping off a few other layers, as well." His gaze focused on her chest.

It lingered there for several seconds.

You wish. She kept the thought to herself as her mind took a leap backward to their first meeting—his hand on her breast and the heat of his body burning against her hip.

This wasn't good; sex had no business rearing its ugly head when she had to concentrate on learning everything she could from this guy. Darn you, Kurt Jellic. Why d'you have to be so gorgeous? she thought.

But Kurt had moved on. "How are those glacier glasses going? Not too loose, I hope. Did you remember to put the spare pair in your pack?"

Great! Any notions of sex went straight out the window when he treated her as if she was still in kindergarten. "The glasses are fantastic—nice and firm but not rubbing—and yes, I have the spare pair in my pack. I'm not a child, Kurt. You don't have to keep checking on me all the time."

"If you were a child things would be easier all around."

"What is that supposed to mean—things would be easier all around?" She mimicked his serious tone.

"Come off it, Chelsea. Keep beating around the bush if you must, but the attraction between us is no secret. The kind everybody knows, but no one wants to be the first to mention out loud. Okay, I'm attracted to you."

Secrets? If only Kurt knew. Chelsea's career depended on it. She'd sworn never to reveal the contents of any document she translated or anything she heard in the IBIS ops room. That meant she couldn't afford to be as open as Kurt about her life.

And she couldn't afford a hormonal distraction that would shorten the odds of her making it through this week. Because of her inexperience, the odds were already on Kurt's side. Animal attraction would have to wait.

His steely expression didn't look promising. It showed he

had a streak of hardness at his core that he didn't want anyone to breach. "Well, I guess the secret's out now. But—"

"Well, keep that secret in your pants for now, Jellic. I've no intention of freezing my butt off for any man," she said, taking attack as being her best form of defense.

Kurt laughed. "So the lady knows how to get down and dirty. I'm amazed, and fascinated. I only wanted to reassure you that I wouldn't be trying to jump your bones."

Typical male. *I'm attracted to you, but not enough to do anything about it.*

It was another twenty minutes before he spoke again. "Time to show me what you can do."

They were on solid ice now. They were the only two people in the empty white space, but the noise of shifting ice was constant.

"What? No demonstration?"

"Would I do that to you? Come closer."

Chelsea moved up next to him as he brought up the ice axe looped around his wrist. They had used the long handle like a walking stick crossing the rocky valley at the foot of the glacier, and even with her crampons digging into the frozen snow, it had helped to keep her balance.

"Okay, as you can see, the slope is becoming steeper. Crampons aren't going to be enough on their own. Normally, as leader, I would cut steps and you would follow in them. But what happens if you're on your own?"

A rush of coldness whooshed up from her toes and settled near her heart. Panic? "But you're not going to leave me up Mount Everest on my own?"

"Never say never. I didn't think I'd be coming down on my own and leaving Bill and Atlanta up there. I'm just covering all the bases."

Self-confidence had a way of slipping that could leave peo-ple—namely Chelsea Tedman—flat on their back. It didn't matter that an accident had brought her there. That it could happen to her or Kurt hadn't entered her tunnel-vision mind.

He swung the ice axe and carved out of the ice a step big enough to fit one large foot. Then he stepped into it. "See how I'm not just relying on the crampons on the sole of my boot. I'm digging the spikes on the front of them hard up against the back wall of the step."

Stepping back down and out of her way, he instructed, "Now you try it."

Chelsea looked down at her foot as she bent her knee. She had big feet—size nine and a half—but she knew it was one of the costs of being a tall woman and until now had let it bother her only when shopping for shoes. Now her long, nar-row feet were encased in double plastic climbing boots with fully insulated overboots on top. Kurt had insisted she get used to the full deal, and her toes did feel warm and toasty—hot even—but he'd assured her that when they climbed higher, sometimes three layers of liner socks over the ones she was wearing now wouldn't be enough. All she could see when she put her foot on the step was that it looked huge.

She dug her toes firmly into the back of the step.

"Good." Kurt's hand was touching her calf urging her weight forward onto her toes. He seemed so indifferent, her leg might be a part of the masses of climbing equipment he carried. "Now you cut the next step. Don't make it too far up so it's difficult to reach. That's the way to overbalance."

She dug the other crampons into the slope as she swung the ice axe and cut a step the way Kurt had done. Except that it took her longer to get the shape she wanted.

Sweat gathered in the small of her back, and the coil of rope lying against her hip bumped her leg with each swing, as if marking time, but at last she was done. "There." She sighed. "Finished." Pulling her toe spikes out of the icy slope, she took a step onto the fresh hollow she had hacked out.

One annoying thing about men like Kurt was that most of the time they were correct. She had made the next step too high. Oh, she reached it, all right, but she hadn't taken the weight of her backpack and ropes into account. Her foot stayed on the step for about two seconds, then with her equilibrium out of kilter she slowly toppled backward.

Chelsea felt Kurt's arms gather her in, but she was no lightweight. He went down, as well. They slid a few feet farther, her feet waving in the air, until Kurt dug in his ice axe and arrested their slide. Gurgles of laughter she was unable to control bubbled up inside her. She hadn't laughed since before she'd heard the news about Atlanta. A sobering thought.

Released from his arms, she twisted and, grasping for purchase, took hold of his jacket. Looking into his face, she risked her equilibrium for the second time in the space of a minute. His harsh breath grazed her cheek. His features could have been carved out of the icy slope. She panicked and fought to get to her feet. Kurt grasped her arms and held her. She couldn't move.

"Hell's teeth, woman! Be careful with those crampons. If you spike my leg we might as well book our flights home now, for we won't be doing any climbing."

She went still in his grasp. Embarrassed, not knowing where to look, she shut her eyes. Next thing she knew, he was pressing her face into his shoulder. His voice sounded as rough as the whiskey they'd shared a lifetime ago. "Don't take on more than you can handle. If it means cutting extra steps to be safe, be safe."

The thud of his heart echoed in her ear while he paused for

breath. She had no excuses. Kurt had warned her and proved that climbing wasn't a game.

As if to reinforce the gravity of her mistake, he said, "Say we'd been two, maybe three hundred meters up even without a vertical slope—you would have slid right down. The momentum would have carried you away and me with you. Later I'll teach you to self-arrest."

Chelsea had gone through life expecting the unexpected. That was how she'd ended up studying languages at Harvard and had fallen into her job at the embassy, ending up with IBIS. But Kurt's gloved hands cupping her face as his mouth descended toward hers was more than just a surprise, and his "Damn you, Chelsea," shocked her.

At the same time, his freezing lips were both soft and firm and his mouth hot enough to melt a glacier. The kiss went from gentle, exploratory, to hard and urgent in ten seconds flat. Then as if her time was up he lifted his head.

"C'mon," he said. "Let's get you back on your feet. Turn around, dig in your crampons and I'll push from behind." Which he did with deceptive strength. Chelsea knew she was no lightweight, yet one second she was on the ice, and the next she was holding out a hand offering to help Kurt to his feet.

Kurt didn't need her help. He was as agile as a mountain goat on the ice. One arm snaked around her shoulders. She could feel its weight on her backpack as he walked her back to where they had started the exercise. The kiss was never mentioned. She certainly didn't intend bringing it up. It was one of those incidents that needed careful consideration—privacy, even. She'd save that task until she was back in her sleeping bag, where she could analyze each short second of his kiss.

Though she didn't need to seduce him now to get her own way, she wondered which one of them would have won.

"Back to business. Let's see you do that again. And no, I don't mean the part where you tried to flatten me. It's one thing you trusting me to take care of you, but have you ever considered taking better care of yourself?"

Kurt's gruff suggestion wasn't something that occurred to her very often. She went her own way, did her own thing. Even at IBIS they knew whatever she put her mind to she did well.

It had been a long time since there had been anyone she'd really mattered to, who cared even a little. She had always felt that Atlanta had abandoned her when she got married, but didn't feel so bad about that anymore. Losing the sister who'd mothered her through childhood had hit her harder than she'd realized. But the letter she'd received from Atlanta had put a new slant on her memories of that earlier time.

And now Kurt, too, cared for her, if reluctantly.

Who'd have thought?

Chapter 5

Kurt closely observed Chelsea's brightly clad figure. Her work had become sure and methodical. This wasn't the worst slope they'd face, but he was pleased to note she made no more errors, didn't try to take on more than she was capable of, or misjudge the length of her stride. "Not far to go."

He followed her up the ice face, reassured that was one mistake she would never make again. "You're doing good work, but don't try to rush it."

She didn't reply, but he hadn't expected her to. She was saving her breath.

Overhead, the sky had formed a huge blue bowl frosted in white around the rim. They were treading through a dangerous, almost barren landscape where man's voice was a pitiful thing compared to the groans of the icefall, which at times reminded him of a whale breaching.

They were close to the top now and going easily. He issued

an occasional instruction, but took care not to take Chelsea's mind off her task. He knew from personal experience that cutting steps in the ice was hard, tiring work—just what Chelsea needed to build up her stamina.

Now and again he pondered whether she was used to men suddenly kissing her without warning. She hadn't lost her temper, dramatically told him to unhand her, or slapped his face.

All of which she'd been entitled to do.

No, he'd been the one who was angry. He could still feel pinpricks of memory, buzzing like gnats inside his skull, taking him back to the day he'd lost Bill and Atlanta. Lost them for all time.

It wasn't anything visual, unless you counted the stark sheet of white ice in front of his eyes as he'd heard those sounds.

They'd reminded him of skimming flat pebbles across water as a boy, counting each bounce across the surface. The dreaded word *avalanche* had opened a crack of terror in his thoughts as he'd recalled hearing another climber telling about a close encounter with a rock shower. Chunks of ice had spit off the ice face as he'd rammed the spike of his axe in as hard as he could, waiting to be tossed around like a rag doll at any moment.

Then he'd heard it fly past to his left.

Bill and Atlanta—still roped together, spinning after each bounce like the weighted ends of a bola. Down and down…

God! He had to stop thinking about that day before it drove him crazy. Had to stop second-guessing himself, looking for an answer that would have made a difference.

Chelsea's determination had infected him till he felt a new urgency to retrieve his friends' remains—the last act of friendship he could make for the friends who had trusted him to get them to the summit.

Kurt lifted his gaze and watched her reach the crest and disappear like a glowing orange sun setting behind the ridge. A pang of fear slammed into his gut with her out of sight. He increased speed until he caught sight of her as she stood panting, dragging in scads of thin air. Climbing at these altitudes deprived the human body of oxygen needed to fuel it. And it would only get worse.

"How are you feeling, Chelsea?"

"I'm tired but exhilarated. And I've discovered that the climber who said he wanted to climb a mountain because it was there was an idiot. He didn't explain the half of it." The palm of her hand skimmed the scene below as if it were a painted canvas she could touch.

"I know we haven't climbed anything like the heights waiting for us on Mount Everest, but this is wonderful. It's not only reaching the top, it's looking back where you've been and discovering just how beautiful planet Earth is."

God help him, she was hooked already.

"Tell me that when we get to the end of our week here. More important, how are your feet holding out in your new boots? Any blisters?"

Her joyous expression took a dive. "None that I can feel." She lifted a foot and glanced down at her yellow-and-red boot topped by black overboots, gaiter-style, that reached to her knee. "My boots feel pretty comfortable."

"So they should. They cost enough. It would have been wiser to break them in first, but since we didn't have time…" He let the rest of the remark hang. No sense in reiterating the obvious. "The condition of your feet is vitally important. When we get back to the shack I'll get out this stuff that will help harden them up for something more than walking around carpeted rooms wearing stilettos."

Her smile faded as his gibe hit the mark.

Who was he kidding? He hadn't been making a crack at her expense. He'd been protecting himself.

That kiss had been a blunder.

Letting loose the reins of the attraction they felt had been another. Two more to add to the mistake he'd made by agreeing to take her on this outrageous adventure. She was a rookie, for God's sake. Her life was at risk, and heaven only knew what it would cost his soul if anything bad happened to her.

Face it, Jellic—you agreed to be her guide only when she suggested flying someone in from the States if you turned her down. He couldn't stand the thought of another man being alone on the mountain with her, touching her. It was sheer unadulterated jealousy that had driven him to agree to this crazy stunt.

"Now all we have to do is get back down. This part should be a cinch for you, so let's see how you belayed down that climbing wall in the Parisian gym." He knew he was doing it again—emphasizing the difference between them, between the lives they led. By rights they should never have met.

He stood aside, watching her deft handling of knots and carabiners. Finished, she pulled out the gadget to stop her gloves melting on the line. She didn't make a wrong move. And he didn't know whether to be happy or annoyed that, apart from her earlier mistake, she was passing his tests with flying colors.

All he said when she was finished and he'd anchored the line was "You go first. I'll follow."

She stared at him. "Don't you trust my knots?"

This was one of those moments when the glacier glasses were too dark. He wished he could see her eyes and know if she was teasing. "Like everything else about you, the knots are perfect."

He should have known Chelsea wouldn't let him get away with that remark. She hooked on to the line, took a good grip and just before she stepped back over the edge she asked, "Does that intimidate you?"

Hell, yes, it disturbed him. He'd already discovered she could twist his insides into knots much less perfect than the ones she'd tied. Being with Chelsea was starting to feel like stepping off a high ridge without ropes. Flying without wings. Great until you came down to earth and crashed.

Chelsea couldn't remember the last time she had felt this tired. But it was a good sort of tired, bone deep with contentment now they were back at the shack. Knowing the Sherpas were camped outside and would do all the cooking sure helped.

She pushed back into the wall at the corner of her bed, her down parka between it and her back, happy to have succeeded with only one small learning curve to blot her record.

And one huge discovery—she enjoyed being kissed by Kurt. She relived the moment. His lips had tasted sharp and icy, worlds away from the heat his mouth and tongue had generated.

And had he enjoyed kissing her? He was the one who had brought up the attraction between them. What had she done apart from falling into his arms that had startled that curse out of him? *Damn you, Chelsea.*

He'd been blowing hot and cold from the first, telling her "No," then changing his mind, but she had put that down to her persuasive talents. Not this time. Kurt was an enigma that she might be better to leave unsolved.

The door opened and the man in her thoughts appeared holding a steaming basin. "Dinner?" she asked.

"The meal will be ready soon, but before then, let's deal with your feet." He set the aluminum basin down on the crushed-rock floor. Water slopped back and forth and a few drops went over the side. Light wisps of steam wafted in front of his tanned face and tangled with his lashes as he hunkered down in front of her bed. His beard had grown thicker and darker. She called up the memory of the soft brush of stubble against her cheek, the feel of it tickling her lips. A swift heat spike impaled her down low.

Kurt brought her back to the mundane. "Okay, let's take your socks off."

Glad to have an excuse for the flush she felt suffusing her face, Chelsea hit him with an indignant "Why?"

"I'm going to wash your feet."

"No need—I'm a big girl. I can wash my own feet."

"The last thing I expected from Chelsea Tedman was coyness. C'mon, Teddy bear, it's something you can't afford on a climb when you're dependent on one another."

"What did you call me?"

"I called you Teddy bear, Teddy. Did no one call you that at school? I'd have thought with a name like Tedman…" He let his words taper off and replaced them with a grin that made her insides curl. She saw it so infrequently. "You do the growl so well, and I always manage to make you bite," he added.

"Huh, I'd like to bite you right now!"

Silence rocked the shack. The heat of his gaze burned where it passed over her, a startling, pathetically vulnerable and all-feminine sensation that made her limbs go weak, until he blinked then said, "So let's get to it before the water cools. Not that it takes long to heat at this altitude, but fuel costs a bomb to transport."

Realizing she had no choice, Chelsea wiggled forward on

the makeshift bed and hooked a finger in the top of her thick wool sock, thankful she'd changed them when she'd freshened up. She'd been limited to four pair, and each night she hung the ones she'd removed outside to air. Washing them was out of the question.

"Both socks. There's room in here to soak two feet at a time."

Did he remember how big her feet were? She pulled off the last sock and gingerly slipped her toes into the water. It wasn't as hot as the steam implied. The weary soles of her feet felt the warmth and she sighed, as if he'd handed her a delicious Belgian chocolate truffle. Her favorite.

He gazed straight at her, all business. "How does that feel?"

She closed her eyes, as if her pleasure was private. "Great. I like getting spoiled." But her eyelids snapped open again as water cascaded over the high arches of her feet, directed by a trickle from Kurt's hand. He scooped up some more, skimming skin dampened by his last effort. His touch set up a tingle in her belly, as if he'd touched her up there instead of three feet lower. She squeezed her knees and thighs together to ease the needy ache. It simply added to her awareness of him.

Chelsea wiggled her toes and stretched them out straight when she wanted to curl them under. They were the only muscles she dared move as tension from the water massage built inside her. How humiliating. She couldn't let him see how deeply he affected her

He tapped her left foot. "Okay, give me this one."

Startled by the request, she obediently did as he asked, placing her foot in his hands. "What are you going to do?"

"Examine it for bruises and blisters. You have an even bigger day ahead tomorrow. Can't be too careful."

He ran the palm of his hand along the sole of her foot and

up around her heel, massaging the hollows on either side of her Achilles tendon. She shivered. "My feet are very sensitive."

Sensitive! Who was she trying to fool? She'd always been ticklish, but she had just that second discovered how sensual his touch felt as his thumb prodded the base of her toes. Much more of this and the top of her head would blow off. She would give him a hundred years to stop what he was doing.

"It tickles because of all the sensitive nerve endings, like at the tips of our fingers—probably something we needed while we were swinging around in the trees." Kurt smiled, looking really relaxed. If it weren't for the facial hair he would have looked younger, boyish. "You Jane, me Tarzan."

"Wrong continent. And I seem to remember a dearth of trees in the neighborhood."

He perched the ball of her heel on his knee and began checking her other foot. "Spoilsport. I was just warming to the subject."

Warm? She was red-hot. She leaned back on her hands and turned her gaze to the ceiling as he gave her second foot the same treatment as the first.

Her heels sat on the long, lean muscle of his thigh, its strength pronounced by the way he crouched, all his weight on his toes. She heard the basin scrape the floor as he slid it to one side. Next moment he was drying her feet, carefully attending to each toe in turn.

Didn't he know what he was doing to her?

Or was Kurt Jellic simply a tease?

"Right, that's done. Swivel around and put your feet up on the bed. I've got some liniment that will toughen them up."

Liniment. She thought of the stuff she'd used on her horse. There was nothing sensual about that smell. Her mood was blown.

"Thanks for looking after me." Chelsea swung her feet up onto her bed and tucked the foot of her thick sleeping bag over them to keep them warm. The air chilled quickly as soon the sun began its journey behind the mountains.

"No problem." Kurt uncoiled his legs and stretched his arms. As he straightened, she got her first real indication she hadn't been the only one turned on by his efforts. She saw him catch the direction of her glance. His mouth twisted to one side as he scrubbed at his beard, his fingers rasping against his hair-roughened chin, but he didn't embarrass her by mentioning it.

"If there's any hot water left, maybe you could shave."

He flung the towel on top of his sleeping bag and retrieved the basin from the floor. The look he sent her was strictly unapologetic. "No point."

Did he think she was propositioning him? Sure, she'd enjoyed his kiss. That didn't mean she was up for anything more. Not even a fling. She wasn't ready, wasn't sure she'd ever be ready to get that intimate with a man again. Jacques, the Frenchman she'd thought she was in love with, had shown her that throwing caution to the wind led to disaster. She had let him into her bed, into her heart—a heart that had been vacant since the day Atlanta had married Bill and left her in the hands of a cold, imperious father who thought love was for the masses.

Hence the arrangement he'd made for her sister and Bill Chaplin.

Of course, she'd rebelled. Their family life had become so acrimonious, her father had shipped her off to school. It wasn't a particularly happy period of her life. All that had kept her going had been her horse and knowing that in a roundabout way she had won.

What a little stinker she had been.

Atlanta had tried over and over to tell her she really did love Bill, but all Chelsea had seen was her father's manipulations.

She had been blind to the manipulations of Jacques.

At least the wedding ring hadn't been on her finger when she'd discovered Jacques's extracurricular activities. And she'd been saved from paying out the alimony he'd planned to live on once he had divorced her.

As Kurt had discovered today, she learned from her mistakes, didn't make them twice. With Atlanta and Bill dead, she might be twice as rich as she had been before. She hadn't really given it much thought until now, but some people might think it made her twice as attractive.

For her it meant double the trouble.

Kurt heeled the door shut with his boot and announced, "Dinner is served." He proceeded gingerly into the room, a food-laden metal plate balanced in each hand. On top of that he held the neck of the liniment bottle in the crook of his little finger.

He moved carefully, mindful that the forks tucked in his waistband would stab him in eight places if he leaned too far forward.

Chelsea sat on the bed hugging her knees with her arms. She shuffled into a sitting position on the edge of the bed as he said, "Pick a plate—any one." Then he passed one of the forks over and sat on the other bed facing her, the plate balanced on his knees. No chance of getting burned. The food had already cooled.

"Eat up while it's still slightly warm." He held up the liniment bottle. "This can wait until after the meal."

He watched her eye the bottle, a hint of suspicion in the lift of an eyebrow. Sometimes Chelsea was so easy to read.

"You're not expecting me to drink that?"

Tipping it back, he read the label with as much attention as he'd given to the bottle of Pinot Gris in the hotel restaurant.

"Well, it does contain alcohol, but are we really that desperate? There are other components in the mix that could turn the hardest stomach."

He saw her eyebrows rise as if to say, "What, exactly?"

"No, don't ask. I don't want to put you off your food." He was simply mucking around, but knew he hadn't fooled Chelsea.

"And what's in this?" She poked at the one-pot mix on her plate with her fork. "Anything I should be wary of?"

"Nothing but rice, onions and a few almost fresh vegetables. Any lumps in the mix are probably tofu. It keeps better than meat. You need to increase your protein intake. Don't think calories, think energy."

Chelsea stared at the bland-looking lumps on her plate, stirring them with her fork. Kurt quickly shoveled in a couple of forkfuls. "Actually, it doesn't taste half bad. Enjoy it while you can. It has the value of looking a lot tastier than some of the freeze-dried stuff we'll end up eating if you ever make it up top."

She took a mouthful and swallowed, followed by another. When Chelsea looked up and caught him watching her, she nodded. "I've tasted worse. I just cannot, for the life of me, remember where."

"Have you never gone anywhere that wasn't first class?" He had no agenda this time, hadn't spoken his thought aloud to emphasize their differences.

Her mouth quirked at the corners. The rest of the smile was in her eyes. The gray in them lightened, sparking as she said, "Does cleaning out my horse's stall count? I can swing a pitchfork as well as you handle an axe."

Kurt didn't believe her for a moment. Why would she work when chances were she owned the stable?

Part of him wished he'd never brought up the thorny subject of attraction. But he believed in being honest with his clients, and the sexual tension they generated sparked between them as if a live transmission line had broken loose.

The kiss should never have taken place. But then, he'd never sunk into the mires of temptation until he'd met Chelsea. God, he loved the way she growled at him. At times her vociferous reactions held all the fear factor of the Teddy bear he'd teased her with, though he didn't think she'd appreciate being told she was cute.

Damn, he knew better than to act on the attraction.

But then, everyone was allowed one slip.

A ball of pain gathered inside Kurt as he cupped his palm and gathered the liniment into it. The next few minutes would be like the night of the living damned. "Okay. Let's get to it."

"I could do it myself."

He sniffed the liquid in his palm and canned that scenario. "No sense in us both ending up with hands that smell like a spicy mint julep." The light from the kerosene lamp Kurt had lit earlier chased shadows into the corners of the room, but instead of feeling cozy they hung like venomous bats.

If this was how abstinence made him feel now, God help him in the coming weeks.

It wasn't as if he was hung up on sex, but he'd had his moments. What man of thirty-four hadn't? It had been easy doing without when there was no female within twenty miles that he wanted. No sacrifice.

But he wanted Chelsea.

Damn straight he did.

And that hurt. He didn't mean just because he was turned on most of the time he was around her. Human nature was to blame for that. All Chelsea had to do was look at him a certain way, or brush against his arm or thigh accidentally.

Blast! She was the first woman who looked as if she'd been made for him. The first woman who came higher than his shoulder and whose body looked designed to take his weight.

Chelsea's eyes snapped wide and her nose twitched. The map she'd been looking at dropped from her hand. He noticed a flicker of apprehension in their gray innocent depths, or maybe it was just that her hair was tousled and made her look younger than her twenty-eight years. "Just be glad you don't need to use that stuff as aftershave." She cocked her head to one side and studied him. "Men are lucky they can grow beards."

A bellow of laughter ripped out of his throat and slammed against the rough stone walls.

"For warmth," she said, as if trying to qualify her outrageous statement.

"Believe me, Teddy bear, that's the last thing I'd wish on any woman. You're better off making do with a scarf."

"Don't call me that. I hate being patronized."

She kicked out at his knee and he squatted back on his heels. "Now see what you made me do. I've spilled liniment on the floor. How about I call you Teddy, then? That way we can pretend you're just one of the guys."

He stood so he could scuff the stain on the floor with the toes of his light hiking boots. Changing tack, he sank onto the end of her cot. "Here goes. The smell isn't too unpleasant."

Refilling his palm, he thought to warn her. "It will be cold at first because of the alcohol. Don't jump when I touch your feet."

Chelsea leaned back on her hands, pointing one set of toes at him. "This high enough?"

"Sure, as long as you're comfortable. Maybe you'd be better lying down." *Wrong thing to say.*

He watched the smile freeze on her face as her foot slowly began to sink back down. "Look, forget that heat-of-the-moment kiss. It never happened. I don't want to pounce on you."

He cupped her heel in his dry hand and began working the liniment into her foot, hoping he'd done a better job of convincing Chelsea than he had himself. When she shivered, he said, "Don't worry. This stuff warms up on your skin."

And beautiful fine skin it was. His callused fingers and palm had felt scratchy by comparison when he'd bathed her feet. "It's almost a crime to try toughening your feet—like turning a silk purse into a sow's ear."

He got no argument this time, just a lazy murmur as if she hadn't been listening, and by the time he got to her second foot, she looked as if she'd fallen asleep. He would have liked to think it was his ministrations that had zonked her out, but poor kid, she'd put in a good day's work. She deserved her slumber.

Tomorrow would test more than her stamina. He'd already given a couple of Sherpas orders to go out ahead of them in the morning with some of the aluminum ladders they'd trekked in. On Everest, most of the crevasses they had to cross would already be bridged. All part of the $65,000 fee it cost to use the fixed lines that had been laid out before the season proper began.

He'd told them to look for a crevasse that wasn't too wide. It wouldn't pay to scare Chelsea before she'd gained some confidence in the process. But where they had to climb to locate Bill and Atlanta was away from the preformed trail, which took the Lhotse Face to the South Col, then the Hillary Step to the summit.

Once they left the glacier West Cwm, they'd be on their own. Just like last time.

"What are you thinking about?"

"I thought you'd dozed off, but if you must know, I'm thanking God you don't have the same ambition as Bill. His idea was to follow the route of the U.S expedition of 1963. They conquered Everest via the more difficult West Ridge."

Yeah, he was thankful that this time they only had to reach the bodies. That would be more than enough for a rookie like Chelsea.

"Was I that bad?"

What could he say? That he hoped she had half her sister's agility. "No, but tomorrow we'll be crossing a crevasse on the rungs of a narrow ladder. If you're anything like your sister it won't be a biggie. She almost skipped across them, said all her years of ballet had helped. If she could keep her balance on the tips of her toes, she said, how much easier were huge climbing boots?"

"She was good. I used to love watching her on stage."

"I can't understand how she lost her balance and took Bill with her. It was the last thing I'd expect."

And it didn't make sense.

"Tell me what you do at the embassy," he said, to change the subject. "Is it interesting work?"

Chelsea lifted one eyebrow and matched it with a curl of her lip, and then her eyes narrowed. She looked almost threatening. Then her spontaneous grin turned it into a joke. "Don't ask me. Then I won't have to lie."

She might be useless at ballet, but she was a damn good actress. "You mean if you told me you'd have to kill me?"

She pointed a finger at him and laughed as she took aim. "Right first time," she said as her laughter turned giggly. "Really I'm just a lowly translator. But it gives me an excuse to live in Paris, and that I love."

Chapter 6

Chelsea's week was almost up.

Yesterday she and Kurt had climbed to the highest point of the glacier—16,500 feet—where they had camped overnight.

Up here, everything they did sucked up just a little more energy. And it would be worse when they climbed above the Western Cwm. She was thankful they wouldn't have to go as high as the Death Zone. Simply thinking the name made her shudder. Somewhere along the line the competitive gene must have been left out of her makeup. Well, except maybe when it came to horses, though winning had never been the be-all and end-all of riding in gymkhanas. She had always gotten more pleasure out of the feel of the horse under her, muscles rippling with strength and vigor.

Her mind went blank for a second as sensation took over and the whole segued into a vision of Kurt naked, all ropy muscles and male strength. Darn—not the best moment to become aroused, with Kurt belaying her down from the top, and her trying to cope with a greater degree of difficulty than she'd faced until now.

She ripped the picture of him out of her head.

Her feet touched the shelf. It was narrower than it looked from above, barely five feet wide. The way up, walking the top of the ridge had been longer, but an easier ascent.

She waved to Kurt. "Your turn." She watched him start down. He made it look so simple. His big body didn't bend to the will of the glacier; he used his skills and technique to overpower it. But then, he had made climbing his life. That was another of the differences between them. Sure, she gained pleasure from each new achievement, but aches and pains dulled the edge of the splendor laid out in front of them with each ridge or icefall they conquered.

Conquered, hah! Her mother's family had followed in the footsteps of the conquistadors. In this age there were few places on earth men hadn't been. Goodbye the moon, hello Mars.

Her mother's bloodline must have been well watered down by the Tedman half, for at one stage her mother had dominated the riding circuit. Agueda Filipa y de la Chavez, *star,* became Agueda Tedman, second wife, mother and *star.* Chelsea had a collection of videos of her mother eventing at places like Badminton, but she'd destroyed the one where her mother had broken her neck at the water jump. The way her father had destroyed the horse.

Taking riding lessons at boarding school had been just one more way of defying him.

He had been wise enough to let it go, knowing depriving her of funds would have no effect—not when half of her mother's fortune had come to Chelsea without strings or restrictions.

Yes, if she'd inherited anything from her mother's blood-line it had been willfulness.

She wasn't going to climb halfway up Mount Everest for a prize or trophy. No, the moment she had started her quest, she had begun to suspect that Sydney Carton from Dickens's *A Tale of Two Cities* must be one of her ancestors.

It is a far, far better thing I do…

Obviously she had more of her father in her than she had so far acknowledged. She was making this sacrifice for his business. To make sure it didn't go under in a huge scandal that would take thousands of little, ordinary people with it.

And the funny side was, there *was* a funny side to all her meanderings. She looked down at the huge vista in front of her and began to laugh, holding her ribs and chortling out loud, "Good grief, will you listen to yourself?" The thin air had to be responsible for all these delusions of grandeur.

She was still laughing when Kurt landed beside her.

"What's up?"

"Nothing that will translate. Let's just say I suddenly realized I was taking myself far too seriously. If there is one thing climbing mountains does, it is show you how small a part you actually play in the continuum."

Her hand swung in an arc that took in the whole view. "Look out there. Is it any wonder we came past so many monasteries on the way to Syalkyo? This place makes you believe in God."

"You mean you didn't before?"

Kurt's smile didn't patronize. It held understanding and a certain something that made her insides tremble, but most of all, it was if he was telling her, "Been there, done that."

He was already reeling in the lines to use on the next step of their descent. Kurt had an effortless way of doing things that made them look simple. But she recognized now that spoke of self-confidence and a vast experience in everything he did to keep them both safe.

"I did believe, but more in a general way. Up in these mountains it's as if you can see the hand of God. That's what makes the difference."

"Welcome to the club. But I should tell you that the Sherpas believe *he* is female, a goddess."

Chelsea didn't have to reply; her smile said it all as the feminist in her won the day. So the Sherpas took comfort that the mother of all gods was with them on their perilous climbs into her lap.

Once Kurt had fixed the lines for the next section of their descent, he grinned at her and said, "Ready, Teddy?"

His teeth were a blinding white against the darkness of a beard he'd never gotten around to shaving. She was sure that behind his ski goggles his eyes were alight with enjoyment…and something else, something more elusive. They might not be having sex, but the attraction Kurt had spoken of the first morning on this glacier hadn't gone away. It had as much of a physical presence as the safety line that more often than not was strung from Kurt to her, keeping them together.

How long had she been staring at him? Quickly she caught hold of the line and took up the little joke that for some reason she had started letting him get away with. "Ready, teddy, go!"

Back at the rim of the ice shelf, Chelsea took the same kind of nervous leap her heart had been taking during this week she'd shared with Kurt—off the edge of the world.

Kurt looked back over his shoulder. Thin, see-through clouds that resembled huge wedding veils were building up over the glacier. The wind had been steadily picking up, strengthening its tug. Even now as he turned to look back, it lashed his face with the ties of his hood, and dragged the air he was trying to suck in away from his mouth.

He switched his ice axe to his other hand and tucked the strings under his chin, slackening his speed until Chelsea caught up. The rope from one belt to the other lay in slack loops on the ground. "We need to step it up. Can you manage?"

"I'm feeling no pain. You set the pace, and I'll follow."

They were roughly a mile from the shack and had left the icefall behind. The surface underfoot was mainly ice and rocks brought down by the glacier over millions of years. A lot of damage could be done in the time it took to walk the distance to the shack, while the wind was doing forty-five, maybe fifty knots, growing stronger every minute.

"Take a look back there." He turned her, looping an arm around her shoulder, pointing up where they'd come from. Chelsea turned, the side of her pack pressed tight against his chest and her head almost touching his shoulder as she followed the straight line of his arm with her eyes.

"See those clouds swirling near the top? Most of that white stuff is windborne snow scraped off the glacier. We don't want to be out in the open when that hits. Be glad we kept our warmer parkas on this morning instead of changing."

Twisting her head to face him so her words couldn't be torn away by a wayward gust, she cupped her mouth to be heard. "You mean be glad it felt too cold on the ice to change out of what we'd slept in."

"That, too," he said, grabbing her arm as a huge gust rocked them together. It was the closest he'd voluntarily come to her since their kiss. Maybe he should kiss her again, just to take the significance out of it only happening once.

She pushed against his arm, cupping her mouth again. "What are we waiting for? Let's get out of here."

When they eventually reached the deserted shack, the ground around it was bare, wiped clear of the tents and paraphernalia the Sherpas and porters had used. Not a scrap of paper or can littered the ground. He ought to be pleased the men he'd employed this time knew how he felt about conservation. But another thought overshadowed it. How was he going to get through the night without touching her, or repeating that kiss?

Chelsea drew up beside him. "I never thought I'd be so glad to see this shack."

"I see that being in the mountains has downgraded your expectations somewhat."

"The Ritz by any other name, you mean?"

Kurt nodded. Last night he and Chelsea had slept side by side in a tent on the ice at the top of the glacier. Another new experience for her, one she would have to become accustomed to.

When they'd finished their descent of Ama Dablam, he'd unwillingly conceded he was going to have to make good on his promise to take her up Everest. Damn, at least another month of keeping his hands off her. In a fit of exuberance when he'd told her, Chelsea had flung her arms around him, but he'd dragged her arms away and told her, "Don't thank me yet. This isn't over—it's just the beginning."

He'd a notion that his deliberate withdrawal of anything physical was the reason that a mere meeting of lips continued to loom large in his memory.

He'd begun to look at her in a new light since she'd pointed her finger at his chest and pretended to shoot him. Whether she was an actress or comedienne, he'd gotten the impression that there was more to Chelsea than met the eye. That she wasn't simply a rich woman enjoying the prestige and perks that came through working in the American embassy. That the supreme confidence he'd taken for bossiness came not through being rich, but also from making her life count.

Kurt pressed his shoulder against the door. "Looks like we're definitely on our own. How are your cooking skills?"

"Nonexistent."

"Then it's just as well I can throw something together if need be."

If he discounted the sometimes virulent whistle of the wind, the area around the shack seemed oddly quiet. No chatter or pots rattling. He looked at his watch. "I wonder how far our team got before this struck."

Rei and Ang Nuwa, his cousin, were to have packed up, then joined the others on the trek to Base Camp, where everything would be set back up before he and Chelsea reached it.

Now he wished he could call them back.

Come off it, Jellic—be a man. It's only one night.

And it was going to be a long one.

He swiped at the powdering of snow coating their shoulders. No point in taking it inside. When he released the handmade wooden catch, the wind flung the door open. They tumbled inside full of breathless laughter as they jostled each other to be first, bumping against the sides of the door frame in their rush to escape the wind.

Shrugging off his backpack, Kurt dropped it where he stood, then braced his back against the door to force it closed. The gusts were growing fierce and he was glad of the roughly cut lengths of wood that held the door shut. Even then the wind buffeted the door hard enough to make it shake.

Daylight was minimal. For a change, at this time of day, the sky was dark. Larger windows might have made a little difference, but not much.

The odd giggle disrupted the huffing and puffing caused by Chelsea's exertions. He heard her pack hit the floor, then the zipper on her anorak slide down. Kurt tried to ignore the sexual ingredient of her stripping in the dark. Instead he concentrated on the damage that would be done if one of them tripped over their carelessly discarded packs.

On Everest the effects of any injury increased tenfold. Lack of oxygen stressed the body to its limits without adding the pressure to heal itself onto its struggle to survive.

One more danger to add to a long list. One more set of odds to beat, as he pitted his luck against the mountain.

"God, I think it's still too cold to take my jacket off," Chelsea said.

"Yeah, the temperature is plummeting, but shelter will soon take the edge off it. Offhand, do you remember where your headlamp is stashed? I feel a sudden urge to be able to see what I'm doing."

"No problem. I rolled it in a T-shirt on the top of my pack."

"Get it out, will you?" Kurt asked. "And check what they left behind in the way of food. I noticed a pile of stuff between the cots as I was blowing through the door." Kurt stripped off his gloves, then raked around in the pockets of his pack for the matches and lamp they'd used in their tent, a task made a whole lot easier once Chelsea retrieved and switched on a headlamp.

She totaled their resources. "They've left us the small kerosene stove, some bottled fuel, but not a huge lot—though I guess that's not really important, since most of the food they've left is freeze-dried. There are protein bars and some snacks, plus the bottled water. Also a few plates and a pan for using on top of the stove." The beam of light turned in his direction. "I've got my mug and some extra tea bags in my pack."

"Anything else? Any more protein bars or candy you haven't eaten? I'm asking because I'm not certain that this wind is going to die down overnight. I'll try to get a report on the satellite phone, but the link could be closed out by the storm. I'm worried that if there's a lot of weather coming our way, we'll need to conserve what supplies we have."

He took the gas mantle out of its protective case, fixed it to the gas cartridge and set it on the floor to set it alight. The match flared and in an instant they could actually see. For all they'd just gone through, Chelsea still looked damned sexy. Not an idea to reflect on while being shut up in small space with her for God knew how long.

Kurt made his thoughts do an about-face. "I've got a couple of gas cartridges. Are you carrying any?"

"I know I've got a partly used one, and I've the makings for a cooking top that it fits, still in the box I bought it in."

Kurt crossed the room. Their last mile back to the shack hadn't been a pleasure stroll. Twice he'd had to stop to refasten Chelsea's hood. He'd pulled her woolen ski cap down level with her goggles, but knitted balaclavas that covered everything but the eyes and nose would have done better, if they hadn't been somewhere near the bottom of their packs.

Damn, he should have known better. He was in charge of seeing no harm came to her, from him or anyone else.

"Let me see your face. Does it sting?"

Pink half circles painted the creamy cheeks where her snow goggles had finished. Kurt rubbed at them with the backs of his knuckles. "Just checking for windburn."

Her lips were very close to his. He held back, though that most natural of caresses had set off an explosion of heat inside his groin.

Oh, yeah. Circumspection had added to instead of subtracting from the attraction she wrought in him.

Testosterone, long denied, was having a field day.

Time to step back.

"How are you fingers and toes? No numbness?"

"I'm fine—honest. I'd tell you if I had any problems."

But would she? She was bright and gutsy, never seeming to let anything get her down for long—not anything she'd show him, at least.

Chelsea had secrets and they weren't all connected to her job. At times she'd begin saying something, mainly about Atlanta or her father, then she'd stop abruptly, pretending she'd lost her train of thought.

He'd come to realize there was some mystery, something so private that only Chelsea and Atlanta had known, and she wasn't about to confide in him.

But with the news rife with stories of child abuse these days, he'd begun to wonder. He'd refused to jump to any conclusions, though. It wasn't misery he saw smudging her gray eyes as she shut him out—more like fiery determination.

The same kind of spark had appeared this week with each new step he'd used to test her endurance. To all intents and purposes they might still be strangers, but if he'd been less cautious they might have been lovers.

Time was what he needed to earn her trust. The clock was ticking and there wasn't a lot of that commodity left between now and the end of the season. Standing here while they both froze wouldn't advance that goal. "Okay, before the wind gets any stronger, I'd better go out and hunt and gather."

Chelsea smirked. She always teased him about acting like the chief of his clan as he organized the Sherpas.

"There's a pile of juniper stored in the lean-to at the back of the shack," he said. "I didn't want to touch it, but what we have going now qualifies as an emergency."

He eased the hood of his dark green parka over his head and pulled the drawstring tight. "Close the door after me. I'll thump on it with my boot to be let back in, but it could take three trips, maybe more."

He eased his gloves back over his fingers, and before he reopened the door he teased, "While I'm out hunting and gathering, why don't you do the wifely thing and prepare something to eat?"

She tilted her chin at the challenge. Next second, Kurt was outside and the wind whipped away any smart-ass reply she might have made as she shut the door.

How many translators did it take to light a kerosene stove? One. There were no more available. Chelsea reasoned that if the porters could get it to light outside in the wind, she could do it inside. She put a lot of effort into pumping the fuel the way she had seen it done, then lit the match. It took, the fumes caught light and she sighed as if it was some great achievement. She could translate four other languages besides French, do the sort of task that required skill and speed, but so far the bureau hadn't asked anything more from her. She shrugged off the discontent niggling at her. So she would never set the spy network on fire the way some of her companions at the bureau did. Had she ever expected to? God help her if she had leaped into this adventure to retrieve Atlanta not without a second thought, but as a way of proving her worth. How utterly naive would that be? Jason Hart, chief of IBIS, had told her up front she would never be called on to work on a clandestine op. Her money, if not her face, made her too memorable.

How calculating if she was the sort of person motivated by nothing but personal glory. If any hint of selfishness lingered in her subconscious, she dismissed it now. Simply being here, seeing that money didn't matter that much when you were up against the immense challenge of the mountains, had changed her already.

By now, her compassionate leave had segued into AWOL. She had to get in touch soon or IBIS would send someone out looking for her.

When Kurt kicked at the door after his fourth trip outside, she had water heating on top of the stove and the two freeze-dried food packs warming in it for dinner.

Chelsea rushed to open the door once more, stepping back quickly as he was blown through the opening.

The scratchy juniper branches were soon added to the pile, and looking at the size of it, she wondered if Kurt knew something about the conditions he wasn't telling her.

"I reckon that will about do it. I lost as much as I managed to carry this time. The wind snatched off the top of the bundle and whisked it away. I think we can thank our lucky stars we're not perched on top of Ama Dablam in a tent."

Chelsea had been so lost in thought as she worked that the increase in noise in the past half hour hadn't sunk in until she tried to hear Kurt over the shrieks of the wind.

"Will the roof hold?" She looked up at the ceiling. If it fell in on them, she could stop troubling her conscience with wayward thoughts she couldn't control. More important, if anything happened to her, cousin Arlon would come into everything now. There was no one else. She should have told someone at the bureau about Atlanta and Maggie and the letter before she set out on her harebrained scheme.

"Don't worry about the roof until you see something flapping. Then it will be time to duck. Flying corrugated iron can do a lot of damage to the human body."

Chelsea's jaw dropped. They could die and he didn't seem the least concerned.

Kurt worked as he talked. His anorak came off, followed by his ski cap and goggles. Then he looked at her face. "Hey, I was joking. This building has stood up to winds like these for a lot of years and still looks sturdy. We need to be aware of the dangers, but not blow them out of proportion."

He wrapped an arm around her. "I'm sorry, real sorry if I frightened you. You act so tough most of the time, as if you could walk through flames and come out holding a toasted marshmallow, I forget to allow for a woman's vulnerable side."

"It wasn't your fault. I guess Atlanta's death has finally got through to me. I mean, how we can be here one minute and gone the next? Standing up on that ledge today really showed me how small I am." And how careless she had been by keeping everything to herself. She would call Josh McBride—Mac—at the Paris bureau first chance she got.

Standing there enclosed in Kurt's hug, she noticed that the front of his sweater was coated in a strip of dried juniper needles. At least this was something she could deal with now. "Keep your chin up, Kurt. I'll get rid of these prickles before they present a bigger danger than flying corrugated iron."

She had almost finished—only a few in the neck band of his sweater to go—when she remembered the food. "I'll be done here in a second, just in time for dinner. I'm not dead certain of the contents of each sachet, but we can share if one is better than the other."

"Sounds good to me." He looked down.

She caught a sparkle in his dark eyes—eyes hidden from view most of the time by glasses or goggles, along with the many subtle nuances of conversation. Not to mention warnings.

"Keep your head back. Just a couple more," she ordered.

"I think a few might have worked into my beard. Care to take a look?" Chelsea tossed the last of the needles into the cold fireplace, knowing he was teasing, wondering if she would take the bait.

His beard was softer than she'd imagined as she ruffled it with the tips of her fingers, smiling when her attentions drew a rumble from deep in his throat, like a tiger purring.

The tremors of her own reactions began way down past her larynx. The tips of her breasts peaked, drawn into tight beads that scraped the inside of her bra. If she'd been the type of woman who liked to ponder the whys and the wherefores, she'd have been out of luck. The moment Kurt's palm slid under her hair and curved around the nape of her neck her breath snagged in her throat. His hand was so big it was no effort for his thumb to tilt her chin higher.

His eyes blazed so bright the juniper might already be alight, spilling its reflection into his irises. That bright ember made her rise to her toes. His other hand caught her to him by the waist until not even the wind could pass between them.

She gasped, sucked oxygen into her starved lungs. The wind had dried her lips, but she resisted the desire to lick them. If this kiss was going to happen it had to be at Kurt's instigation and without her tempting him.

A hundred silly things teased her brain. Her hair needed to be washed, she smelled as sexy as a yak and hadn't a lick of makeup on her face to hide its imperfections. Kurt, if he wanted her, would have to take her at her worst. And he did.

His thumb moved from her chin to her lips, brushed across them as if they were made of satin, not dry as parchment. The warmth of his breath on her face caused her eyelids to flutter, to slide down, so heavy she couldn't hold them open.

A roaring noise that couldn't be blamed on the wind echoed in her ears as he angled his head, bumping noses, adjusting to fit. At the last minute her tongue slipped out to moisten her lips and touched his.

Kurt's arm tightened, gathered her closer than she'd thought possible. She stopped breathing. If he didn't cover her mouth with his soon, she would swoon away like a Regency heroine.

And then it happened.

Gentle at first, then hard, this was the kiss she remembered, had craved without rhyme or reason in her heart of hearts. This was the need she had tried to deny.

Then it was over.

Finished as suddenly as it had begun.

Kurt freed her from his embrace and her head spun from loss of equilibrium. This had never happened to her before. She placed her palm against his chest as if he was the only one holding the world steady.

He plucked her hand off his sweater to lift it to his lips. The kiss he dropped in the center of her palm was short on length, but long on intensity and sweetness. And when it was done he placed her hand on his cheek and rubbed lightly.

"Thanks for that. I had an itch that was driving me crazy."

He didn't say which itch she had scratched, but she'd bet her last dollar that it wasn't the one on his face.

He drew her with him until they were standing over the kerosene stove and a pan that had almost boiled dry. "Looks like dinner's ready. You did well while I was acting the alpha male."

Again there was more to his meaning than could be translated by ears alone, but his body language spoke volumes. He hunkered down and turned off the stove, then pierced the top of the foil on each packet with the knife he always carried on his belt. "Smells good. Guess this week's proved you're more than a pretty face."

Chelsea had no mirror to gauge her appearance in, but she knew that under no circumstances could anyone in his right mind use the adjective *pretty* to describe her. Kurt had to be blind not to see her as a tall, practically lanky woman in need of a haircut and facial. Blind, but which of the *L* words had put out his eyes? Was it lust or…? And did she really want to know one way or the other? After all, what did she really know about him?

Circumstances had thrown them together, but for all that, Kurt was still a stranger.

Chapter 7

As the wind strengthened, it found gaps around the window frames invisible to the human eye. Drafts whistled through the cracks and teased the hair on the back of Kurt's neck as he hunkered in front of the fireplace. Although the meal had warmed his insides, the air on his face and hands was decidedly chilly.

He'd waited as long as possible before lighting the fire. Their supply of wood was limited. But sleep would come more easily if they were already warm when they slipped inside their respective sleeping bags.

The needles took the flame first, cracking and hissing, licking the gnarled twists of wood with greedy ardor. As the first branches caught he tossed on two more.

Kurt heard the swish of nylon against nylon as Chelsea walked up behind him. A mug of tea appeared in his peripheral vision, so he held out a hand. "Thanks."

Turning, he lifted his gaze higher. Chelsea had both hands cupped around a similar mug as she shrugged her shoulders. "Sorry I can't offer you sugar or milk—not even powdered milk."

"No problem. The tea is hot and it's wet. That's what counts." He saw Chelsea shiver as she looked over his head at the flames. "It's not throwing out much heat yet, but once the stones warm up it will get nice and warm in here," he added.

"What I wouldn't give for an armchair to draw up in front of the fire." Chelsea sighed. "I have this sudden longing for creature comforts. I know it sounds ungrateful when I was the one who made all the demands to come here, but my bones are aching for a cushioned place to sit."

"Culture shock—coming from a five-star hotel to a shack in one easy leap." With his mind's eye he took stock of what was in the shack, wondering if he could do anything about it.

"Nowhere did I mention the word *easy*. Hard work yes, easy no. But it was worth it to hear I passed all your tests," Chelsea said.

She had at that, but in the forefront of his mind was the kiss they'd shared after she'd tweezed the juniper needles off his sweater. The feel of her mouth had been better than he remembered, its textures softer, silkier than any woman had a right to be after a week on the ice.

He'd been wrong. A second kiss hadn't been the answer.

"Tell you what. Why don't you hop into your sleeping bag?" he suggested. "Take the tea with you. The beds are the most comfortable spot around and an early night won't go amiss after a week testing whether or not you would make the cut."

He gazed down at the flames—safer than watching Chelsea's face, her lips, her lush mouth. He could still taste the idea of it. "I wouldn't say no to an early night myself," he went on. "And if the worst happens and we don't get out of here tomorrow we'll be conserving fuel." Conserving his sanity.

"Good idea. I am rather tired, and you are one-hundred-percent correct about me being strung out all week."

He heard Chelsea rustling around as she slid alone into her sleeping bag. Don't even think about it, Jellic!

He stayed where he was looking at the fire. It wasn't so much a case of out of sight, out of mind as out of temptation's way.

It was going to be one hell of a long month.

Surprisingly, for all the noise, Chelsea slept the whole night through. However, she could tell from the moment she blinked out of sleep that they wouldn't be going far today. Kurt was still asleep. No point in waking him, she thought. She hadn't heard him go to bed, but it was probably later than the early night he had mentioned. The man got by on only a few hours a night.

The day stretched ahead endlessly. Just the two of them, all day and all night in this small box, with nowhere to go, nothing to do. She closed her eyes and tried to compose her thoughts so she could fall asleep again. It didn't take.

She had no control over her mind or her body. It was if something had sent them a message that, *tick, tick, tick,* her biological alarm clock was about to go off.

Get a grip, Tedman. You should have more control.

But she didn't. She did have this feeling, though, that if she didn't commit murder first, she would very likely jump Kurt's bones.

"Another cup of tea?"

Kurt turned swiftly and nearly bumped into Chelsea. Although this was a small place, she managed to creep up on him easily. "Not this time." A beer sounded better, or even a shot of rotgut whiskey—anything that would take the edge off his nerves.

Chelsea had tidied everything in sight, swept up the ash in the fireplace and made cups of tea as if prohibition had been declared in Nepal. He raked in the pockets of his pack and found an old paperback mystery novel. The book curled at the edges from the way he'd shoved it into his pack.

He threw himself down on his bed, one arm behind his head, the paperback blocking his view of the rest of the shack. He'd read the book three times already, but so what? If he could lose himself in the story it might take his mind off losing himself in Chelsea.

Chelsea had found a small Swiss army knife with a manicure file in her toiletries bag. She sat on the edge of her bed, bent over her nails, filing them to within an inch of their life, continuously checking one hand against the other to see if they were even.

Neither of them had thought to bring a pack of cards, and they had run out of things to talk about two hours ago. She looked at her watch again. Too early yet to make the dinner—maybe a snack?

She threw down the file and shot to her feet.

Next moment Kurt followed her. "What?" His eyes darted, searching the shack. "What is it?"

She let out a little shriek. "Oh! You startled me."

"No, you startled me." His hands grasped her shoulders. "I thought there was something wrong. That you'd cut your hand with that nail file or something."

His hands slid down her arms and he lifted her fingertips to examine them. "Pretty, but wasted here."

She could feel the heat radiating off his chest. Smell him.

His scent acted like an aphrodisiac. Her eyelids drooped till she had to tilt her head back to look at him. Heart pounding, she resisted the urge to reach out, to lay her hands on him. "I was going for a snack. Want one?"

His pupils almost blacked out his irises, proving he was just as aroused as she was. Chelsea felt his hands slip farther down until his fingers circled her wrists. Her pulse juddered, missed a beat, then raced ahead of thought or reason. She swallowed, stating the obvious. "We shouldn't be doing this."

A pulse hammered in Kurt's temple, tapping out all the reasons she was right. It didn't mean he had to like them. He released her wrists as the fury of the wind gathered in a howl above the shack, echoing the feral baying in his mind, like a wolf deprived of its prey. It colored the tone of his voice, bleeding with sarcasm. "Babe, if we were doing anything, you wouldn't get me walking away like I'm going to now."

He turned his back on her and stepped away. Four paces and there was nowhere left to go but out into the storm. He thrust his hands into his pockets and reached for calm—a stupid thing to do, as it tightened his pants against an erection that was begging to be set free.

On the floor at his feet his big climbing boots sat with the satellite phone poking out the top of the left one. It gave him the excuse he needed to do something else with his hands and take the thunderclaps of tension roiling in the small room off his mind. "I think I'll check the weather, see how much longer this is going to last."

He didn't put a name to what he was referring to. The weather would change—it always did—but the need to make love with Chelsea didn't feel as if it was anything he could stick a use-by date on.

* * *

The twitchy feeling under Chelsea's skin was getting so bad she was glad to have the domesticity of heating food for their evening meal to keep her busy.

Kurt had already lit the lamp. It hung on a string from a beam on the ceiling, swinging gently in a draft whistling through one of the chinks the windstorm had exposed in the walls.

Her resistance was weakening. She had begun wondering what they would be doing now if she hadn't put the brakes on earlier. Would she be lying sated in his arms...?

Her brain did a double take as the word *sated* slipped into the silent conversation she was having with herself.

When had she ever experienced *sated?* Certainly not with Jacques. He would never occupy space on a list of legendary lovers. His talents were more cerebral than physical—but then he had been more interested in her money than her body. In fact, when the suave, handsome Frenchman with all his flattery had first invited her out, she'd had the uneasy suspicion that maybe he was looking to discover some of IBIS's secrets during pillow talk.

But all Jacques really had wanted to talk about was Jacques.

More to the point, was she going to let Jacques affect every relationship she went into? That would be giving him more relevance than he deserved.

Now, if she could only resolve Kurt's reservations so easily. To do that, she would have to know what these reservations were; so far he hadn't actually come straight out and told her. He had been up front with her when he acknowledged attraction zinging between them as if they were hot-wired together. It was the assurance that he wouldn't act on it that had begun to rub on her nerves.

She took a quick glance through the steam. Kurt was rebuilding the fire with the last of the juniper branches. The swinging lamp turned his crouched figure into a bright image one moment and a blurred one the next. Is that how she wanted to go through her time in this world, with only a blurred memory of Kurt? Or did she prefer the full Technicolor one?

The prediction he had received from the weather bureau was turning out to be a good one, Kurt thought. The wind had begun to die down.

Though he always checked the forecast, he didn't always trust them. Mainly because of what had happened to friends in New Zealand. They had set off to walk a ridge with an assurance of bright weather. But when the cold clear air flowing from the Antarctic crashed into warm moist winds from the Pacific Ocean, the unpredictable happened. Within fifteen minutes they were in the middle of a weather bomb. Less than an hour later they had almost died from hypothermia.

Thump. The toe of Chelsea's boot kicked his. Kurt grabbed the plate balanced on his knee and looked up and lost his bet with himself that he could spend the rest of the evening thinking of anything but Chelsea. "What?"

"Something dreadful just occurred to me."

"You came to Nepal and left the iron switched on?"

"No, silly. I don't do things like that. I wanted to tell you I've actually enjoyed my dinner."

Kurt looked at the few forkfuls left on his plate and at Chelsea's empty one. "They do say hunger is the best seasoning you can get for a meal, and we haven't exactly been digging in to the supplies," he said, then quickly finished eating before the rest of his food got cold.

"We didn't have a lot to begin with, but since it looks like we're going to be out of here tomorrow, I've decided to allow myself a chocolate bar," Chelsea announced.

"Women and chocolate. I never met one who didn't love it." He got to his feet and held out his hand for her plate. Cleaning up would give him something to do that would keep him out of mischief, out of Chelsea.

She tilted her head up and to one side, her eyes wide, bright and luminous in the gaslight. She licked her unpainted lips, which added a soft sleek glow to their fullness. Her eyelashes fluttered, shading her cheek. "Didn't you know that some of us think it's better than sex?"

He didn't know what kind of game she was playing, but he decided to join in. He studied her intently, letting his gaze travel from the top of her head to the soles of her shoes. "Then you've been sleeping with the wrong men." Kurt hunkered down and dropped the plates into the pan of water Chelsea had used to heat their meal. As he stood again, he asked, "Fancy a drink of brandy to go with that chocolate? Somewhere in my pack I have a flask, and if you're going to act the sinner you might as well sample them all."

"Well, I had thought of making tea...." She hesitated, but didn't look away.

There was something going on at the back of her eyes—more games? When he played he played to win, but maybe this was one time he should disqualify himself.

"What kind of brandy is it?" She tossed the question into the gathering silence.

"Good stuff. Bill gave it to me. Said it was medicinal."

"I'll get the mugs."

She was holding them up in front of her when he turned around with the flask. He shoved into his pants pocket one of the packets he'd found beside the brandy.

He looked down into the blue mug and began to pour. The sound of the liquor hitting the bottom took him straight back to the night she'd come sneaking into his room at the tavern. He straightened the flask, flipping the lid shut as his eyes left the mug and the contours behind it filled his mind. His vision grew fuzzy as he recalled the feel of her curves in his hand.

"This one's mine." Blindly he reached for the mug and tossed back the contents. Then he dropped the flask, took her cup and threw both mugs down.

Chelsea's bottom lip dropped as the mugs hit the floor. He took the step that brought them thigh to thigh, heart to tripping heart, and finally mouth to mouth. He wrapped her in his arms and gave up the fight to ignore the attraction that had made him scratchy and frustrated. And horny as a goat since he'd realized the consequences of giving in to the allure of the stranger who'd come looking for his help. Let her keep her secrets. For now he'd be satisfied with her body.

The moment his arms enfolded her, Chelsea knew this was what she had been angling for all along with her quips about sex and chocolate. She just hadn't known he would be so fierce, so thrilling. His mouth tasted heady from the brandy. She supped it from his lips, his tongue, sucking until she was drunk on sensation and wild enough to throw caution to the wind.

The kiss went on and on, never ending. She never wanted it to end. Her arms slid around Kurt's back with breathless haste.

She hugged him tighter, felt the urgency of his erection pressing her belly. So what if she'd known him only a few days? The rough kindness she had met from him reassured her that even at fever pitch Kurt would take care of a more delicate partner.

Wanting, needing closer, she hooked one leg around his while her hands worked at pulling his shirt and undershirt out of the back of his pants. Just to touch. She had to touch.

Her hands slid up the wide expanse of his back and found a spot that made him groan aloud—music to her ears. Chelsea sighed as the sound rippled through the palms of her hands. "I didn't know skin could feel so good, so warm and sleek."

"I always thought your skin would feel creamy, and velvety, like magnolia petals." Kurt's hands dived under her shirt. "And it does."

His fingers slid around the bottom edge of her sports bra. "Front fastening?"

"No fastening. It's a pull-on."

"Then I guess it will have to pull up."

She almost fell as his hands covered her. His fingers plucked at her nipples, and her breasts responded.

His mouth was on her neck, kissing her seductively until her sanity shivered with pleasure. They went into overload when he slipped one hand down the front of her pants and caressed her.

"I'll give you a hundred years to stop that," she whispered achingly.

"Not long enough." Kurt gently bit down on her earlobe and felt her squirm with delight. He drew back. "You taste so damn good, Teddy bear."

He could tell she was ready for him, hot and wet, from the moment he'd touched her below. He slid a long finger inside her, rubbing her with the heel of his hand. She pressed closer and he held still a moment. Damn it, he was shaking. He needed her, and he needed her now. Slipping his other hand around her back to pull her closer, he tilted his head back and released the deep-throated rumble of possession that had been ripping his chest apart.

Her lips were warm on his throat, her teeth sharp on the

cord of his neck as she fought for his attention. "I can't wait. I want you now."

He started to say he wasn't prepared, then remembered the packets he'd found beside the brandy flask. As soon as one problem was solved another cropped up. "Damn, we're both wearing boots. They'll take forever to get off."

"Mine are unlaced. This is no time for niceties—just one will do."

With Chelsea's "Hurry up" ringing in his ears Kurt reached behind him and pulled off the boot she dug into the back of his thigh.

"Look in my pocket. Protection."

"My hero," she whispered.

The wait became more agonizing as her slim fingers searched his pocket. "I thought you were in a hurry?"

Damn, he wanted to feel her breasts against him, to see the nipples that had tightened in his fingers. He didn't have enough hands. "I want to feel you against me."

"Next time. Lean back so I can cover you."

Her hands were at the waist of his pants. Kurt's breath locked and held as her hand wrapped around him. Eyes scrunched, he shut out everything but the sensation of warmth, her touch. He shook at the intensity of her touch. He'd wanted Chelsea from the first moment he'd held her, and reality far surpassed anything he could imagine.

Taking Chelsea at her word that niceties had gone out the window, he grappled with pulling down her pants. Her skin was hot as his big hands cupped her bottom, hoisting her up against him as he twisted. Heading for the nearest wall, he crushed her back against it and thrust inside.

Hot, wet, pulsing, his climax was racing toward him like hell on wheels. He needed to slow down to make it good for

Chelsea, but the way her muscles squeezed he was fighting a losing battle.

He covered Chelsea's mouth with his, filling it with his tongue as he thrust once, twice. On the third stroke he swallowed her moans, and on the fourth they reached the top and crashed over the edge of reason.

Even as he spilled inside her he recognized this hormonal-driven frenzy had been madness. Now that he knew how fantastic making love to Chelsea felt, would he ever be able to give it up?

Chapter 8

The second time, they made it to the pile of mattresses and sleeping bags Kurt had thrown onto the floor. Their clothes followed, tossed in an untidy heap, and they were both unashamedly naked.

Chelsea assessed Kurt's magnificent body with her eyes, touched the long ropy muscles with her hands, kissed his neck and the width of his shoulders, shivering in awe at what this fantastic man could do to her. How he could make her feel.

Had she ever felt more like a woman?

Of all the men she had ever met he was the strongest in both body and mind. And for tonight he was all hers.

She laid her hands on the sides of his face, pulling it down to hers for his kiss. As their lips met, he asked, "What's my name?"

"Kurt."

"Remember it, Teddy bear. I want to hear you shout it when you come apart in my arms."

Just the thought almost made her climax again.

He sank onto the sleeping bags with her, holding her as if he never wanted to let go. It made her feel so wanted. No one had wanted her like this before. Not ever.

A juniper branch on the fire spat oil into the flames. Out of the corner of her eye she saw sparks fly up the chimney. Then their lips met and the flames were inside her. A burning passion she hoped would never die.

He parted her legs. She let him in, reveling in the weight of his body on hers. He thrust, as if laying claim to her, *Chelsea*, the woman under him. Making sure she'd always remember him.

Squashed tight against Kurt in his sleeping bag, Chelsea sighed as she awakened, remembering the comfort of her big soft old-fashioned bed with its squishy pillows and feather quilts in her Paris apartment. They could stay there for days. Kurt had such stamina.

He didn't seem able to get enough of her. It was as if he expected them to say goodbye when they left the shack. But that wouldn't happen. He'd promised to take her up the Southwest Face, and she trusted him to keep his promise.

He had treated her with a courtesy she hadn't met in a long time. Certainly not from Jacques, who hadn't cared if she found satisfaction from his lovemaking. Of course, she hadn't known then he was only using her. They hadn't even decided on a wedding date and Jacques had been planning how to compromise her. Planning to pay one of his friends to ensure he came out as the wronged husband, with his pockets stuffed with Tedman money.

Funny how she had managed to fall for two such dissimilar men. Chelsea found no humor in the thought that she might have married Jacques, and therefore, never met Kurt.

"You okay, Teddy?" Kurt's voice was relaxed and sleepy.

"Mmm I'm nice and warm and pleasantly surprised that your sleeping bag could hold both of us."

His mouth breathed next to her ear. She had enjoyed the soft shooshing noise he made as he slept. Now he whispered, "Listen."

"I don't hear anything."

"The wind has died down. Looks like we're good to go."

"It's arrived far too fast."

"Yeah, but at least we had last night."

She hated the finality in his tone. It frightened her. She shivered, but before she could say anything he had rolled over so she lay alongside him.

"God, Chelsea," he began. When he didn't use his nickname for her she knew it was going to be bad.

"You know it's never going to work. Us. The way we met is against it. There would always be someone willing to point the finger. Money can bring more problems than it's worth. Trust me, Chelsea. Even people who have known me for years were looking at me sideways when those rumors started spreading. I have no witness, no proof of how the accident happened. Only my word."

Air locked in her burning lungs at the thought of Kurt giving her up. *Was she being used again?*

"Your word is good enough for me." The declaration was as close as she dared come to saying she thought she was falling for him. Kurt had enough on his plate without discovering he might be breaking her heart.

One thing for sure—Jacques hadn't managed to break it. He'd only made her spitting mad.

"Thanks for the vote of confidence, Teddy. I don't know what I did to earn your trust, but I sure as hell won't break it in a hurry."

Chelsea fizzed with frustration. Her words hadn't changed the stubborn set of his mouth.

It had taken all her energy to prove she was fit for this climb, knowing that if she had failed even one of his tests, he would have turned her down.

Then where would she be? Stuck at the foot of Everest, with the key she needed to save Tedman Foods fastened to a chain around Atlanta's neck halfway up the mountain. That's where her priorities should lie. Not in wondering where the next kiss was coming from.

Well, at least she had discovered right away that nothing to do with Kurt was going to be easy. Forget sex, absolutely fantabulous sex, the best she'd had in her life.

From Kurt's comments it was obvious there was something he didn't want to tell her, some reason for him to be almost paranoid about the damage rumors could do. Yeah, Kurt did have a secret—one he didn't trust her enough to share.

And that hurt.

Then it made her wonder if he was in the least concerned about the secrets she was keeping from him.

Kurt glanced across the room at Chelsea. She was shrugging into her pack. Their backpacks were much heavier than the ones they'd shouldered back from the glacier, and even though he'd taken the bulk of extra weight, it still bothered him that he had to ask her to carry more.

"Can you manage?" He should have helped her into the pack, but the memories of last night were too fresh. Too hot. How could he touch her without pulling her into his arms?

She patted the belt across her middle into place. "Teddy's ready to go." She grinned, using his pet name for her. Why had he even thought that was funny? It was the sort of thing that could give the extent of their relationship away to other people.

Kurt was finding it hard to meet her eyes this morning. Not that he felt guilty over what they'd shared. Asking her to deny what they'd shared stuck in his craw.

But how to make her understand without letting all his dirty family secrets hang out? Though he supposed if necessity drove him to it, he'd have to tell her about his father. That would make her think twice or maybe three times about wanting more from him than his services as a guide.

Hell, he remembered the first time some TV documentary on bent cops had brought it all up again. The story about Milo Jellic had barely resurfaced when his brother's fiancée's father had done his damnedest to break the engagement off. It didn't help that the guy had been Drago's boss, as well. In the end her father had gone to the length of contaminating fifty thousand gallons of wine and blaming it on Drago. He'd blackened his eldest brother's name in the wine-making industry. By rights, Drago should have been making his own wine, not writing articles and books about other people's.

He knew as soon as he spoke she was going to flash him one of those looks that said he was being a pain in the ass, but he couldn't stop himself. "You okay about leaving everything that happened last night behind us once we close the door of the shack? From then on, all we have is a business relationship."

As he'd expected, her mouth tightened. He hoped once they began mingling with the other climbers at Base Camp she'd be more adept at hiding her emotions.

"You don't have to tell me again, Kurt. I get what you are saying. I don't understand it, not unless you get some sort of sadistic pleasure from depriving us of a little harmless sex."

Hell, he would never understand women, but this one had

a way of getting under his skin and making him squirm with anger as well as lust. "Let me reiterate as succinctly as possible. Bill and Atlanta were rich. You stand to gain by their deaths. I was there when they fell and died, but I had the misfortune to survive. All it needs is for us to start cozying up for someone to start whispering collusion. Now do you understand?"

She nodded.

"Good. Let's hit the trail. Close the door behind you on the way out."

"Sure thing. We wouldn't want the mice to get back in."

He let her get the last word. It was the least he could do, and since she was behind him she couldn't see his wry smile. If anything, her remark highlighted the differences in the lives they'd led and the homes they'd lived in. Chelsea had no idea that mice didn't need an open door to get into a house, even one built of stone.

In just the same way he'd tried to harden his heart against Chelsea, yet she'd managed to squeeze in under his defenses.

They got to Base Camp on the second day. The high winds had brought a lot of climbers back to the tent city. Steam and smoke curled up from myriad cooking fires surrounded by porters and Sherpas making the most of the downtime to sit around and talk.

Almost all the tents were the same dingy yellow color, broken up here and there by a national flag—Japanese, American, German, Swiss—indicating which team had claimed a piece of the rocky landscape. Kurt couldn't remember if he still had a New Zealand flag amongst his equipment.

Passing the piles of cans and rubbish on either side of the track awaiting transportation back down the mountain, Kurt walked into the camp feeling edgy with frustration and cursing under his breath. "Where in all hell has Rei parked our gear?"

Chelsea tugged on his elbow. "Something wrong?"

Was she never going to learn not to touch him? He shrugged her hand off by pretending to resettle his pack. "Every man and his dog is in camp today. If I can't catch a glimpse of Rei we'll have to wander around this lot searching for him."

He hoped he'd prepared Chelsea for the snickers and sly comments, and that she'd maintain a professional distance. Getting to the top shouldn't be a competition, but there were those who couldn't stand knowing that a good reputation for summitting meant more than money. Clients were willing to pay for the best. Well, they'd be laughing up their sleeves that his reputation was in tatters, cut to pieces by innuendo.

"Let's try this way first. Chances are Rei looked for the space he helped clear when we were here with Bill and Atlanta." Damn, gruffness clogged his throat with choppy emotions he wanted to escape. He glanced down at Chelsea. She'd walked for a day and a half after a night of strenuous lovemaking.

No good blaming his mistake on the fire and the warmth. Temptation in the shape of her womanly curves had come calling and he'd sunk into its snare without a backward glance.

All he'd wanted was one night with Chelsea, and he'd had his wish. Now he felt as if he'd spend the rest of his life paying for it. He couldn't see himself finding another like her. Every other woman would be fool's gold compared to twenty-four karat.

Heads turned as they found a route between the tents, and an occasional Sherpa or porter waved a hand in recognition. Unlike some of the guides who'd turned a cold shoulder his way as if his reputation might rub off on them, the indigenous population didn't lay blame. If someone was hurt or died, had some misfortune that prevented them reaching the top, it was the goddess's doing. Man proposes and the goddess disposes.

Kurt caught sight of a South African flag tangled with a twist of juniper smoke from a dying fire ringed by stones. They wended past the site, carefully avoiding sharp rocks that had been removed to create a flat surface under the floors of the tents. Any one of them could cause a twisted ankle.

On the far side of the fire a familiar bull-shaped head popped out of one of the unzipped flaps. "Hey, Jellic, man. I thought you were long gone. Word was that you'd gone back to New Zealand."

Basie didn't say *with your tail between your legs,* but Kurt got the message. Obviously that was the latest story circulating in the camp.

"Not a chance. I've work to finish here."

Basie scrabbled out of the tent to stand beside them. He was a big man and had a laugh to match. "Ms. Tedman. I see you got what you wanted. I wish you luck." His almost colorless blue eyes narrowed as he assessed Kurt, but it was Chelsea he was talking to. "You're going to need it. The season will be rushing to a close sooner than we thought if last night's winds are anything to go by."

"I've every confidence in Mr. Jellic," she told Serfontien.

It struck the right note as far as Kurt was concerned. He didn't mind the formality one bit. It meant he'd gotten the need to protect her reputation through to her.

"So, Kurt, your team came ahead. You managed without them?"

"We found a roof to shelter under. I've been coming here for a few years. There aren't many villages on the route where I haven't made friends." Let Basie make what he could of that.

No one needed to know where he and Chelsea had stayed, or what they had done during the windstorm. "So, you've seen Rei? Did you notice where he set up? Am I heading in the right direction?"

"Your Sherpas arrived yesterday. We saw Rei on our way back down. It wasn't weather for camping on a narrow ledge, though I've done it before. We spent half the night with our backs to the tent poles propping them up. Now we're ready to rest."

Kurt couldn't be bothered commenting. He'd been through windstorms—he knew the routine. Besides, it was Chelsea Basie was trying to impress. "Whereabouts did you see my team?"

"Where you were set up before. It's a good spot, but nobody was keen to take it over while you were gone." He turned to Chelsea. "Some guides are as superstitious as their Sherpas."

Chelsea passed the insinuation off with a tired laugh. "Good thing I'm not. All I can think of right now is taking this pack off and finding a seat and a hot cup of tea, in that order."

She was doing well, making out that the trip up had been hard on her, when in fact all her walking and climbing muscles had been broken in during the past week.

Kurt could be just as formal as Chelsea. "Not to worry, Ms. Tedman. My team have worked with me on and off for quite a few seasons. If I know them, they'll have seen us coming. It might be a long way from the Peaks Hotel, but I can assure you my men will treat you right and see you have everything you need."

She took the cue and kept up the act like an old hand. "Great. I can't wait to see what the inside of my tent looks like." She glanced over to the opening Basie had appeared through. Her nose curled as if all her aristocratic Spanish ancestors were ranged behind her.

Kurt followed her gaze. Inside, Basie's tent looked like the scene of a typically untidy, all-male occupation. "Don't worry, the tents are roomier inside than they look from out here, and you'll have it all to yourself."

"That's a relief." Her gaze held Kurt's and added another meaning to her next comment. "I'm not used to sharing."

"No problem there. That was never part of the deal. And now I know where Sherpa Rei has camped, you'll have that hot drink before you know it."

He thrust out a hand to Serfontien, who shook it and slapped the top of Kurt's arm, laughing again. "Good luck, my friend." He gave Chelsea a sideways glance as if he meant *Good luck with that one.* "I'll see you on the mountain."

"Yeah, see you around."

"But not if we see you first," Chelsea muttered as soon as they were out of earshot.

The darn cheek of that man!

"I'm glad Basie Serfontien wasn't available when I asked him to take me up the mountain. He actually feels sorry for you."

She could tell Kurt wanted to smile. It was in his eyes, if not on his lips. "Wasn't that the whole point of the exercise? You play the shrew very well."

"I've had a lot of practice. Does that make you rue the day you decided to take me on?"

"What do you think?"

They were passing a group where a Japanese flag flapped occasionally in the stuttering breeze that wasn't even a thirty-third cousin of the winds they'd had a few night before. She didn't think they would understand the discussion, but just in case she sharpened her tone. "That's no answer. Tell me the truth—do you wish you'd never met me?"

Kurt didn't reply straight off and when he did, compared to her voice, his was pitched low. For her ears only. "I could wish we'd never had to meet this way. That it hadn't taken the deaths of Bill and Atlanta to bring us together, because what happened to them is the reason that keeps us apart, and nothing you can say will convince me otherwise."

For a second she saw heat in his gaze, hidden just as quickly behind his thick dark eyelashes before her eyes could respond to their smoldering fire. Her body had no such reluctance. Her breasts peaked and grew full, tight.

Her step faltered, letting him get a couple of paces ahead. Just as well, she decided. She would get her female instincts under control only by keeping away from him.

If this was an example of camouflaging their regard for each other, the next few weeks were going to be hell. Kurt might think she was a good actress, but from the moment she'd heard of her sister's death she'd been ruled by her emotions. She was only ever going to be as good as her turbulent feelings let her, and there was one question that needed answering.

Just one.

Then she would let it go, she told herself.

She could see Sherpa Rei and the others just ahead. If she didn't ask him now it would be too late. She lifted her hand to snag his arm, and then remembered how casually he'd shrugged off her touch when they first arrived at Base Camp.

"Kurt!"

He swung around, frowning. He hadn't looked at her that way since he'd quietly taken command at the hotel and insisted on paying for their lunch, even though he'd just told her he was short of money. That was when she had discovered, like it or not, Kurt would be the man in control of their lives for the duration of their agreement. She had backed down then, and for the first time had been glad to leave all the arrangements to him. To discover how it felt not to have the stress of always having to make the right decisions for herself, by herself.

"Sorry. You were walking too fast. There's just one more question I need to ask, and then I'll let it drop. Do you regret what happened?" She held her breath, waiting for his reply. It seemed to take forever to come and when he spoke, his face was drawn and strained as if it hurt.

"No regrets. How can I regret the best night of my life? And I know you're having trouble with my decision never to let it happen again. I know it's hurting you. But hell, Teddy, you've no idea the agony it causes me just being around you."

His smile was tight and flat as he took a step closer, one small step as if he couldn't resist. Then he whispered so softly that if the breeze had come up at that moment, it would have carried his words away. "If we were alone, I'd take your hand and show you an example of how I feel, and that's just from looking at you. I want to kiss your face, taste your lips and be back inside your healing power."

He sighed, a rueful noise that matched her feelings as he said, "But it's never going to happen. Not in this lifetime. It can't. You've trusted me to protect you. Let me do my job."

The rough cadence of his whispers built into a growl. She saw a nerve pulse in his temple as he leaned toward her. Anyone watching would think they were arguing. "So, damn well drop it, Ms. Tedman, and let me get on with the work you're paying for."

She watched him turn on his heel and walk away, his boots throwing up small chunks of rock as he quickened his stride.

You just couldn't leave it alone, could you?

Subdued, she slowly followed in his wake, taking time to think. There had to be a way around his fears.

Surely once this was all over… She closed her eyes, unable to bear that it might be otherwise. If she put her mind to it she would find a way for them to be together—if not here, then Paris, the States, or New Zealand. Whatever it took, she was going to find the solution to the mess her life was in, not only with Kurt, but with cousin Arlon and IBIS, as well.

Chapter 9 ·

Kurt had a bad case of déjà vu. It didn't seem long ago that he'd sat around this same fire, planning the route to the top in a huddle with the Chaplins, Paul Nichols, Rei and Ang Nuwa.

This time to complicate matters, two of the original party wouldn't be going home under their own steam, and that would take careful preparation.

He counted heads—Chelsea, Rei and his cousin. The odds weren't on his side with only him, two Sherpas and a complete rookie. Not a combination to inspire confidence in anyone. He gritted his teeth, but it didn't prevent a worry gremlin taking a sideswipe at his worst-case scenario.

What if his luck was no better than last time and they came up one, or even more, short again on the way down?

He blinked the thought away. It was hard to keep a positive attitude, and he couldn't prevent sudden flashes of concern from popping into his consciousness. It wouldn't do to let these concerns filter through to the others.

"Right, let's talk about safety. We stay roped together most of the time, and use ascenders where we can on the fixed lines. In other words, we take no risks." He nodded to Rei and Nuwa. "Yes, I mean everyone."

"Anything you say, boss."

"You count on us, Kurt sa'b." Nuwa grinned. "We take no chances with pretty lady."

"Hey, guys, I'm sitting here. Talk to me, not about me." Chelsea softened the demand with a smile. She got along well with both the Sherpas.

"We take no chances—full stop—and make sure we come back down with everyone we went up with, plus two bodies. Our biggest problem, once we recover them, is how we get the Chaplins' bodies to Camp Four. The route up the Southwest Face isn't a place for porters." He nodded over to the group of men around a second fire heating up the midday meal. "In all probability, some of these guys will feel the bodies should remain where they are, in the lap of the goddess."

He hadn't discussed this next detail with Chelsea, but he hoped she would agree with the point he was going to make and that the Sherpas would pass it on to the porters. He glanced at her before he began, and as the explanation took shape in his mind he realized it probably wasn't far from the truth. "Chaplin sa'b and his wife were very important people in America. There is much money involved, but the lawyers won't be able to agree to anything unless we recover their bodies. They'll want proof."

Kurt hated to put a mercenary connotation on Chelsea's insistence that Bill and Atlanta's remains had to be recovered. He'd heard the worst stories of hassles over the division of family property and the feuds that could result.

An icy coldness filled his insides as if the goddess herself had come down from the mountain and put her hand on his innards.

He'd watched Chelsea fool Basie Serfontien.

Was she a better actress than he'd thought? Had he been manipulated by a pro? Seduced into helping her? She'd been very quick to tell him she didn't know who would benefit from the deaths, as if it didn't matter to her.

Damn, he didn't like the direction his thoughts were taking. Just as well he had called the shots and said their relationship had nowhere to go. He might have made an even bigger fool of himself, with the way she made him feel.

Look before you leap.

Hell, for all his protests he'd jumped in boots and all, with both feet. When Drago's plans had fallen apart, their grandmother's philosophy had been *Money begets money, boy. You didn't have nothing but your brain and a nose for a good wine. It wasn't meant to be.*

All Kurt had was a run-down lodge and the will to make it work.

It was time he remembered that.

But he'd give half of all he owned to know why Chelsea was so insistent on risking her life to help recover her sister when she had the money to pay other people—people like him—to do the job for her.

Finished with her meal, Chelsea went back to the tent where she had slept alone last night. After sharing the one-room shack with Kurt, a guy who took up a lot of room, she felt the tent left too much open space around her. At last she'd borrowed the satellite phone from Kurt and had the privacy to use it. All she had to do was explain why it could be another month before she returned to work, if ever.

Since they had reached Base Camp, with Mount Everest looming ever larger, her experience on Ama Dablam felt like dipping her toe in the sea to find out if she could swim.

What if, like Atlanta and Bill, she never came down again? Atlanta had made sure cousin Arlon's misdeeds would be punished by passing on the knowledge to her. She needed to do the same.

There was only one man she could think of to tell. Mac. Those who knew him thought Mac was part of the embassy staff. Fewer than six people knew he was one of the top agents IBIS had, and *they* weren't allowed to tell anyone. No one would dare—the punishment was too severe.

She had made sure to wait long enough to make up for the time difference, and even if she was a little early she was sure Mac would be at his desk. He lived and breathed for the bureau. He might not approve of her plans but she needed at least one more person in the loop—and who could you trust with a secret if not a guy who lived by them? She might not be a field agent, but she learned all the secrets as she translated them into English and from there into code to be passed on to Jason Hart in Washington, D.C.

It took a few minutes to get through to Mac's number from the embassy operator. His extension number changed randomly every few weeks, and she had no idea of the new one. Collecting Mac's number in case she had to call him hadn't been top of her to-do list before she'd hightailed it onto the first plane to Bangkok.

Mac McBride looked up from the computer screen and gave in to the insistent ring of the phone. "McBride here."

"Mac, is that really you?" The voice had a hollow echo to it—must be a bad line. "This is Chelsea Tedman speaking, I didn't know your new extension and it feels like I've been through a dozen operators. Are you still in Paris?"

"Hey, Chelsea. Never mind about me—are you back? We expected you a week ago. Jason's in town and he's a bit antsy about you not calling in." Mac swiveled his chair slightly to look over his shoulder. Jason Hart was silhouetted in the blue-gray light of more than a dozen computer screens. The Intelligence Bureau for International Security was Jason Hart's brainchild. They had offices and agents all around the world and were opening more. The agents came from a group of aligned nations, which had come together to fight terrorism of any form both within their borders and without.

"I'm not. I'm halfway up Everest. And in case something happens—"

"What do you mean, in case something happens?" Mac kept his voice low but urgent as he straightened in his chair and swiveled back to face his desk. "Are you in trouble?"

"Maybe, I don't know. See what you think. Let me tell you the reason I'm about to climb a mountain." She then proceeded to tell him about the letter, Maddie and the circumstances of Maddie's death. He already knew about her sister and Bill. The news about cousin Arlon really snagged his attention. "Damn it, Chelsea. Why didn't you come to me about this before you left?"

"I thought I could handle it. You know me...."

"Yeah, I do. You never ask for help unless you're forced into it." He glanced over his shoulder. Jason was heading toward him, drawn no doubt by edgy vibes he was giving off. The guy missed very little. That's why he was the best at what he did.

Chelsea began to explain. "On the flight to Kathmandu I started thinking what if it wasn't an accident?"

Jason's shadow crossed Mac's computer screen. He looked up at him and mouthed, "Wait one" as Chelsea carried on. "I'm sure I can trust Kurt Jellic, the guide who climbed with Atlanta and Bill, but I didn't think it would be wise to mention the key to anyone."

"You've done the right thing. Best to keep knowledge like that to yourself. Of course, you've realized what this means or you wouldn't be there." He signaled to Jason to pick up the extension as he said, "Tedman Foods have processing plants in nearly every state. If it goes down we're talking major disaster."

"I'll give you all the information I have on the safety deposit box, and if the worst happens you can deal with it."

"Jason's listening in. Do you have time to go through it all again?"

When she'd finished, Jason said, "You know, Chelsea, we could do this without you climbing Mount Everest, could have done this without you traveling to Nepal."

"I knew you'd say that. Maybe that's why I didn't call sooner. But my sister and I have unfinished personal business between us needing attention. And this is the only chance I'm going to get."

"Okay, we won't pry, but like your sister said, watch your back. I'm no more a believer in coincidence than she was, and this scenario stretches beyond that. I'm going to hand you back to Mac now. Tell him what you need and when you need it."

"I can pay."

"I know you can, Chelsea, but you're one of us, and I think what you're working on just might come under the heading of a national emergency. Tell Mac the rest and let him deal with it."

"Okay, Mac, I need to find out about helicopters. I saw some at the airport at Shyangboche when I arrived. I'm not sure how high those babies can fly. I know they'll ferry supplies up as far as Base Camp where we are now at five and a half thousand meters, but I'm not sure if the air will be too thin another thousand meters or more higher. That's where the bodies are lying. Once I've done this, I don't want to come back and leave my sister and her husband on the mountain, and the terrain is pretty difficult—crevasses and such."

"Chelsea, I always knew you had guts. Don't worry, I'll make inquiries and find you that helicopter. I know the French make the Alouette III, which is used in the Alps. Hell, the bureau might have one. If that comes up trumps, I'll make sure it stands by at Shyangboche. I'll get back to you as soon as I have any news, and you remember to keep me in the loop. No matter how small, if anything changes where you are let me know."

"I will if I'm able. This isn't my phone. I'm hanging up now."

When the line went dead Mac turned to Jason Hart. "What do you think?"

"I think our Chelsea is in heaps more trouble than she realizes. Money and power—they're at the root of the world's problems, and our job is to solve them. So get to it, Mac."

Mac had an odd compulsion to say, "Aye, aye, sir," but then Jason's orders always affected him that way. First things first, though. He'd just run a check on this Kurt Jellic to see if the guy was as trustworthy as Chelsea thought.

Chelsea depressed the button and cut off her link with the place she'd called home for the past few years—Paris. It seemed like another world, and more than half a lifetime away. She had packed so much into the ten days since arriving in Namche Bazaar.

Pushing up from her cross-legged position on the small

folding stool a porter had produced, she heard Kurt call her name. "Chelsea, Ms. Tedman. You decent? We have a visitor."

A visitor? She heard the rough burr of voices outside her tent, one with a definite South African cadence, and she shuddered at the thought that Basie Serfontien had come calling. After her talk with Mac, she wasn't in the mood for any of Basie's hearty humor.

"Chelsea, this is Paul Nichols. I've told you about him."

Paul was the antithesis of Serfontien—lightly built yet muscular, dark haired and olive skinned; his blue eyes caught her attention. He reached for her hand. "My condolences on your loss, Ms. Tedman. Bill and Atlanta were good people."

His accent wasn't as strong or rough as Serfontien's. "Thank you. I'm sorry to say I didn't know Bill real well. I live in Paris mainly," she said to excuse the omission.

"I've felt terrible that I wasn't there to help when it happened. You know how you start thinking maybe something I could have done might have prevented the tragedy. It makes me feel a bit of a wimp to admit that food poisoning kept me back in camp."

"What brings you here this time, Paul? I thought Kurt said you'd gone home."

Paul's blue eyes regarded her sharply for a moment, though his reply was pleasantly modulated, almost cheery. "Only as far as Kathmandu. When I got back to Namche Bazaar, I ran into Kora, Sherpa Rei's sister, in the marketplace. She told me Kurt had gone back to Everest, so here I am."

Chelsea looked from Paul to Kurt and back again. "And?"

Kurt spoke first. "And Paul's come to join us. We could do with another pair of experienced hands."

She took a sharp breath. "Oh." Meaning *Oh, you didn't ask me if it was all right to bring a stranger among us.*

If only he'd arrived earlier she could have asked Mac to screen him. Maybe he would anyhow. She'd told him Nichols had been part of the team when the accident happened, but she hadn't known he was South African. In fact, she'd taken it for granted he was English. The guy just had one of those names…

Paul explained. "I'd like to finish what I started."

And just what did you start?

Darn, her conversation with Mac had her seeing shadows out of the corner of her eye and spies behind every bush—make that every tent.

She tried another angle. "I would have thought you'd team up with your countryman, Basie Serfontien."

"I wanted to last time, but he said he wasn't equipped to cater for another climber, and then, lucky for me, I ran into Kurt. He said he had space in his tent. And the Chaplins didn't object last time—"

"Oh, well, if my sister didn't object, why should I?"

She could see now what Kurt was up to. He thought if he had someone else sleeping in his tent, she wouldn't be tempted to sneak in and join him in that big sleeping bag of his.

As if she would.

On the other hand, she might have. She had just been too tired to think of it before now.

She handed Kurt the phone. "Well, I'm sure Mr. Jellic has a lot to fill you in on, and you won't need me."

She wouldn't say anything to Kurt about the helicopter until she was sure it would be possible. "And since I have some spare time on my hands, I'm going to find some hot water and tend to my personal hygiene while it's not too cold."

Let Kurt Jellic think about that while he was bringing the new member of their party up-to-date.

* * *

The woman sure knew how to make a snit last, Kurt decided as he showed Paul where to stow his gear—which didn't consist of much more than removing his sleeping bag from his pack and retrieving his favorite mug.

"I thought you would have broken that thing by now."

Paul tossed the mug into the air, then caught it. "Guess it's looking the worse for wear, but you know, it's my favorite. Tea tastes better in it."

"Must be all that tannin coating the insides, but since you've got it handy, let's see if we can find some of that hot water our lady climber mentioned and drink a cup while we talk."

Chelsea had looked chagrined, but Kurt was glad to have Paul back. It would take some of the pressure off being almost alone with Chelsea—if you could call it "alone," with two Sherpas and a dozen porters around. But when he thought it over, he realized it wasn't until the others had left them by themselves at the shack that he'd let down his guard.

"I could do with some strong tea. All that talk about ladies seeing to their personal hygiene brought me out in a sweat."

"Tell me about it." Kurt remembered his own first meeting with Chelsea. "Just keep in mind that she is the lady with the checkbook and treat her with respect."

"No chance of anything else. I can see she's a woman with a mind of her own, and they always scare me. Did you notice she was taller than me?"

Kurt nodded. Paul was only five foot nine and always measuring himself against everyone else. "I noticed, but there is no mistaking she's a woman."

One of Paul's best features was his wide grin. It split his face like a band of white against his tan. "I noticed, and that scares me, as well. I'll bet she's a tiger in bed."

Kurt couldn't find it in him to blame the guy. Besides, getting uptight over the usual male camaraderie might give the game away. He settled for "Guess that's something we'll never find out."

It shocked Chelsea how quickly she had gotten used to rising three hours earlier than normal. She had surprised Kurt, too, when she was outside before him and Paul, waiting, already halfway through the protein bar and her mug of tea.

They came out of their tent into the black of a Himalayan night, headlamps on, each looking like a Cyclops with a gleaming eye. "Good on you, Ms. Tedman. You beat us to it this morning," Kurt congratulated her, but whispered in a low voice as he passed by, "Showing off to the new boy, are we?"

What did he mean by that? she wondered. Kurt couldn't possibly be jealous of Paul. In her eyes there was no comparison.

"Why don't you two men start calling me Chelsea? Soon we're going to be like triplets connected by an umbilical cord, and if there is an accident waiting to happen, I'd rather you didn't waste time by shouting Ms. Tedman, look out, when it's quicker to say Chelsea, look out."

"Chelsea it is. Feel free to call me Kurt." She hoped he was silently applauding her for slicing through one of the links in the chain of formality he'd been using to keep his distance. Each time he called her Ms., she wanted to grind her teeth. Wasn't it enough that she was in that tent alone, missing the companionship they'd shared in the shack? She missed hearing about mountains he had climbed and adventures he had shared with her sister and Bill. Stories that made it easier to fall asleep.

Now all she had was the rustle of the porters moving about and the murmur of Kurt and Paul talking in the other tent.

She missed Kurt.

And she hated having to lie in her sleeping bag with her thoughts going around in circles. She hadn't heard from Mac yet, but nothing was ever easy. Maybe he'd call by the time they reached Camp Two, where they aimed to acclimatize for a couple of days before moving up to the next one. The plan was to climb up and down between the camps until they were no longer fighting for every breath. Once that was accomplished, Kurt said he'd establish a second base camp at the top of the Western Cwm. Then it would begin again, up and down, taking relief from the better oxygen levels before climbing back to the top of the Cwm.

Kurt hadn't said it would be easy, but then she'd discovered that nothing truly worthwhile was a cakewalk. The human condition was such that it thrived on challenge.

Ang Nuwa had left before them with a string of porters, and others would follow them up—they didn't have the same problem with thin air, having been born high above sea level.

Kurt took the lead, with her in the middle and Paul and Rei behind. The ground beneath their feet was still the gray mountain rock they had been camping on, but by the time the sun rose they'd face the treacherous Khumbu Icefall.

Then she'd see whether the work she'd put in was enough.

To keep her mind off the ice ahead—ice strong enough to pop huge slices out as if they were pieces of toast and open up huge blue-green crevasses too deep to see down to the bottom—she sang out, "Kurt, you've been up Mount Everest a few times. Have you ever seen one of the fabled yetis?"

"Paul heard all the tall tales last time—get him to tell you about it when we reach the camp. Until then, save your breath for climbing. You're gonna need it." So much for distraction.

Behind her, Paul cursed as a rock spat out from under his boots, reminding her to take care.

The hairs stood up on the back of her neck. She pulled down hard on the bill of her cap, but it didn't help. Maybe it was because of the stranger trailing her. For all the gossip they had slung around last night, she knew no more about him than she had yesterday when he'd arrived.

His lean, tanned features and dark hair would automatically typecast him as the guy wearing the black hat in cowboy movies.

Ahead of her the headlamps of other teams no longer stood out like bobbing yellow strands of thread in the darkness. Morning was a pale shade of gray tinged with pink at the top of the mountain where the sun rose on Tibet, making it simpler to see where she was heading. And what she was heading into.

Her stomach clenched with excitement at the thought that she might actually achieve the task she'd set herself. But then, didn't she always back herself to win?

All she had to do was keep reminding herself that this was no worse than the first time she'd ridden her horse up to a six-foot hedge. The other side was just as unknown, but she had gotten over it then, and she would get over it now.

It was a pity there was nothing she could do to prevent the little voice that had spoken to her in the dead of night coming back to ask, *"But what if you don't?"*

She consoled herself with the fact that if like her sister she didn't make it back, at least Mac was all set to put a spoke in cousin Arlon's wheel.

Chapter 10

How could anyone ever become used to the white, cold beauty of the icefall? Every time he started to climb it, Kurt was struck by the otherworldliness of the fall, as if he'd stepped onto another planet, or had suddenly been transported to one of the poles. No wonder most climbers regarded Everest as the third pole. Its landscape was equally bare. No plants clung to these magnificent slopes, no birds dared these frozen heights.

It should have been a silent waste ground, but a war was being fought under their feet, a pushing and shoving, weight tipped against weight, until the groans of the struggle could be heard on the surface.

Some blocks of ice they passed were five or six stories high. Any one of those giants could fall over and crush them. Those were the risks climbers took on the Khumbu Icefall.

The wind of a few nights ago was nothing but a memory,

and the other struggle played out against it, by him and Chelsea, would have to remain just that, a few moments in time never to be repeated.

The scrape of their crampons on the ice sounded weak and tinny compared with the creaks and groans of the icefall. No one spoke, all saving their breath, apart from Rei. One reason Sherpas easily managed the thin air was that they breathed more rapidly.

Behind him Kurt could hear Chelsea give the occasional soft cough like a baby seal, through lack of oxygen. Paul's bark was deeper, more like a sea lion. He'd call a proper halt soon and give them all a chance to replenish their fluids. He remembered Paul having trouble adjusting the last time. Strange why he'd choose to come climbing when his body's resources were clearly more suited to the flat tablelands of Africa. And though neither of them had mentioned it in that context, it could be that the stomach infection had saved Paul's life.

So why was Paul back, willing to go through it all again? *Why?*

Maybe both he and Paul needed their heads banged together to let the message through. Damned if he knew what drove them to reach for the heights. Could be that their sensible gene was missing—the one supposed to warn the brain not to push the body beyond its limits.

He tugged on the connecting line to warn Rei, who'd changed places with him at the lead an hour ago. "Time to take a break."

Rei came to a halt, leaning his backpack against a convenient block of ice until Kurt caught up, and by the time Chelsea and Paul came level, the Sherpa had lit a small kerosene stove to heat water. Chelsea unbuckled her straps, slipped off her pack and sat down on it. "Ooh, that feels so good."

His mind leaped back to the last time she'd uttered those words with heartfelt gratitude. Only, then he'd been deep inside her bringing her to climax, and he'd thought it felt damn good, as well. "Tired, are you?" he asked.

"I thought you were never going to call a halt."

"We've done well," Kurt said. "Made good speed. It helps that these first stages we have precut steps and fixed ropes. And by the time we attempt the Southwest Face, barring accidents, we should be in good physical condition to go on. Our breathing will get easier and we'll have learned not to overtax our lungs and our muscles."

With her backpack keeping her off the ice, Chelsea downed the dregs of her tea. Had anything ever tasted so good? she wondered. Mindful of Kurt's story of Atlanta leaving one of their precious supplies of ropes behind, she had made sure they were still secured to the belt that took some of the pack's weight off her shoulders.

"Time to move on," Kurt ordered.

Paul straightened out of the hunkered position he favored for resting. "Right with you, man."

Chelsea saved her oxygen ration for something important and began to pull on her pack. Tired this time, she was struggling not to let it throw her off balance when Kurt came over.

"Let me help you with that."

Kurt stood in front of her adjusting the shoulder straps so the padding on them sat more comfortably. He bent to fasten the belt at her waist, bringing his face close to hers.

For days he'd kept his distance, and now this. "I can manage," she murmured, breathless from the close-up, not the thin atmosphere.

On the cold, crisp air she caught his scent and a flush raced across her skin. He stared into her eyes, and behind the lightly tinted lenses of his glasses she saw his pupils dilate. She felt so hot, she wondered if he could feel the heat surge through layers of thermal wear, anorak and the padded glove touching her waist above her belt.

She put her hand above his and pushed it away. "I thought you said I had to learn to cope."

He drew back his shoulders, the width of them hiding her from the others. "That's when you were the student. Now you're the client."

She tilted her chin, forced to look up now he'd straightened to full height. "I'm paying now—is that what you mean?" She kept her voice low but spoke quickly, her words tripping over each other in their haste to make her point. "Kurt…you can't keep doing this. Either touch me or leave me alone. I need to focus my energy on the essentials if I want to survive this experience. You were right to pooh-pooh my climbing-wall boast."

She began to cough and covered her mouth with her hand. Her glove was as cold as the air temperature and was just the nudge she needed to finish what she'd started. She had to keep finding her sister and the key to the forefront of her mind, not let her body sidetrack her by putting its wants and needs first.

She hungered for just one more taste of his lips, the feel of his body covering hers with its supple strength. But he'd been right when he'd talked about rumor and innuendo. It had been rife, sizzling in the air around them at Base Camp each time he introduced her to anyone who stopped by their site and they learned who she was.

Time to nip sex in the bud.

"No one who has never been in this environment can know what it is really like. No matter how fit one is—and believe me, I was fit—acclimatizing is never going to be fun. So just don't help me. Unless I'm hanging halfway down a crevasse on my safety line, let me manage."

She watched him turn pale. He was angry and she didn't blame him, but if her ploy worked, well and good.

He stepped away, his mouth grim. "Don't say anything like that, not even in a joke. And don't worry—from now on, I'll be sure to keep my distance."

He strode away, clipped on the safety line and never looked back. Chelsea sighed as she watched. She'd learned manipulation in her cradle by watching her father, but even her late father couldn't get it right every time. Choosing to bring his cousin Arlon into Tedman Foods because her grandmother had thought it the right thing to do had been like springing a viper on his unsuspecting company. When she got home she would have auditors go right back through the books, back to her father's time as head of the company.

Arlon hadn't learned to plunder Tedman Foods to the extent that Atlanta's letter had indicated unless he'd started small and been working his way up to the big haul.

She clipped her ascender onto the line and grabbed her ice axe to steady her when they crossed the rough parts, which was most of the time. Kurt didn't appear to be having the same problem. She mulled it over and decided it had to be his big feet. It was only what you would expect from a man his size— big feet, a long blade of a nose, big hands, big… Darn, she hadn't intended to go there, but she just had to look at him and the word *sex* shimmered on the edges of her vision.

As last she made out some yellow splotches on the horizon. "Are those our tents?" she called out.

Kurt turned, "Yeah. Nuwa's crew has made good time. And if we're lucky he'll have a special treat ready. Coffee never tasted so good. At eighteen thousand feet it tastes like ambrosia."

They weren't the only teams camped there. Basie Serfontien and the South Africans had set up their tents close to theirs, and a Russian outfit was settling in on the other side.

She watched Kurt frown. He turned to Paul. "Slightly overcrowded up here."

Why was Kurt so annoyed? To her inexperienced eye there looked to be loads of room. "What does it matter?"

"It's a matter of hygiene. Some climbers aren't too careful about where they empty their waste. That's probably how Paul got sick last time, and at this height it's damn dangerous."

She noticed Paul quite often went over to talk with the South Africans and sounded homesick when he came back.

"Tedman Foods has a plant near Port Elizabeth. Do you know it?" That set Paul off. Soon he was telling her stories of South Africa, and again she wondered what the mountains of Nepal had to tear him away from home.

After a day and two nights they moved on to Camp Two, still on the icefall. She hadn't expected to find so much traffic on the mountain, but the season was closing in and with it the chances of some climbers missing out on reaching the summit.

So far, she had adjusted well. Running had expanded her lung capacity and taught her to control her breathing. She was sure that helped. But climbing to the next level was like starting over.

Kurt was as good as his word. He let her manage her way. But she'd have had to be blind not to react to the man who'd taught her so much about herself without realizing it.

She was a product of a privileged upbringing.

It was hard to turn all that around in a few weeks. Sure,

she worked for IBIS, but she wasn't a field agent. Some days her hours would be long, but mainly she could have been working in an office. In Paris she'd run, gone to the gym and worked out on the climbing wall, pitting her skills against the most difficult runs. But when she had finished, she'd had a shower, gone home, or maybe dropped into a fashionable beauty spa to have her hair and nails done.

She had never had to face the day-to-day slog that was needed to become a successful climber. In these surroundings there was no such thing as a comfy bed like the one she had pictured sharing with Kurt.

It didn't take long to realize her sister had become a whole person long before Chelsea had discovered such a state existed.

She was tired at the end of the day—a good tired. One she'd earned by pitting her mind and body against nature in its most primitive form.

Not the exhaustion of staying up half the night dancing at some function attended by people just like her who had no idea this type of life existed—or if they did, didn't care to try it.

Her experiences gave her a better notion of what it took to be a Sherpa, and live year in, year out in Sagarmatha National Park.

About midafternoon Kurt stopped until she and Paul drew level. "We're coming up to the last crevasse on the icefall. You'll remember it, Paul."

He paused a minute before going on, looked at her and said, "This one's the biggie, but I know you can cross it. You've taken the others in your stride and this next one is exactly the same, just a little longer. Don't let the distance bother you. It's just a few more steps."

Chelsea pushed her glacier glasses onto her forehead and rolled her eyes. "If that speech was supposed to be encouraging, Kurt, don't take up brain surgery. Your bedside manner stinks."

He did the same—pushed up his glasses and gave her a smile that turned her bones to water, as if Paul wasn't standing right beside her. What had happened to being careful not to let anyone know there was anything between them? She supposed Paul didn't count. Had Kurt discounted Paul as the person who had started the vicious rumors about him?

She had to admit it was difficult acting like virtual strangers 24/7.

"Are you trying to tell me my tact and diplomacy need work?"

Darn, she wished he wouldn't smile at her that way. His habit of quirking his mouth to one side made her insides quiver. She should have foreseen his response before the words *bedside manner* left her lips. "All I'm saying is you need to learn how not to scare people half to death."

Paul started chuckling on the other side of her. "Heh, heh, she's got you there, man. You've got me thinking twice about that crossing now."

Kurt punched Paul on the arm. "Cut that out. Chelsea I might manage to carry across on my back, but not you."

"What do you mean?" Paul looked her up and down. "She's taller than I am."

"Yeah, but haven't you noticed? She's a woman."

Indignant, Chelsea tried fisting her hands on her hips, but it was difficult with so much equipment hanging from her belt. So she stamped a boot, just missing the loops of nylon safety line they were all attached to. "For goodness sake, leave it alone, you guys. I can manage, and you both know it. I can pull my weight. I don't need any man to carry me."

Paul slipped an arm under hers and pulled her closer. "We know that. We're teasing. It doesn't do any harm to release a bit of tension. How would it have looked if we'd started laughing on the edge of the crevasse?"

Kurt slipped his glasses back down his face and began shaking out the line to prevent knots forming. "Nichols might have gone chuckling off the side of the ladder to his doom. This guy has kept me awake with his never-ending supply of sick jokes, and he finds it impossible not to start laughing before he gets to the punch line."

"I've heard him."

"See, Paul. You've been keeping Chelsea awake, as well. Let's move on out before she starts snoring."

If anyone kept her awake, it was Kurt. She'd never felt so lonely as the times she slept in her tent alone, never felt so cold without Kurt near her. She missed him.

Not just his lovemaking, wonderful as it had been, but simply hearing him breathe as he slept.

Instead of sleeping, she had lain there with her eyes closed, speculating about the future. What happened after they recovered her sister and Bill Chaplin?

Did he really expect them to part and go on with their lives as if this mad passion had never taken hold of them? As if he'd never tumbled her into his warm embraces, making her cling to him as she had never clung to another man in her life?

She, for one, couldn't take that step backward. At the first opportunity, she would resign from IBIS.

And then what?

It was in the lap of the gods, or maybe the goddess. She hoped the local deity was looking down at her with favor. Hadn't she asked for her help the day before they left Base Camp? The porters had erected a post and strung prayer flags from it. Afterward, the lama had arrived, offering prayers as he banged the traditional bells together. Before they finished they had all thrown barley flour to the wind and burned juniper as an offering, then white and cream silk scarves had garlanded their necks. A pretty ritual, all the more blessed because of the hope it brought in its wake.

Kurt crossed the crevasse first. From the far side she watched him slide his hands along the ropes. His long-legged stride hit every second rung, the fragile bridge dipping under his weight. The bridge consisted of three aluminum ladders knotted together with cord.

Surely someone could come up with a better rig than that?

In compensation, though this crevasse was wider than the others she had crossed, an icy protrusion balanced one side of the ladder halfway across.

"Okay, Chelsea, you now. But take your pack off. I'll come back for it once I have you safely on this side."

Paul helped her off with her backpack. Chelsea shivered straightaway, missing the pack's weight and warmth. "Don't be nervous," he said. "It's no different from any crossing we did on the way up here. Just put one foot in front of the other, and soon you'll be on the other side."

He gave a gentle push on her back. "Go on, now. Take a deep breath and set yourself up."

All right for him to say "Set yourself up." He wasn't staring at a hundred-foot drop so dark green the bottom looked like deep water—but she *knew* it was a darn sight harder.

She took a couple of breaths and steadied herself. Calm now, calm. Her thoughts took the shape of the words she used with her horses. All she had to do was throw her heart over and follow it.

"You're doing great," Kurt called as she reached the halfway mark, but she kept her head down as if her life depended on that next step.

From behind her Paul shouted, "Not much farther. I knew you had it in you. You're a right little battler, Chelsea."

Ten more feet and she'd be across.

Ten more of her steps.

She counted them. One, two…eight, nine. She glanced up as she went to put her foot on the last rung and saw Kurt waiting, arms outstretched ready to grab her.

All of a sudden she wanted him to do just that—grab her, hold her and never let go. She laughed. "Here I am, K—" But she never finished the sentence as the last rung disappeared under her weight and her right foot flailed at fresh air.

The blood drained from her face.

Off balance, she dropped through the gap. Her automatic reflex was to let go with her right hand to stop her face bashing into the ladder. The judder went straight up her arm. Luckily she didn't let go with her other hand. It tightened on the rope.

A lifeline.

No shouts of dismay battered her ears. Somehow the shocked silence was more terrifying. In the longest moment of her life she was haunted by the thought that she might end up an ice maiden, forever swimming in the green depths of a crevasse.

The safety line at her waist was forgotten as the ice reached up to grab her. She felt a jerk as the line locked up.

Kurt began reeling her in. Then, placing his hands under her armpits, he pulled her into his arms, holding as if he would never let her go.

For long minutes Kurt held Chelsea against his chest, though they weren't as long as the mind-numbing seconds when he'd seen her fall. Instead of his past life flashing before him, he saw his future, barren and empty without Chelsea.

Once he'd regained enough composure to let her go, he yanked off one of his gloves with his teeth. He had to touch, to feel the heartbeat that proved she was alive. Cupping her pale face in his palm, needing the closeness when he found his voice, Kurt asked, "Are you okay?"

Tell me you're all right.

"I'm fine…just breathless," she said at last, then ducked back into the security of his chest.

He felt her breasts rise and fall as if she was sobbing, but she didn't utter a sound. With his back turned to the others, he hid her from curious eyes. "I think our secret just got out."

She looked up at him at last. Her eyes were slightly puffy, but not too bad. He glanced over his shoulder as the ladder rattled. Paul was sliding across the gap after her.

"I can pretend I've been crying. No one will blame me."

"God knows you've a right, but it's not your style, Chelsea, is it?" He put her aside. "Take a minute to get it all together again. Any bruises I should know about?"

"Nothing I want you to rub. That could be more dangerous than bridging the huge crack in the ice that Paul is scampering over."

He turned. With what appeared to be more luck than judgment, the South African was almost across. "Mind that rung at the end."

Paul was panting, but for a change still had breath to talk. "Hell, Kurt. I figured she was a goner. What a lucky break. I was sure we were about to witness a repeat performance."

Kurt held out his hand to Paul. "You didn't see it last time."

Paul's hand locked with his, then the smaller man leaped over the gap. "I know, but I feel as if I had. Remember, it was me who met you coming back down."

"Yeah, I remember. You said you felt better and decided to follow us. That was dangerous to do on your own, almost as dangerous as the way you came across that bridge."

"That piddling little thing doesn't faze me. I spent years in the South African navy."

"You never said." Kurt was struck by the thought that though Paul often talked about his homeland, it was mostly superficial, nothing personal or revealing. What did he really know about this guy? Was Paul pissed off enough over missing his chance to get to the top to have planted the rumor that questioned why he, Kurt, had survived when they'd all left camp roped together?

"You never asked. But never mind that. How's Chelsea?"

"A little shaken, but pulling herself together just fine. See for yourself." He turned to see Chelsea calmly sitting on top of his pack. Absolutely amazing, no one would believe she'd nearly fallen to her death and taken his heart with her.

That's why he couldn't resist teasing her. As Paul walked over to Chelsea, Kurt called out, "If she needs another shoulder to cry on, you can provide it. I'm going back to collect her gear before Rei comes across."

Well, she was the one who'd brought up pretending to cry.

When Kurt reached the other side Rei asked, "How is the little miss?"

"She'll survive, Rei." He knew Rei liked Chelsea, and thought it was funny how the Sherpa, who was a head shorter, saw her as utterly feminine and in need of protection, like the fragile flowers that bloomed only occasionally in this frozen environment. What was even funnier was that for all Chelsea's tough streak, she'd become someone whose life Kurt was driven to protect with his.

Chapter 11

Chelsea had been climbing mountains for over a month if she included the time spent with Kurt on Ama Dablam. She was counting on this being the last time she would have to climb back to Camp Three. The fragile aluminum bridge had lost all its terrors now that she'd crossed it so often.

They were in the Western Cwm, a silent place compared to the icefall. Huge crevasses striated the flat floor of the valley, but there was no need to cross them. The snow was thick, squeaking under the weight of her boots. This was the only part of the route where Kurt didn't insist on her being roped to him and she could walk by his side instead of staring at his back.

The temperature in the valley was up in the nineties because of the reflection off the snow. They had all stripped down to their undershirts and wore silk and cotton squares draped under their baseball caps to keep the sun off their necks.

A few days ago they had been in Base Camp, recuperating and doing housekeeping chores before starting back up. She smiled as the memory teased her. "You know, Kurt, if I told any of my friends at the embassy that I'd gone almost four weeks without a shower, they would think I'd gone mad."

His mouth quirked, making her certain he was winking behind the dark goggles. "Yeah, just when you've gotten used to the smell, you have to start again."

"For all its meager dribble of barely warm water, it felt like the best shower I have ever taken."

Kurt looked behind him. She turned, as well. Paul was fifteen yards back. The soft dark hairs on Kurt's forearm brushed hers as his next step brought him closer. Without easing his pace, he said, "I enjoyed my shower as well, but yours was sheer torture for me. Guarding the screen and knowing you were naked behind those thin squares of cloth was the worst kind of temptation. I get hard just thinking of you all wet and slippery."

He glanced down as he finished speaking.

She flushed, knowing he would see the telltale signs of her reaction to his words. Her breasts felt too big for her bra and the tips were like little bullets trying to pierce their cotton confines. But the wet and slippery place was between her thighs.

"Don't say things like that to me when you know there is nothing we can do about it. It's been so long since we made love, it's been more than torture. It's been hell."

"Join the club, Teddy bear. When we get out of here I'm going to take a room at the Peaks Hotel close to yours and hope nobody sees me creeping along the corridors in the dead of night."

She pouted. "I can't wait, but I'm sick of all this sneaking around when we really have nothing to hide."

"I've told you, I can't be sure that it wasn't Paul who

started the rumor. It's okay to act friendly, though. After more than a month in each other's company that's only natural. But we can't let it go any further. So don't you go thinking about my great body and making google eyes at me while we're eating dinner or you'll give the game away."

Chelsea burst out laughing. The brute. Kurt had done that intentionally to cut the tense atmosphere that sizzled so strongly Paul could probably see waves of heat rising. "Could be it's because you took a shave and I can see what a stud you are under your beard."

"Remind me to shave every day."

They were both chortling loudly by the time Paul caught up with them. "What's so funny?"

Kurt answered, still grinning, his teeth like a slash of the pristine snow they were walking on. "You had to be there."

Chelsea decided to take pity on Paul. She quite liked him despite Kurt's suspicions of him. "We were talking about what some of my friends would think if they knew how bad I smelled before we hit the showers at Base Camp."

Paul gave a short bark that passed for a laugh. "Not to worry. I always thought you smelled sort of young and cuddly."

She felt Kurt stiffen beside her, and a quick glance told her the hairs on his arm were standing up like a dog's hackles rising. Well, she had no intention of becoming a bone of contention.

"You mean like a baby. I have to thank Kurt for that. He was the one who put me on to baby wipes. Even gave me his last box. I just hope they're not all gone before we finish here."

"Maybe it won't be too long now, Chelsea. I think we're pretty right to go now. What do you say, Kurt? Do you think we have enough fixed lines and anchors out to reach that little couloir? It's only a tiny corridor compared to the Hornbein Couloir."

"You're right—hardly a squiggle on the map of Everest, but tough enough. As far as the lines go? Yeah, I think we've pretty much put out all the fixed line we can. The good thing about it is we only have to carry enough rope to take us from the couloir down to where Bill and Atlanta fell. That doesn't mean it's going to be an easy climb. Are you sure you are up for it? No matter that we've taken all the safety precautions possible, climbing the Southwest Face is never going be anything but risky."

Kurt stopped talking. She heard him catching his breath to finish speaking. When Paul began to say something he waved him off. "The stakes for us taking risks are higher. Chelsea and me, well, we really need to do this thing. But you, Paul, don't put your life on the line when at the end of it we won't summit."

"I want to do it, Kurt. I need to. I've always felt if maybe I hadn't got sick they'd still be alive. You're pretty offhand with me sometimes, man. But I take that with a grain of salt, for I've a feeling you blame me, too. The Chaplins had become my friends, so I'd say my stake in this is higher than you think."

"Have it your own way. But don't say you weren't warned."

Chelsea slid her arm through each of the men's and pulled them with her. "Enough with the serious talk. We were having fun and you've both poured cold water on it."

She could feel Kurt's skin ripple where they touched, as if a growl ran under it. "Okay, we'll leave it for now, but it was going to have to be said sometime," he retorted.

Chelsea slipped her arms away from the men. "Hey, look. Rei is waving at us. I can see the tents. Last one into camp gets the cold coffee." She got ahead slightly, but she was never going to win. Kurt's stride was too long. And even though Paul was smaller than she was, he had a slim, wiry build that moved easily through the thick snow. In the end, they all reached Camp Three together.

The coffee was hot, but it couldn't shift the burgeoning fear at the back of her mind. Not for their safety. It was the finality of finding Atlanta that scared her.

Once they found her sister, Atlanta would really be dead.

Seeing *was* believing.

And that meant the problems with cousin Arlon would have to be tended to next. She had heard Mac had gotten her a helicopter, but not if it had reached Shyangboche. Communications were difficult—something to do with sunspots affecting transmission. And if she couldn't tell Kurt they had a helicopter, how would they get her family down from the mountain? No matter how many Sherpas and porters Kurt had standing by, the task would be gigantic.

Paul sat across the small fire from Kurt and Rei, watching them talk. Kurt had not given Paul an inch of slack since she had almost fallen down the crevasse. She had asked why, but Kurt wasn't a man who opened up his emotions to close inspection. Not even to her, who had been as close to him as another person could be.

But then, she had her own share of secrets, the helicopter being the least of them. So how could she blame Kurt?

She had a sinking feeling she was falling in love with a man who would never share his innermost thoughts, even with the woman he loved. Was that something she wanted to live with?

For the rest of her life?

Kurt watched Rei nod in agreement, but could see the Sherpa wasn't happy. Hell, he didn't feel like laughing either. Retrieving the bodies was going to be dangerous.

Chelsea didn't know it, but among the supplies he'd had delivered to Base Camp—snacks, candy bars and other essentials that everyone had fallen on with cries of joy—were two body bags in extra-strong plastic. In some places, like the couloir, it was going to be impossible to carry the bodies. Instead, they'd have to drag them up behind the team or let them slide ahead.

He didn't like it, but he couldn't see any other way around the problem. The couloir went straight down. Below it were a series of crevasses deeper than those on the icefall. The bodies had halted their downward rush on the rounded lip of one of these slashes that traveled the mountainside.

"Don't look so worried, Rei. We will make an offering to the Mother before we leave and let her decide." When Sherpas said it was in the lap of the gods, they really meant it.

"We will ask her to protect us."

"Good. I want you to come with us. Nuwa can organize the others while we're gone."

Kurt finished the dregs of coffee in his mug. The liquid had cooled long ago, but the caffeine still did the trick. "That's it, Rei," he added. "We'll see how it goes, my friend. A few of the porters already here can follow us to the couloir. Chelsea has the money—she'll make it worth their while. They can help transport the bodies once we get past the worst ice and hit the smooth downward slopes where the fixed lines are anchored."

Chelsea has the money.

Was that why Paul took every opportunity to flatter her? Admit it, Jellic, you're acting like a dog in the manger. You've been so busy trying to look out for both your names, and Paul's seen a gap that he's ready and willing to step into.

Even without all this rumor nonsense, what chance had he with a woman like Chelsea? On her mother's side she was descended from Spanish aristocrats, one of the first families of Argentina, who owned vast tracts of land. He owned a half-built lodge. She had money and he had debts. It could never work.

Didn't mean he was going to give Paul a chance to step into his shoes. And he would continue to keep a close watch on him.

Kurt uncrossed his legs to stand, looking down at his feet as he rose. He then glanced over at Paul sitting with Chelsea. No way could that little guy ever fill his size twelves.

He continued to watch as Paul followed suit, rising at the other side of the cooking pit. Kurt saw him murmur something to Chelsea as he left, heading away from the campsite. A quick glance over his shoulder and he knew the reason. Basie Serfontien had arrived.

Paul must be feeling homesick again. There was no other reason that Kurt could see why the younger guy would choose Basie's company over theirs. The big fair Afrikaner was all hail-fellow-well-met and shouted his business to the world, while Paul was full of secrets.

It was Paul's secrets that bothered him most.

It was the wind that woke Chelsea.

She knew that when the air grew cold and heavy at night the winds might descend from high on the mountain. But this blast, this buffeting and rocking of her tent, was loud enough for jet-stream winds. *Oh, please don't let this hold up our plans. Don't let anyone get hurt.*

Ashamed of her selfish little prayer, she cowered inside her sleeping bag, willing to put up with the terror as long as the result didn't mean another trip down to Base Camp.

The next time the tent tipped, Chelsea decided she couldn't just lie there. She sat up and scrabbled halfway out of her thick, quilted sleeping bag. Both hands searched the nearby floor for the stretchy band attached to her headlamp.

Success.

Her fingers latched on to the elastic strap, but before she could flick the switch, she froze, desperately aware of another noise outside. She recognized the sound the zipper on her tent made when it stuck and needed an extra tug or two. Someone was outside.

Were they intent on rescuing her?

Was the situation out there that bad?

Fumbling with the cold headlamp to locate the switch, she pushed herself upright. Darn blasted thing, she cursed as the switch toggle didn't connect the battery with the lightbulb.

Then when it worked, the light blinded her. In a rush she aimed the beam at the entrance. Through the dazzle of red spots she made out a bulky white arm. The light flashed off steel.

A knife. Chelsea screamed as she grabbed the first thing to hand, a boot with crampons still attached. Her violent throw lost her the headlamp and all sight of her target. In the second or two it took to retrieve the light, the arm had disappeared through the yellow flap as though it had been a figment of her imagination.

She screamed again, this time from sheer bloody temper. No one raced to help her. The winds were too much competition for one little voice. Their roar dominated everything, her cry in the night included.

Her fingers shook, and stretching the lamp over her forehead suffered from the more-haste-less-speed syndrome. In another few minutes she had pushed her sleeping bag off and slipped her warm sock-clad feet into her boots. She had worn the thick socks and everything but her quilted jacket to bed.

Quilted parka—where was that? Oh, yeah, her pillow.

Since the intruder hadn't bothered to refasten the door flap, leaving her tent was the least troublesome task she had to perform. But as soon as she tried to stand upright, the wind ripped the breath from her throat. Bent double, making a smaller target for the gusts to bowl over, she set out. As she stumbled across the rocks of the cooking pit, shapes much like her own, heads lit by yellow Cyclops eyes, flitted past in the darkness.

She didn't approach them, couldn't abolish the fear of running into her knife-wielding intruder.

Her goal was simple. She wanted Kurt.

Chelsea couldn't miss his tent, not with the light on inside. The flap was partially open, and in less than a heartbeat she dragged the zipper to the floor and crashed straight through.

She let out a huge sigh. The sight of Kurt's red anorak did everything to confirm her faith in him. Whoever was out to get her couldn't be Kurt. Until now, she hadn't admitted that when she saw the knife her memory had flashed back to the day she and Kurt met. And farther, to Atlanta's warning to watch her back.

Kurt, like Rei, was propping up a tent post, both men pushing their weight against the pressure building outside. They faced her from opposite sides of the basically flimsy structure. She heard Kurt laugh as she dragged her last leg through the gap.

The tent floor was cluttered with sleeping bags and camping gear. Candy wrappers spilled from a bag filled with rubbish. As if they'd been having a party and Chelsea hadn't been invited.

One look at her stricken expression and his laughter disappeared. "Chelsea! What's wrong? Has this wind trashed your quarters? These gusts are stronger even than Ama Dablam."

Ignoring the mess on the floor, she trampled across it to throw herself at Kurt's chest. "Someone tried to break in to my tent."

His arms came around her. "Teddy, honey, it was probably a mistake. All the porters are out checking that the tents don't blow away. Most of these guys are reinforcing the rocks weighing down the guy ropes."

"Do they need a knife to do that job? I only saw a white arm, no face. The hand was holding a knife, but it disappeared the moment I flashed my light at it. Why? I've never given any porter reason to be frightened of me."

"You sure you weren't dreaming? Maybe one of those stories Rei and Paul have been telling about the yeti played on your mind, and the noise of the wind exacerbated the dream."

Her temper flared. How could he doubt her this way? "It wasn't a yeti, or a dream! It was a man. I saw his arm…and his gloved hand…and the knife."

"I heard you, but none of our guys wear white. We'd never see them against the snow and ice." He hugged her closer. "Do you want to spend the rest of the night here with us? I can get some porters to stand against the walls of your tent. It'll soon blow away with only the weight of your backpack and a lady's accoutrements to hold it down."

"No. And I don't have accoutrements, not that I know of. And to hell with what people think. I want you in my tent with me. Your extra weight will be all it needs. My tent isn't nearly as large as this one."

"As soon as Nichols comes back to relieve me, I'll take you back to your tent. Hopefully the porters have secured it well enough to last until then."

Chelsea let out a gusty sigh as if she she'd taken some of the turmoil of the storm inside her. "That's great. I always feel much safer with you around."

"Listen, don't you go trying to make me hero. All I do is what it takes to get by. Nothing heroic in that." Kurt's hand clasped her shoulders as he put her at arm's length. "If you want to make yourself useful, find a post to lean on before Nichols returns and sees us. It'll only take one moment of weakness and our efforts of the past few weeks will have been for nothing."

Chelsea crossed the equipment-strewn floor more slowly than on her arrival, but she did as he asked—put her back to one of the curved posts. The light swung back and forth on its hook at the top of the tent, and every time it lit up Rei's face, she could see him grinning at her.

It didn't take a clairvoyant to work out what was going on in his mind. Throwing herself at Kurt had outed her.

A blind man could have seen she had feelings for Kurt.

At least Rei was one person they could trust not to let them down by carrying tales. At the core of his character the Sherpa had an essential honesty. Rei would never have deigned to spread the rumors bothering Kurt so much.

And once she got Kurt by himself, maybe she could work up enough courage to tell him about the key. How else could she get him to realize she had not imagined the knife-wielding hand? Come to think of it, the hand had been white, as well. Whoever had broken in only had to lie in the snow to become invisible.

Telling Kurt about Atlanta's letter and cousin Arlon wasn't going to be easy. She didn't want him to stop trusting her or think that her motives were all about money.

Hard as it might be for Kurt to believe, she had this horrible feeling someone up here on the mountain might want her dead.

What was a man to do when a woman literally threw herself at him? Kurt's mind was abuzz as he tossed his sleeping bag inside and stepped into Chelsea's tent. If anything was needed to show how much he wanted her, his body had gone hard, ready to mate from the moment her thighs and breasts pressed close.

His needs were secondary now. His first task was discovering if Chelsea had just missed being a victim of a guy with a knife. And if she really had seen it, if it wasn't a dream, what were they going to do about it?

His thoughts kept returning to the incident on the aluminum bridge on her first climb up to Camp Three. Why had only that rung been so worn it had given way? He'd checked the others as he went back and they were fine.

Rei had fixed the rung with some wire he had in among the bits and pieces in his pack, kept for just such an occasion. One rung out from the end was the point where people stopped looking down and fixed their eyes on their goal, solid ground.

Like him, most men with their longer stride would probably take the rungs two at a time. Sherpas were shorter, lighter, but he'd seen them cross like Nichols—forget the rungs and slide their feet along the sides of the ladders.

He heard Chelsea enter behind him and the sound of the zipper being closed. "Leave that, but stay where you are until I light the lamp."

Kurt clamped his teeth on the middle finger of his glove and hauled it off to search out the matches. Soon the lamp was shedding soft light, making it possible to see farther than their headlamp's narrow beams. The floor was tidy compared to his quarters, but then, Chelsea wasn't bunked in with Paul and Rei. Nuwa shared with the porters, making them his responsibility, but his old friend Rei was with him for his climbing expertise. With Chelsea's experience no more than minimal—

only what he'd taught her so far—and Nichols in his first season in Nepal, Rei's input was definitely needed. If the going got too rough, Kurt needed to know there was someone he could rely on.

The tent rocked as if they were at sea in a storm instead of 21,000 feet above that level. He tossed Chelsea's sleeping bag at her. "Here wrap that around you if you feel cold, but leave your boots on in case we need to make a hasty exit," he said.

"I want to talk about what happened." She stood three feet away, making it impossible to miss her tight-lipped frustration.

"I was getting to that. Any reason why you can't be comfortable while we do it?" As another gust hit the walls he thrust one hand against a post, putting all his weight behind it. The worst blasts were hitting eighty knots an hour and more. "Hang on to your hat—this one's a doozy. Get your weight onto the outside edge till it passes." He had to shout to be heard.

The light swung, lengthening then shrinking their shadows on the yellow bowed walls, while the top of the door flap bounced up and down making an annoying pit-a-pat, pit-a-pat. Kurt flung an irritated scowl in its direction, expecting it to rip apart any minute. It would be his fault. He had stopped Chelsea closing it fully. The wind whistled in and out of the opening as if expelled from a giant bellows, and he watched it lift the floor.

One of Chelsea's overboots slid into the middle of the floor, accompanied by something else—a knife.

Not the stuff of dreams after all.

"Take a look near the door. Can you see what I see?"

"One of my boots and… My God! I threw my boot. It must have hit him." She broke away from the wall and made as if to get it.

"No, Chelsea, hold it. All the proof in the world won't do you any good if we get blown off the side of the mountain."

Neither of them said a word. They both stared intently at the knife on the floor, as if the moment they took their eyes off it, the six-inch blade would disappear.

Eventually the wind died enough for the post behind Kurt to stop shuddering. "You got a plastic bag?"

Chelsea's eyes flicked away from the knife. "What for?"

He nodded in the direction of the knife. "This could be evidence. Did I ever tell you my dad was a cop?"

She licked her lips, then pressed them together. In the low light her gaze was uncertain, as if she was weighing up the odds before she spoke. He didn't blame her after the reception he'd given her news earlier.

Eventually she came out with "I think the guy was wearing gloves as well—white ones."

"What the hell is going on?" He shook his head, but couldn't shake the notion that someone wanted to kill her. But why?

For an age neither spoke—they simply looked at the knife, their expressions fixed. He hated seeing Chelsea this way. She had enough to worry about. Getting her sister off this mountain, for a start. He wanted to take that look off her face. It was the only way to explain his inane comment. "White gloves? Couldn't have been a yeti. I hear they're wearing black this year."

From under her eyelashes Chelsea cast him a glance that needed no translation. She took a step toward her backpack. "I have a plastic bag holding my brush and comb."

He picked up the knife between the thumb and forefinger of his gloved right hand, keeping the tips on the narrow edge of silver above the bone handle, and his heart sank as Chelsea said, "Uh, Kurt? It looks just like yours."

He slapped his other hand on his hip where his knife usually hung. He wasn't wearing it. Kurt groaned out loud. "Damn. I swear to God mine is in my tent. I don't sleep with it on."

"I know it can't have been you. Not dressed in red."

He wished she had a better reason for believing in him. "I could have stripped it off" was his grim reminder. He didn't feel like joking anymore.

Chelsea huffed out an extra-long breath. She touched his arm. "Do you want me to suspect you?"

What he wanted and what she needed to do were at opposite ends of the problem. She needed to look at every angle, every single one. "I need you to take nothing for granted, not even me."

The door flap began flopping up and down as the wind got up again. No peace for the wicked, as they said.

He bowed his shoulders to keep his head from scraping the roof and let his headlamp shine on the zipper. He moved it up a couple of notches, then stopped midclick. "There's blood on the side of the zip and it's still red. Looks fresh."

She came closer to look at the zip. "That would be when I threw my boot at him. The crampons must have nicked him."

A second later the boot was in her hand. "Look, here it is."

She showed him the front spikes designed for climbing an ice wall. All it took was a toe kick to hold fast. She pointed at one of the three hefty spikes on the front. "There's blood on this one. I must have better aim than I knew. It pierced his glove. No wonder he dropped the knife."

Kurt held the blade up to take a good look. Like his, it was a hunting knife, a heavy bone hilt with a six-inch blade. He didn't need any tests to know how sharp it was. "He might come back looking for it."

Lips parted, she looked up at him. He was close enough to make out the dark gray ring circling her irises. She never even blinked as she asked, "Do you think?"

"What I think is you'd better tell me why you aren't more surprised that someone obviously wants you dead."

Chapter 12

Chelsea no longer had any choice. She was going to *have* to tell Kurt the full story, and it was going to hurt both of them.

Why, oh, why had she let the situation drag out so long without coming clean? Atlanta had said in her letter that she felt nervous, as if someone was watching her.

What if that *someone* was still here on Mount Everest?

"Kurt, there is something you should read." Stalling, Chelsea began to unzip her anorak in excruciatingly slow increments—*click…click.* Chelsea Tedman, this procrastination isn't like you, she scolded herself. Just get on with it. Tell him. *Now.*

Frankly, sometimes she wondered if she understood her own motives. Was this fear? She had always considered herself to be a feel-the-fear-and-do-it-anyway type of person. What had changed?

Don't mention it and it will go away.

When had she become a coward? What was different with

this situation, this problem, that she couldn't just throw her heart over the obstacle and take the leap after it?

Why hadn't she turned to Kurt for help? Turned to the one man to truly make her feel like a woman, the man who had done his utmost to protect her good name?

Instead, she had asked Mac and the bureau for help.

Would Kurt consider her actions a slap in the face?

She removed her synthetic gloves, pulled Atlanta's letter from her inside pocket and puffed out a cloud of air. "This is the letter I received from Atlanta shortly before she died."

Kurt slipped the knife into the plastic bag and tossed it down beside her backpack. The headlamp's beam shone through the flimsy lightweight pages limp from excessive handling—softened by oil on her skin as she read the letter a hundred times or more. At each reading she searched for an elusive clue, expecting to find it written between the lines, only to come up blank.

That had set her wondering about Maddie's letter. Where was it hidden? Would she find it among Atlanta's possessions, in her pack, on her person? If only her sister had been more explicit about Maddie's missive.

She watched Kurt flip the final page, his fingers scrunching the lower corners together as his hand dropped to his side. "Damn it, Chelsea. You should have given me this information earlier." The words escaped between his teeth, exasperation underlining each one. "Can't you see that the more people who know about the threat the less power it has over you, and the greater your protection is?"

His eyes were dark, hot, midnight-ebony from deep emotions. Red-hot fury was no more than she had expected. She asked the question anyway out of a need for affirmation. "After reading that letter, can you still believe that Atlanta's and Bill's deaths were an accident?"

"Is that what's really worrying you? That the Chaplins were murdered? Who by? *Me!* Is that what you think?" His chest expanded as he dragged off his knit cap. Over the rough edges of his breathing she heard it land softly, but her eyes were on the fingers he dragged through his flattened hair.

"Oh, yes, you're cool. You could think that, yet lie naked beside me, take me in your arms and let me make love to your body. Pshaw." He spat out his disgust. "How could you?"

"Kurt, no!" God, she had made a mess out of her search for answers, and now he hated her. "I never ever thought it could be you. They were your friends—you couldn't speak of them the way you do if you had killed them. I would hear it in your voice."

She blinked her eyes shut, but couldn't confess her sins blind. He had to look into her eyes and know what her penitence cost her and hopefully find his answer there.

She opened her eyes and laid her hands on his chest. "Kurt, unlike me, you haven't a deceitful bone in your body. Whereas I *am* willing to do whatever it takes to protect this knowledge from getting out. Even if lying to you was what it took. It comes with the job description. I wasn't kidding you. I work for an organization that you won't have heard of because it's covert. But I didn't deceive you because I suspected you of being in cousin Arlon's pocket. Your integrity is bred in the bone. It shows."

His hands covered hers. A shake of his head said he didn't know what to do with her. "Shows what you know. But this isn't the time for any you-show-me-yours-I'll-show-you-mine nonsense."

Her breathing was shallow, abbreviated, but began to race with the previously forbidden contact. She trembled at his closeness.

It felt a lifetime since she'd felt his breath tickle her face. Only two days since he'd last shaved, and already his skin prickled with black stubble. She wanted its roughness to sweep across her cheeks; she wanted to touch it with her hands.

Could Kurt read her face, know what she was thinking? Know she wanted to be the only Teddy bear he cuddled up to?

"You and I have been as intimate as two people can get. I would have known." She smoothed his chin with the tips of her cold fingers, and let one dip into the dimple. "You have to believe me, Kurt. I never really considered you a threat to *me,* not even when you held a knife at my throat. And once I knew you, it was obvious you couldn't kill in cold blood."

"Don't be too sure. I could kill, but to protect what's mine, never for money." He paused a moment before going on. "That's what we're talking about, right? You think this cousin of yours, cousin Arlon, could have put out a contract on Bill and Atlanta."

"Yes."

"Forget it. Your cousin may have paid someone, for all I know, but that's not what happened up there. Couldn't. I saw them fall, heard the screams, and never saw another living soul until I met Nichols on his way up the face to join us. Whatever you may think, it was an accident."

Chelsea scowled and he said, "And don't look at me that way, as if I didn't know what I was talking about." His lips tightened as if to lock the words behind him. "I heard them hit, not just once but many times. Bill was silent, but Atlanta screamed as they flew past me. I can still hear it. I had to climb down to be certain. They were both dead—not a pulse between them."

She wanted to hold Kurt, comfort him. Wanted to take him in her arms and take away his pain, fix the genuine grief she heard in his short brutal explanation of what had happened. But all she felt entitled to do was stroke his face and rub his shoulder with her palm. "I'm sorry. I truly am sorry."

He shrugged her hands off as if it was too late for her condolences. *Too late for the two of them, maybe.*

"What I don't get is why Atlanta didn't tell Bill. It's okay—I can see you not trusting me with the information. We were strangers." His voice grated, no more than a whisper. "But Bill was her husband. How could she keep him in the dark?"

"You read her letter." They were both whispering now. "She wanted him to have the climb he had been dreaming about. Bill had as much money, if not more, than her. I can understand her motives. What else could she give him that he couldn't buy for himself?"

Kurt's jaw worked. He took a deep breath and fixed his gaze on her mouth as he spoke. "Love. She could have given him love."

"He already had that."

"It would have been enough for Bill. He was that kind of guy."

Somehow, the moment they lowered their voices they had drawn closer, their bodies automatically leaning into the other as if seeking the intimacy they'd shared at Ama Dablam…a million years ago. That's how it felt.

Kurt reached out and cupped the back of her neck, pulling her closer still. The wind buffeted the little world they were in, making their shadows dance on the wall of the tent.

"Kurt, we can be seen from outside."

The letter fell to the floor as he reached up and extinguished the gas lamp. He was breathing hard. His musky-male scent escaped the neck of his anorak as he bent his head. The beam from her headlamp struck at his eyes and she turned away, but he whipped the stretch band off her forehead and sent it the way of the letter. The only light in the tent shone upward, beaming onto the roof like a faint searchlight.

"I can hardly see you, Kurt."

"Soon that won't matter."

His other glove was added to the pile on the floor. She felt his hands cup her cheeks. Was there ever a more cherished feeling than a man holding your face in his hands?

"Love would have been enough for me," he murmured against her lips. She had no time to think what he meant by those cryptic words. No time to wonder if he was talking about her love. The moment their lips touched, she could no longer think, only feel. His hands on her face, his mouth, his tongue, the rough with the smooth; it was all about two people, starving one for the other.

"I want you," he said as they sank to the floor, entwined.

"Take me. If your need is as great as mine, this is long overdue." Chelsea was on such a sensual high that she didn't notice the rocks under the thick nylon flooring. She was aware only of Kurt's weight, his heat, the hard thrust of his flesh against her stomach.

His hands stripped her and she helped. Who cared about cold air when you were burning from the inside out? All she wanted was Kurt. He was all she would ever need.

Her bones melted beneath his touch. Their anoraks were spread open, the rest of their clothing pushed out of the way. Again they ignored the niceties of romance. "Oh, how I've missed you, missed this."

He cupped her breast, put his lips to its curve and groaned, "Teddy, you taste like heaven."

The wind howled outside the tent as if jealous of the heat they generated, flesh to flesh, pulse to racing pulse. Their cries were their own to share, hidden by the raging storm, an unwitting conspirator keeping watch outside their secret rendezvous.

"Now!" His breath was harsh as he entered her.

Her sighs were softer than a whisper. "Yes, come into me. Come out of the cold into my heat where you belong."

After weeks of abstinence they were one.

Completion took her in a rush that showed her all the stars hidden behind the wind-borne snow flurries skimming the top of the world.

She called his name. "Ku-u-u-rt."

Called him to follow. "Come with me."

And as he joined her in that place, time stood still. She wished it could stay this way forever. But reality soon stabbed at her bones in the shape of a rock.

Kurt came to with a rough curse on his lips as he felt the air cool on their skin and Chelsea shift under him. "Blast, I'm crushing you. You'll be black and blue from this night's work. I was in too much of a hurry to tuck you into my sleeping bag."

"Do you think I care? What's a few bruises between lovers?" He heard her giggle as he rolled and pulled her up on his chest. "You were so masterful you literally swept me off my feet."

But she couldn't coax him to laugh. "A real man wouldn't bruise his woman." He trailed his fingers down her back to curve over her butt in an act of possession. He knew he had no rights, but couldn't escape the shout running through his thought banks that yelled, "Mine! All mine."

Chelsea tucked her head into the curve of his shoulder as he let his fingers wander. "Did you know your skin feels like satin? I can't touch enough of it. It's a shame about your butt, though."

She pushed herself up on his chest, her hands splayed across his collarbone. "What's wrong with my bottom?"

"It's gotten smaller."

"Is that all?" She sank back down on him. "I thought there was something wrong with it."

"Nothing major." He'd let her lie there a few more minutes. Delightful though the sensation of her skin against his felt, he couldn't let her get chilled. "Since you don't appear to have missed many meals, must be all the hard work you've been putting in. You've done better than I thought you could."

A muffled "Thanks" came up from under his chin.

"At least your breasts haven't changed. They still fit." His mind wandered, went back a month or so. "I wanted this, wanted you from the moment we met."

She shivered against him. "It showed."

"Ha!" He barked out a laugh that jiggled her against him and he felt she was cold. "C'mon, let's get into our sleeping bags, Teddy. Your skin is getting goosey."

He sat up, pulled her onto his lap and began rearranging her clothes. When her sweater was back in place and the drawstring on her pants tied, she asked, "Can we share?"

Wouldn't he love that—but it was impossible. "We can't. Can you imagine the look on Rei's face if he finds us sharing a sleeping bag when he brings you a hot drink in the morning?"

"I think he knows."

"Well, let's not give him proof. It wouldn't be fair to expect him to keep our secret."

She slid down into her sleeping bag as he shook his out. "Can we at least sleep back to back?"

"Yeah, fine." He spread his unzipped sleeping bag alongside hers and stepped between the thick downy layers to lie down.

In silence he switched off the headlamp and pulled the hood around his ears, shimmying over till his back touched hers.

He heard Chelsea say, "Mmm, nice" as he began to relax, waiting for the black hood of sleep to slide over him.

Half-asleep, he still felt the need to tell her, "I know it sounds weird, but I have this aversion to Nichols knowing about us."

"Paul?" He felt her wiggle against his back and come closer. "Why? Do you suspect him of inventing the rumors?"

"Maybe. He went away from Namche soon after we gave our statements to the magistrate. Then you turn up and suddenly he's back again." The words slurred in his mind. He hadn't meant to bring this subject up until tomorrow in the light of day. "Besides all that, I've seen how he looks at you and I don't want him trying to imagine the two of us together, if you get my drift."

"I don't want him to think of me that way at all. But you can if you like. In fact, I insist."

"Darlin', I've done nothing else but imagine you and me together from the day we met. You fill my dreams."

"And you mine."

He settled down, let sleep claim him knowing that for one night in his life everything was as it should be.

Chelsea was alone when daylight wakened her. She rolled over and felt inside Kurt's sleeping bag. It wasn't dead cold, so he couldn't have been gone long.

She sat up, realizing it hadn't been the sunshine that had wakened her but the lack of noise. The wind had died away, and with it had gone her confidence that the climb would go on now that Kurt knew.

Sure, they had made love, but that had been instinct driving them into each other's arms, not words of reason. What if Kurt thought she'd be safer if he took her back down the mountain and sent her home? She had to convince him that she'd be safer here with him, completing their goal, than in a crowded city where she could face a hired hit man on any corner she turned.

Yeah, even in the unlikely event that the guy she had stabbed with her boot was on cousin Arlon's payroll.

That was the trouble with Kurt thinking they might have an obvious suspect in their camp—the obvious could blind them to the truth. They weren't the only climbers to weather the high winds last night. There were a few other teams who had chosen to stay put. But no one else was targeting the route the U.S expedition of 1963 had conquered.

When she and Kurt headed west, the others would be on their way up the Lhotse Face.

By the time Kurt arrived back at the tent, she had taken a quick sponge bath with baby wipes. For a mind-rattling moment, she had realized they hadn't used any contraception.

The more she thought about it, the less she worried at being cast aside barefoot and pregnant. Kurt wasn't the type of guy to abandon his child. And if worse came to worst, she had money to support a family.

Her humor returned with a sudden surge of self-knowledge. She was putting the cart before the horse. Her cycle had barely begun—another reason for being glad of the shower at Base Camp.

Kurt came bearing gifts. She bet tea would never taste so good. "Thanks," she said, reaching for the mug from her perch on top of her folded sleeping bag. "How did the rest of the team get through the night?"

He hunkered down next to her holding his blue mug. "Well,

I don't think they had as much fun as we did, but the injury toll could have been worse. A few cuts and bruises, nothing major."

She held her breath. "Nothing to stop us leaving tomorrow?"

"Not a thing," he replied. "The weather should be good for it. Clear skies all the way. We'll get an early start, and with the fixed lines we've already put up, we could make it in a day, easy. Though we're going to have to stay overnight where Bill and Atlanta are, and try moving their bodies out in the morning. But I'm not promising anything. I've been trying to work out the logistics, but I always end up with a headache."

"That's something else I need to tell you."

Although his long legs were folded in a crouch, she saw him grow still, as if preparing for the worst. What did that say for their relationship? From now on she would not hold anything back. She didn't dare if she wanted their liaison to grow into something more than a brief association with a mountain. "It *is* good news this time. I rang a contact at the organization I told you about. He promised to get a helicopter up here."

His big fist clamped around his mug, his knuckles white. "And you are just now telling me this. Do you know how difficult it will be? Risky? Expensive?"

"Yes, I do, all of that. The cost doesn't matter."

Kurt didn't say anything, just flicked her a sharp look from under his lashes.

"Don't be like that," she protested. "It isn't about flaunting the money. I might only be a small cog in the wheel at the organization, but they value my skills and want to help. I understand the difficulties of getting their bodies off the mountain, but if this can prevent another death…" She choked at the thought of anything happening to Kurt. The stakes weren't nearly as high for him—was she asking for too much? Was she gambling with more than she could bear to lose?

"You're right. I should have thought of it myself. And I know you don't flaunt your enormous wealth. You don't even think about it half the time, and I wish I didn't have to."

He pushed himself to his feet and stood looking down. "Luckily we're not leaving until tomorrow. I'll get you the satellite phone. Do you think you can get hold of your contact?"

Kurt was already halfway through the door flap before she could reply. "More than likely. But I work with the guy. Don't ask too many questions."

"I'll leave it to you."

While Kurt was away, Chelsea began to pick up around her tent. There was stuff all over the floor, and she tucked her precious baby wipes and her headlamp into her pack.

She had rolled both sleeping bags when she came across the plastic bag containing the knife.

Daylight made it easier to see the lethal grace of the weapon. There was none of the heavy clunkiness she expected of a hunting knife. The blade on this one was finer, as if it had been sharpened often and honed into this particular shape.

There was writing on the blade, but she couldn't make it out through the plastic. Careful not to touch any part of the knife that could hold fingerprints, she held it as Kurt had the night before, with the tips of her fingers on the narrow silver bar overlapping the top of the horn handle.

She twisted it in her fingers and let the bright sunshine from the doorway highlight the maker's stamp at the thickest part of the blade. For a moment as she read everything seemed to go dark as if she might faint. She quickly pulled herself back from the rim of fear and verified what she had read. Made in South Africa.

Everything clicked into place.

Apart from Kurt and the Sherpas, the one thing both climbing expeditions had in common was Paul Nichols.

To think she'd actually liked the guy. It stung to think her judgment was so far off the mark.

As soon as Kurt reentered her tent, she would tell him about the clue they needed to set them on the right track.

To put them on their guard.

For weeks she'd been climbing with Paul behind her, watching her back. It would be torture to keep climbing in that order without spending every minute looking back over her shoulder.

What was the saying—*better the devil you know?*

Her mind buzzed with a million questions. Did they out Paul now, or wait until the next time he attempted something? Her head hurt just thinking of the extra precautions she would have to take to keep safe.

Kurt would know what to do. It didn't matter that her people-reading skills had been off with Nichols—she wasn't wrong about Kurt. She had trusted him with her life and would continue to do so. Nothing would persuade her he wasn't one of the good guys.

Just as she came to that conclusion, that particular good guy entered her tent, his wide shoulders easing through the opening the way he did. The satellite phone was in his hand.

They were shoulders she could lean on, at least metaphorically. She just knew that any moment now Kurt would insist on restoring the status quo, where any physical contact between them was forbidden. At least she'd had last night.

Kurt looked at the knife swinging between her fingers and sighed. "You shouldn't be playing with that. It needs to go somewhere safe until we can have any fingerprints checked out. It'll probably have to be in the States."

"I will, as soon as you've read what's on it. I think the blade itself may be all the clues we need."

After coming in out of the bright sunlight he had to squint to read the maker's stamp. "Well. I'll be damned. This might explain why Nichols was nursing a bandage on his right hand when I went to collect the satellite phone."

Chapter 13

The knife wasn't enough proof in itself for Kurt to send Nichols packing, though he knew Chelsea wanted action, wanted him to do something straightaway. "Problem is, we have nothing else to substantiate that this belongs to Nichols. Have you ever seen him use it? I haven't."

He pulled off his cap and tunneled his fingers through his hair, taking time to think. "It may simply be coincidence. A fair number of people got dinged up last night. And there are enough South African climbers around that the knife could have been found, or even stolen."

"I hadn't thought of that."

"One good thing," he said, his ire at being left out of the loop for so long catching up with him. "Now that I've *actually* been allowed to read Atlanta's letter, not only do I have to plan to stop you falling off a mountain, I'll be the one watching your back. If it *is* Nichols, he won't be able to get away with much with both of us and Rei keeping an eye on him."

"Thanks, Kurt. I know this wasn't the deal you signed up for and I appreciate it more than I can say."

"This is more than a business deal and you damn well know it," he retorted. He reached out, touched a finger to her face, her lips, letting his actions speak for him. All his intentions to keep Chelsea safe from notoriety could burst like a bubble if he wasn't careful. "No one is going to harm you while I'm around. Got it?"

"Got it. Is there any chance you can sleep here tonight?"

He could see Chelsea was hoping he'd say yes. Hell, he'd love to say yes, but that would be letting his hormones make his decisions for him. And they weren't concerned with safety; they were looking to slake themselves in the soft, warm heat inside Chelsea. "The offer is pretty tempting, but I think sleeping in the same tent as Nichols would be a more productive choice. Things start to get out of hand when the two of us are alone at night, and as much as I'd prefer sleeping with you, the only way to keep track of Nichols is by knowing if he gets up at night to take a wander and following him."

Chelsea held her hand out for the satellite phone. "I guess there is nothing much more I can do but call Mac and see where he's at with the helicopter. I hope he has a pilot who knows what he's doing in mountain conditions. I'm still not sure it can be done in thin air."

"What's this Mac guy's job?"

It still rankled Kurt that Chelsea hadn't thought to speak to him before calling this Mac character. He knew Chelsea was used to her independence. Could be it was just as well that when their venture was over they'd be going their separate ways. When he did take a wife, he wanted them to be equal partners, sharing all aspects of their lives, not simply two people living together who never knew what the other was going to be up to or when.

"That is something you don't need to know. In fact, forget I told you his name."

"I just thought he might be able to check out Nichols. Tell him all we know about the guy and see what he comes up with. As for helicopters, if you'd asked, I could have told you that they've gone higher than we are now."

He let out a short laugh as Chelsea pouted. Guess he deserved it. The moment he'd said it his comment had sounded like one-upmanship.

"Well, at least I now know it's possible."

"There are a lot of variables for the pilot to take into account flying this close to the mountain. The bodies are lying directly below the peak, so wind sheer could be a problem. And the amount of lift they can get will also depend on the air temperature. Those Alouette threes have turbo engines, but they're dependent on the tail rotors to maneuver."

Her eyes widened as he explained, and it cut him deeply that she thought climbing mountains was all he knew. "Flying choppers at this altitude takes a really experienced pilot. And I'm not happy about using a pilot who might take chances for the hell of it."

"How many times can I apologize?"

"That's not what I'm after. Go ahead and call the guy." As far as Kurt was concerned, he'd seen enough of death on the mountain to last a lifetime. He didn't want to add a seat-of-the-pants pilot to the list.

And he definitely didn't want to add Chelsea. The thought sent acid through his gut. He could come out of this with an ulcer.

Atlanta's letter had explained all sorts of little things that came back to him now in hindsight. From now on his twenty-twenty vision would be focused on Chelsea, on keeping her alive.

He looked down on her as she dialed out and sat waiting for a reply. Part of him wanted to gather her into his arms and protect her from the world, but trying to wrap her in cotton wool couldn't be called living. She'd really spread her wings since they'd left Namche. As far as climbing went, Chelsea was a natural. They could have been great partners if it hadn't been for all her money.

He looked at her dark hair, watched her hand that wasn't holding the satellite phone move as she talked. Her face was beautiful and animated—she wasn't just a pretty doll to stick on a shelf and admire. A warm feeling filled his gut, gathering into a huge lump behind his larynx.

She was speaking to Mac, but he wasn't really listening. There was something a hell of a lot more important going on inside him. A realization that from now on, anyone who took on Chelsea had him to deal with. Anywhere, any time, he would protect her with his life if need be. And knowing that, how could he bring himself to let her go when their expedition was over? It would be a hard call, but best for Chelsea, if not for him.

He would have to learn to live with the situation.

And without her.

Nervous excitement gathered in the pit of Chelsea's stomach next morning. This was it—what she had planned was about to happen. She was really going to find Atlanta and bring her home.

It was still dark and the stars had been out when she had looked out the flap of her tent, but she was up and dressed, chewing on a candy bar. She'd gotten over the horror of eating junk food for breakfast if she felt like it. Climbing would soon burn the energy off. In fact, her body felt slimmer, stronger and all-around tougher than it had been when she arrived.

She couldn't bear to think that once she got back to Namche Bazaar all this would be over for her. The mountains had gotten into her blood. It appeared she was more like Atlanta than she had realized.

How could she give all this up and go back to working in a city? She had thought Paris was her milieu, but she had been wrong. Visiting the fashion stores and ballet would still be all right once in a while, but not as a constant diet. She had learned to see the world through new eyes, and the mountains filled her with more anticipation than the Eiffel Tower did.

When she'd finally reached Mac yesterday, she'd discovered he had exceeded her requirements. An Alouette III helicopter was standing by at Shyangboche waiting for her call, and he was with it. Mac had probably traveled on one of the Courier-Air Company's planes. They were part of the bureau's cover, using offices worldwide that supplied cover for agents, and the means to cross borders invisibly. No cost had been mentioned, but no matter what Jason Hart intimated, she couldn't let the bureau stand all the expense.

Even before she knew the helicopter was available, she had become torn about her plans—to bury her family where they lay, or risk lives to bring them down. Over the past month she had come to learn the difficulties of transporting bodies down Mount Everest. No wonder the locals regarded the mother goddess as a jealous god who refused to give up those she had taken into her fold. It was practically impossible to retrieve them.

It felt strange to feel she was not the arbiter of her fate, to let someone else take control. Yet in a way it was into Kurt's hands that she had placed her destiny. Did he realize that?

She was glad that he had succumbed the other night to the compelling force driving them into each other's arms. If worse came to worst, at least she had been given what felt like love. He might not have said the words, but it had been in his every touch, every warm glance from his wonderful dark eyes.

She wished Kurt wasn't so determined to play out the forbidden-contact angle to the last. What did her reputation matter if she couldn't have the man she loved?

There, she had admitted it. She loved him.

She was smiling to herself when Kurt pushed back the flap and entered her tent. They both were the stuff dramas were made of, both of them doing their damnedest to protect the other. But putting Kurt in harm's way, by drawing him to cousin Arlon's notice, was far more life threatening than a damaged reputation.

Her smile slid away. The grim expression on Kurt's face could have been carved out of the mountain rock surrounding them. The back of her neck prickled as if she sensed a threat. "Kurt, what is it? What is wrong?"

"Nichols."

She watched Kurt frown as he spat out the name in disgust. "He says his hand hurts too much to attempt the climb with us. I'd like to say to hell with you, buddy, then stay behind, but I don't feel good about this turn of events. It's too much like history repeating itself."

Her natural instinct pushed her to take Kurt in her arms and hug him till his worries faded. She had to steel every nerve in her body to keep her distance from the man she wanted above all else in this world. Even though she'd had weeks to get used to it. "Well, at least his injury means there is no need to let Rei take the lead and put Paul between the two of you so you can keep your eye on him."

"I can't help thinking of how he followed up behind us last time. Yet the accident still happened. I'd feel a lot happier with him in plain sight. Now a part of me wants to call the climb off until he's fit to climb."

"And I feel a lot happier knowing he's not around. Is he going down to Base Camp to give his wound a chance to heal?"

"So he says. I still don't trust him."

"I know the sensation. I can tell you, it shook my confidence when I remembered he came from Port Elizabeth. I was thinking about the coincidence last night. Just last year cousin Arlon visited the Tedman Foods plant out there."

Kurt's eyebrows lifted at that news.

"I remembered seeing it in the company newsletter I get twice a year. It is terrifying how thick and fast the coincidences are coming." She let the angry sigh building in her chest escape. "But so darn frustrating that we still have no real proof."

"No one said it would be easy. It just burns me up to know that I took the guy in when Basie turned him down. At least, Nichols said he had asked to join Serfontien's team. Now I'm not so sure."

She wanted to say, *I love you. Don't worry.*

Would she ever be able to say the words? Her life was in turmoil, and she knew that even when she retrieved the key, her safety couldn't be assured until she had recovered the papers Maddie had left in the safety deposit box, and cousin Arlon, if proved guilty, was under lock and key.

Until then, she would have to part from Kurt.

Separation. The big New Zealander had decided it was inevitable. Only, he thought that he would be doing it for her welfare. Not that she would be doing it for his.

Talk about tragic irony.

But Kurt had more immediate worries than what they would do when this was over. "If there hadn't been a chance it would raise eyebrows, I would have asked Basie myself," he said. "Maybe he knows something I don't. Though he seems unable to keep a secret. The fact that I'd asked would be bound to get back to Nichols."

Chelsea grabbed her pack, and Kurt slung it up on her shoulders. She felt Kurt's assessing gaze on her as she fastened her belt, then bent to retrieve her ice ax.

She looked up.

"Are you ready?" he asked.

She found her smile again and with its reappearance, her confidence. Joking wasn't called for this time. "I'm ready when you are."

He held out his hand and clasped hers, pulling her out of the tent after him into the cold darkness.

Chelsea shivered with anticipation as she watched the first rays of the sun rising over Tibet. The refraction of the light tinted the snow in hues of pink and blanketed the rough-hewn rock faces in shades of purple and red.

It felt like an omen. As if the mother goddess was sending them a sign that the mission would go well.

Then Chelsea turned, saw the silhouette of Nichols watching them, and felt heartsick. She regretted the loss of camaraderie, the bond she had thought was between them—two fairly new climbers battling the odds.

If her suspicions were correct, the most they had in common was cousin Arlon.

Kurt felt a spurt of exhilaration. All the advance work they'd done, putting in anchors and fixed lines, had paid off. The first part of the climb was over without any problems.

He let out a little of the breath he'd been holding. Not all, though. It was far too soon to let down his guard and relax.

"Let's stop here for a break," he gasped out to Chelsea and Rei. Talking was an effort. Every breath contained less oxygen than they needed, even though they were well acclimatized. That's why Kurt was making sure they took frequent rest stops.

On the last part of the journey, barely fifty meters in height had been gained on their transverse of the slope. Below them the ice fell away in white waves that crested the tops of crevasses. Beautiful to look at, they were deadly to cross, but the couloir would take them straight down like an elevator shaft to above where Bill and Atlanta had landed, three hundred meters down. They were taking the long road, but also the safest.

Kurt took out his drink bottle and began replacing his fluids as he looked around. Chelsea flopped down beside him and Rei leaned on one of his ice axes. They'd need to use two of them to grip the ice on some parts of the climb.

Their entry to the couloir was barely fifty meters from its top. That's why Kurt had felt comfortable about leaving Bill to help Atlanta over the edge while he rappelled back down for the bag of nylon line she'd been sitting on at their last rest stop. *Like now.*

Though it tied his gut in a thousand knots, Kurt let his mind's eye visualize the sequence of events.

Bill had followed him over the top, both of them weighed down by the extra twenty-pound bags of line they'd need on the West Ridge. Kurt had dumped his, preparing to open up what they'd need on the next stage, and Bill had done the same.

Slower than the men, Atlanta had been eight meters down when she remembered she'd left behind the bag of line she'd been carrying. It hadn't been Atlanta's fault. Kurt had been in charge. He should have noticed.

The pain of the loss of his friends struck him anew. It had been over seven weeks since he'd been here last. Seven weeks from the accident, and the raw wound of what had happened still hadn't begun to heal. Could be that this journey was as essential to his peace of mind as it was to Chelsea's.

If he'd noticed the missing line, none of this would be necessary. Part of the guilt inside his gut centered on believing that if he'd still been with the Chaplins, their deaths could have been prevented.

Then he and Chelsea would never have met and wouldn't have to face the agony of saying goodbye once they got back to Namche Bazaar. He should have been stronger, should have stopped their relationship coming to this impasse. Chelsea would argue against his decision, of course. He expected nothing less from the woman who had wormed her way into his heart.

But Chelsea didn't know the worst. Didn't know about the kind of man who had fathered him. The Heiress And The Drug Dealer's Spawn. That would make a great headline. He couldn't let Chelsea face the notoriety their connection would bring. Bad enough if anyone caught an inkling of the passion that simmered under each glance or the fact that neither of them could keep their hands off the other.

He shut off his thoughts. Time to move on.

As Chelsea and Rei readied their packs for the next part of the climb, his gaze settled on the top rim of the couloir. "Seems to me that a short climb away there should be at least two, maybe three bags of perfectly good nylon line we can use."

Chelsea's smile rested on him for a moment before she said, "We'll come with you." Would she still smile at him that way if she knew the truth? Discovered what he'd been hiding from her?

Rei seldom said much, but when he did it cut to the heart of the matter. "Too tiring for the miss. I will take her down while Kurt goes for line. Can't have too much line." As if it was settled, Rei began organizing the lines, anchors and carabiners he and Chelsea would need to rappel to the foot of the couloir.

Kurt watched Chelsea open her mouth to protest, then turn mutinous as he cut her off before she could utter a word. "Rei knows what he's talking about. The climb would be needlessly tiring for you. If you want to give that helicopter a chance of reaching us before dark it's better if I go on my own. I'll be quicker by myself."

He travels fastest who travels alone.

A metaphor for Kurt Jellic's life.

Chelsea's breath shimmered white in the cold air as she let out a sigh. "You're the boss. I'll see you down there."

He was halfway up before the others had gotten organized. He'd hammered in an anchor attached to his rope close to where he started. If he fell, the anchor would prevent him from falling. His hands worked smoothly in a rhythm that came from years of experience on ice, using the serrated spikes of two ice axes and the sharp points on the front of his boots.

Two-thirds of the way up, he reached a small shelflike protrusion. It jutted two feet out from the sheer ice face and gave him an opportunity to turn and see Chelsea get ready to step sideways into the couloir while Rei took care of the lines he'd set to run smoothly for her descent.

He grinned, knowing the exhilaration she'd experience— the closest a climber came to free-falling.

The pick end of his axe dug in a foot above the level of the ice shelf, the serrations holding it fast. He pulled himself up where he could see over the small flat platform barely big enough for his boots to fit.

Almost there. He smiled to himself, imagining Chelsea's face if he'd dared to make a race of it. But he wouldn't scare her like that. She would make her way down easily, the way he'd taught her, and that didn't involve taking risks.

He looked up into the endless blue of the sky, unbroken by clouds or the snow flurries that had marred its brilliance the day before. Everything was white and blue apart from a narrow length of black sticking out from the rim. Was Bill's ice axe lying on the rim after all this time?

Kurt knew he'd got it wrong the moment it moved, lifted by a figure in white that had been invisible against the ice and snow, but stood out against clear Himalayan sky. White! Chelsea's yeti in the night! How had Nichols gotten past them?

Over the rim of the shelf that hid him, Kurt saw the guy take aim, not at him but lower, where Chelsea had begun working down the couloir. His heart jumped into his throat, thumping against his larynx, stifling the cry that roared in his mind. His next decision was made without time for thought or his own safety. Kurt lifted the other ice ax, sent it spinning end over end till it struck the guy's shoulder.

The rifle went off, with a whimper instead of the clap of thunder he would have expected to rock the air in the corridor of ice they were in. As he ducked behind the shelf for cover, expecting to be the next target, he heard a yell and a couple of bumps against the ice, like a pebble skimming across water.

He recognized it for what it was, remembered it from the last time he'd visited this spot. Someone was falling.

His heart left his throat along with all the air in his lungs and the sound of her name. "Chelsea-ea-ea!"

He looked down and started to breathe again. Chelsea was where he'd last spotted her, on the end of the line that Rei was feeding out. The guy falling was a blur of white and a curse of screams as he bounced off the couloir walls to the bottom and beyond, the way Bill and Atlanta had taken down to the icefall below.

"Don't move. I'll be with you soon," he called out to the other two. Chelsea had to be in shock. He'd been through that, and wouldn't wish on anyone the frozen numbness that entered one's soul watching another climber fall to his death.

From the flat ice shelf it was a few short pulls and a leap over the edge to the top. The blue bags holding the line he'd been after were frost covered but clearly visible. He pushed up to his feet, began looking around for evidence and spotted a small backpack, white as well. The guy had meant business; but obviously hadn't meant to hang around, as the pack wasn't large enough to carry shelter for a night on the ice.

The ice axe beside it was Kurt's. There was blood on the point of the pick, and some of it had seeped into the snow and was already frozen. Head bent, he hunkered down to retrieve it and the pack.

The second white figure was almost on him before he noticed. Kurt dropped the pack and hefted the ice axe in his palm until the balance and weight of it felt just right. "Don't come any closer. I've taken out your friend and I'll take you out just as easily without giving it a second thought."

The second man immediately raised his arms, one of them as if in surrender, the other pulling aside the face covering masking his features.

"Paul Nichols!" Kurt gasped the name. He'd been certain Nichols was dead at the bottom of the couloir.

And if not Paul, who the hell had he killed?

Chapter 14

"Hold it! Hold it right there. Not another step, Nichols, and keep your hands where I can see them." Kurt sidestepped around the bags of line he'd come after. An icy trickle of sweat snaked down his spine as he took a circular route away from the shaft of the couloir, his gaze fixed on Nichols. Kurt's back was still to the drop into the couloir, and he wasn't at what he'd call a safe distance. Twice now he'd seen that the descent might be quick, but it was fatal.

"It's not what you think, Kurt. I was following Basie."

"What do you mean you were following Serfontien? When we were leaving Camp Three, you were supposedly on your way down to Base Camp with an injured hand. First time you let me down, you were whining over a sick gut. This time the convenient excuse was the cut to your hand that stopped you climbing. How many more lies do you expect me to swallow?"

"They weren't lies—they were excuses." Paul's shoulder

gave a little jink back and forth, making his hands wave above his shoulders. At any other time the shrug might have looked funny, but Kurt wasn't in a laughing mood.

"I've been following Basie Serfontien for well over a year, both here and in South Africa."

Kurt slapped the shaft of the ice axe against the palm of his glove to show what he thought of that story. The sound dropped into the chilled silence with a satisfactory echo. He'd given himself room in case the confrontation developed into a struggle, and now he wasn't more than eight feet away from Nichols, closer than he'd been to Basie, too close to miss.

His eyes narrowed as he surveyed Nichols, a man whom he'd once trusted with his life. "But you must have known Basie was heading up the Lhotse Face. That's well away from the route we intended taking. You could have picked a better outfit to join. I did you a kindness and you turned around and bit me, but good."

Eyeing the distance again, Kurt planted his feet wide, his crampons firmly planted into the ice and snow, solid, in case Nichols decided to rush him. "Another thing—you still haven't mentioned what was so all-fired important that you had to follow him all the way from South Africa."

"It's my job. I was an agent with the South African Truth and Reconciliation Commission until they ceased operations. Now another of our—you could say—more secret South African agencies has commandeered my services."

Nichols paused, but didn't put a name to the agency.

"You might have noticed from his manner that Serfontien was ex-army. Probably came into the career naturally—the name Basie means little boss." One of Nichols's hands edged toward his snug-fitting hood. "Mind if I pull this down? I'm sweating like a pig under here."

"Your choice. Remember that this axe is lethal whichever side of the head it hits. Think about that before you try any tricks."

"I'm not stupid."

The irony of the remark made Kurt's mouth twist into a sneer. "Could have fooled me, mate. But you were in the middle of telling me why you traveled all this way to watch Serfontien."

"He was originally part of a covert counterterrorist group. They took away his commission and booted him out after they suspected him of enjoying his work so much he'd begun moonlighting. As far as we can tell he's responsible for the murders of four young up-and-coming leaders. But knowing is one thing, getting proof is something else."

"And I'm supposed to believe all this crap?"

"I have ID in my parka that will show you I'm who I say I am." Nichols's hand went to his jacket.

"No, you don't. You haven't convinced me enough to allow you to reach inside your coat." Kurt waved the axe at him. "Hands back up where they were. I want to know why you linked up with my outfit instead of Basie's. Serfontien never seemed the kind of guy to let an extra buck or two slip past him. I always wondered why he turned you down."

"The first time I arrived in Base Camp, I went looking for him and caught him spying on Atlanta when he thought no one was looking. That's why I pretended he'd turned me down and asked to join Aoraki Expeditions. Could have been the guy was just a pervert, but I knew from past experience Basie never did anything that wasn't to his own advantage." Nichols's mouth twisted in a cold smile. "And the rest, as they say, is history."

Damned if the puzzle wasn't getting more complicated by the minute. If what Nichols was insinuating was correct, the actions of both South Africans left an unpleasant smell, to his way of thinking. "You realize Basie shot at Chelsea? That isn't history. He damn near murdered her a few minutes ago."

"Well, it had to be something along those lines. Can't see him going to all that trouble on the odd chance of looking down her anorak. From the comments he made about them, I'm not even sure if he liked women. But if he tried to shoot Chelsea, then in my book that's as good a reason as any for taking him down. I like Chelsea, man. I wouldn't hurt a hair on her head."

Kurt hit his palm with the axe handle. "I'm thinking you are just too pious to live. I reckon you'd stand back and watch someone else hurt her to get the proof you're so desperate for."

As Nichols opened his mouth to reply to the accusation, a noise behind Kurt made him turn his head, praying Chelsea wasn't about to walk into the standoff. He smiled as Rei's head appeared above the rim of ice.

The Sherpa had obviously been listening. "Ms. Chelsea's a nice lady. You touch her head and you deal with me also."

"Good man, Rei. Just what I needed—another witness." As soon as the Sherpa's blue shadow fell across the snow beside his, Kurt let go of some of the tension bottled up inside his chest. "Okay, Nichols. You can toss over that ID now. Rei will pick it up while I keep my eye on you."

He brushed the snow off the plastic card Rei handed him and studied the ID with Nichols's photo in the top right-hand corner. Right enough, it said South African Security Services. But, in truth, Kurt was no wiser, never having heard of the agency before today.

"So let's hear the rest. You were making a case that Basie might have been after Atlanta Chaplin, but I was there, mate. I never saw a soul or heard a sound except both of them falling."

"He uses a silencer. You must have had luck on your side today to pick him out before he got his shot off. His camouflage was the best around. I should know—this gear of mine cost a fortune. But this time I was ready and followed his tracks in the snow. Last time I followed his party toward the Lhotse Face before I realized he had tricked me."

"You can have this back." Kurt flicked the ID card back to Nichols. It went spinning onto the snow at his feet. "Why was he after Atlanta and Bill? They weren't South African, hadn't set foot in the country as far as I'm aware."

But Arlon Rowles had.

Nichols crouched to pick up the card. His story had a ring of truth. That didn't stop Kurt keeping a wary eye on him as he straightened. He'd dropped his hands, but Kurt let him get away with it. All the talking Nichols was doing was wasting oxygen and probably sapping his energy.

"I didn't make the connection either until Chelsea showed up. She wasn't married, you see, and the moment I met her it clicked. Tedman Foods. Basie was head of security at their Port Elizabeth plant," he explained, sounding pretty pleased with himself.

Kurt was furious. To think they had broken bread with Nichols, and all this time he had kept that news under his hat. "You might have warned us. Chelsea would have been eager to help. When news of this gets out you'd better start watching your back. She has friends in places you and I never knew existed, and her safety means a lot to them. This is probably the last warning *you'll* get."

Though he wasn't dead certain of his facts, it was gratifying to turn the tables and make Nichols look uncomfortable. To rub it in, he said, "You may act the part of a stone-cold killer, but I'd say these guys are the real McCoy."

"Look, I couldn't tell you, man. It might have given me away."

"Well, I hope you can still look Chelsea in the eye when we get down to where she's waiting. Serve you right if she pushes you off the edge herself once she hears you might have been able to save her sister." He picked up Basie's pack. "If I find anything in here that proves what you said is true, I'll save it for the local magistrate."

He gave Rei his instructions first. "I want you waiting with Chelsea at the spot where we climbed into the couloir. Nichols, you can take the quick route down after Rei. I'll follow."

A replay of the emotions that had pummeled him as he'd clawed on to the face of the couloir filled Kurt's heart and mind while he waited on top for the others to descend. If he'd lost Chelsea, would life be worth living?

He didn't think so.

It had taken a near tragedy to make clear what he should have known all along. He loved her with every particle of his being. Not that he would confess his feelings to her—better to leave them unsaid, make it easier on both of them when he let her go.

As he would.

His decision couldn't put the brakes on his pounding heart, though. Following the others down, he tried to pretend that loving her from a distance would be enough, but neither his head nor his heart believed him.

If she lived to be a hundred, Chelsea would never forget the moment when she hung in midair, nothing but air between her and death, as her anxious gaze searched for Kurt against the continuous dazzle of white ice.

When she'd heard him call her name, she had been sure it

was him who had fallen. Immediately she had been stung by pain and guilt. If Kurt died it would be her fault. Wasn't she the one who had hounded him to bring her back to the scene of the previous tragedy?

Her heart had rolled over, a useless lump of lead in her chest that refused to beat without knowing Kurt was safe. The moment her eyes latched on to his red anorak against the gray-blue shadows near the top, her heart had gone into overdrive, pumping blood to her spinning head. Shock.

Only, Rei had kept her from falling. His voice had come from above her, issuing urgent instructions until he had pulled her, flushed and exhausted, back up to the starting point.

That moment had taken its toll. No matter what Kurt said, or how he much he protested that he was no good for her, she knew she'd never love anyone else with the overwhelming emotions that Kurt evoked. The difficult task would be convincing him of that.

When she was young, if she found that an arduous undertaking came easily to her, then her father would say, "You must have taken shortcuts. Next time do it right." She would let Kurt off the hook until she had fulfilled all her obligations. After that he was hers.

But before then, someone, namely Paul Nichols, had a lot of explaining to do. Now that the incident was over, she was bothered about how her usually excellent skill of reading people had let her down. She hadn't realized Paul could be so calculating, and all in the name of truth and reconciliation.

Well, it would be a cold day in hell before she became reconciled to the thought that Atlanta and Bill might still be alive if Paul had given them fair warning of his suspicions. And it was no thanks to him that she was able to stand here listening to his excuses as he repeated what he'd told Kurt.

A light-headed sensation rocked her the moment Kurt joined them. She sent her thanks up to the mother goddess that Kurt didn't have her death to add to the guilt he was carrying over Atlanta's and Bill's tragic demise. More tragic than they'd realized—their deaths maybe could have been prevented.

Kurt was being strong and silent. He left the excuses to Paul as he looped in the line and issued orders regarding the next descent. "Right, Rei, you go first again, then you, Nichols. Chelsea and I will stay back till we see you've both reached the lower icefall."

No more than three seconds after Paul's head disappeared from view, Kurt called to her, "Come here, and stand by me." He was using one hand to guide the line, while the other encouraged her to step inside the circle of his arm. "How are you holding up, Teddy bear?"

His silly little pet name for her warmed her heart more than any of the flattery Jacques had used on her.

"I'm better now you're here." She lifted her face to his. "I would be better still if you gave me a kiss."

"Much as I would love to kiss you, and let Nichols fall, I'll have to give it a miss. He may be a cold rat fink of a guy, but I've done enough killing for one day."

"I'll settle for the cuddle," Chelsea responded. She snuggled against him. "You saved my life, Kurt. If I get through the next few days and manage to turn around the damage cousin Arlon has done, it will be thanks to you."

"Teddy, you give me too much credit. Keep some of that for yourself. I killed a man today. Easy for Nichols to reckon Basie deserved it, but it was a first for me. Now that all the shouting is over, and I know you're safe, I'm back to doing what I do best with a real bad taste in my mouth."

She reached up, the tips of her gloved fingers grazing the

stubble on his cheek. "You look like a real badass with that unshaven face, but the difference between you and those two, Paul and Basie, is obvious to anyone who really knows you. Because you're a lover, not a killer, Kurt Jellic."

"Thanks for the vote of confidence."

The line tugged in his hands, telling them their few minutes of respite from the others was over. "Right, Teddy bear, your turn to clip on. Take it easy. Take it safe. I'll be back beside you before you know it."

Kurt left one line in case the helicopter didn't pan out and they needed it for the return journey. He wasn't taking anything for granted this trip.

Every time he looked at Chelsea now he experienced a deep-seated sensation of relief. It had been bad enough going through the redundant motions of checking Bill and Atlanta for their pulses the day they'd fallen. If he'd had to do the same today for Chelsea…

He felt sick to his stomach. It wasn't a scenario he could bear thinking of. Not now. He needed some time on his own and the distance to put everything into perspective, a situation that wasn't likely to happen anytime soon.

Chelsea hung back while the others were checking out Basie. Kurt put his arm around her shoulder, propelling her along with him. "C'mon, let's get it over with."

"Do I have to look?"

Hell, Chelsea probably hadn't seen anyone dead until after the mortician had done a paint job on the corpse. Basie would have to forgo the dressing up. It wasn't likely anyone would be putting himself out to see he got back home off the mountain.

"If it's too much, then don't look, but the magistrate might want to ask you about it when we report the death in Namche Bazaar. Don't worry, I'll be right here with you."

He chuckled, a deep husky tumble of vocal cords he hadn't realized he was capable of in the circumstances. "I'll even let you hold my hand."

"Since Paul has more to fear from the media than us at the moment, I accept."

Basie was more banged up than Bill and Atlanta had been, so Kurt didn't keep Chelsea hanging around. Instead he handed Nichols a camera.

Five minutes on, he asked, "Did you take enough photos? Chelsea and I are climbing down to the Chaplins' resting place. I'll need to take some shots of them this time around."

Nichols took the hint. "If you don't mind Rei and I looking for the gun, we'll stay here a little longer." He passed over the camera and said quietly, "I'm going to search the body, and I'd rather Chelsea wasn't around."

For once Kurt was happy to oblige Nichols.

"Right. Chelsea, crevasses on the horizon, so we'll put on a safety line. We're looking for a marker. It's an ice axe with a scarf tied to it. And if I remember correctly it's at least a good hundred yards that away."

Chelsea knew Kurt let her find the pointer. He was being very careful, almost tender in his handling of both her person and her emotions. Too bad it was simply a precursor to what he knew they would find when the marker popped into sight.

The marker of the Chaplin's last resting place was nothing fancy, nothing like what they deserved. No *Star-Spangled Banner,* just a scarf that had frozen to the shaft of the axe and had long since finished fluttering in its spot a few yards away from the rim of a crevasse.

"Here we are, then," she said, and then waited.

Kurt didn't disappoint her. "Okay. Atlanta is the one clos-est. The straps of her backpack gave way, and that's the small snow-covered mound in the middle. Bill is lying facedown. I didn't attempt to move them. All I did was check their pulses to make sure they were dead."

He turned away, and she saw him swipe the back of his glove across his face before he added, "It might seem a terri-ble thing to say, but all the way down, I prayed that they *had* died. There was no way I was going to get them back to camp on my own. And when I found them, I thanked God that their suffering was over."

But not even God could solve the Tedman Food problem, only her, and by proxy, Atlanta.

She slipped out of her pack and knelt beside her sister's grave. Kurt was behind her. "Do you want a hand to uncover her?"

Chelsea glanced up. From that angle he looked very large, and very reassuring, but some things she had to fix alone. The guilt inside her ran deep. She should have taken more inter-est in the company. They both should have, but she was the one who had flitted off to France in search of excitement.

"I'll be okay. You see to Bill. Just one thing before you go." She swallowed the hard lump in her throat. "Will I still recog-nize her? I mean, my sister's poor face—was she…was she bruised?" She was too chicken to voice the words *bloody* or *battered.*

"No, she died before any bruises had time to show, and I shouldn't think that has changed. Don't worry, she still looked like Atlanta."

"Thank you."

She started her work closer to one end than the other, brushing away the snow gently. Her gloved hands uncovered a shoulder first, shrouded in Atlanta's green jacket. She recognized the color from the photos Kurt had shown her. Perversely, she began working the other way, gradually uncovering her sister's body, staying away from her face.

What held Chelsea back was the finality of seeing, of having to believe, that Atlanta actually was dead. There was no road back once she had looked upon her sister's face.

Little mom's face. All these years and finally this was how she would see her again. They hadn't had their shopping trip to the Paris fashion houses, or shared the laughter she remembered from the days before Bill appeared on the scene.

And they never would.

The crampons on Atlanta's boots almost cut through Chelsea's glove, and struck her as a warning that the time for procrastinating was long gone.

She summoned up her courage and began to twist around. But with her weight on her heels the courage faded, and instead she checked on Kurt. Just as quickly, she turned back.

He had rolled Bill over to take photos. Soon he would want to do the same for Atlanta. This was another proof of death.

Chelsea's time was up.

"Hi, honey," she whispered, taking special care as she brushed away the snow from the top of her sister's head. "I'm going to look after *you* this time."

Startled, she jerked her hand away as a clump of stiff blond fringe fell into her palm. Atlanta had had beautiful hair with a natural wave. She would have hated to see it hard with ice. "Sorry, sweet thing." Another of the pet names Atlanta had called her when she was little sprang naturally to Chelsea's lips. "I wish I had a comb to make you look pretty."

She worked steadily, discovering her sister's eyes were shut, as though she had fallen into a magic sleep like the princess in the fairy tale. Atlanta had been the purveyor of wonderful stories. She hadn't needed a mom when she'd had her.

Her sister's nose was just as she remembered—a cute little button nose that went with her blond hair and heart-shaped face. Chelsea had envied that nose, convinced that her aquiline one dominated her face to the detriment of her other features.

Without the smile Chelsea remembered, her sister's mouth looked cold and tired and oh, so lonely. Atlanta was missing Bill.

"Not to worry, precious. You'll soon be together. Chelsea will see to it. I will fix everything." Tears blurred her eyes as she brushed away the snow clogging her sister's neck and shoulders and scooped Atlanta up into her arms.

Her sister was so cold. Cold as ice. Not all the heat in the world could warm her, or bring her back to life. "Hush now."

Chelsea's love was all she had to offer. She hugged her against her breast and began to rock. Atlanta had done the same for her when she was little.

Holding her in her arms, she began singing the lullaby that had been as comforting as could be to a child who lacked a mother's arms. "Hush little baby, don't you cry…" she sang. "Little momma's gonna…"

In the nights after her father had decided they were too old to share a room, Atlanta had sneaked into Chelsea's bed with her once their father had retired to his study.

Every night Atlanta had rocked her, singing her little sister to sleep. She had been the only one to realize how frightened she had been of being alone in the dark.

But Chelsea had had to get over it when their father found out what was happening. Charles Tedman hadn't been a great believer in mollycoddling his daughters.

Where had all that love she and her sister had shared gone?

Had Chelsea killed it by refusing to recognize that Atlanta could love someone other than her baby sister?

Sadness too big for one person to bear ripped a hole in Chelsea's heart. The tears blinding her began to form tiny icicles at the ends of her lashes. Just like Atlanta's eyes. "I missed you, baby. I missed you so-o-o much," she sobbed as Kurt's hand clamped on her shoulder.

"You've got to let her go, Teddy bear. Time to say goodbye." He removed Atlanta from Chelsea's arms and laid her back into the hollow where they had found her.

Chelsea's sobs cracked on the sorrow in her voice.

She took Atlanta's hand. "It's too hard to say goodbye."

"No choice, Teddy bear. If we hold the helicopter up, we'll never get them off the mountain tonight."

"I've been thinking about that. It was selfish of me, expecting other people to risk their lives so I could bury Atlanta back home. I think that maybe she and Bill should stay here together. Could we do that? Bury them here in the snow and ice? Or in the crevasse?"

"Sure we can, honey. But you have to realize that the mountain is always on the move. Sooner or later they'll end up at the bottom of the glacier."

"That's okay." Another tearful hiccup escaped, trashing her fight for composure. "We can come back and get them then."

Kurt didn't mention the presumptuous word *we*. He pulled Chelsea to her feet, balancing her weight between his big hands. "Are you steady enough now to come look at this?"

"Yes—oh, no. I didn't get the key. Imagine." She laughed harshly. "I almost forgot all about it."

He gathered her close. Her laughter sounded a trifle hysterical, even to her ears. She was too strung up to feel anything but pain as her pulse beat hard against her temple.

"Don't worry about it. I'll get the key for you."

"No. No, I will. I must. My sister died because of that key. The least I can do is look after it for her."

She took her gloves off to feel around Atlanta's neck, dreading that the key had somehow been lost during her fall. But it was there, right where Atlanta had told her it would be.

As if she had known that one day Chelsea would come looking.

She stood up and slipped the chain holding it around her neck. Its dreadful coldness burned against her skin. She didn't care. In her head she heard Atlanta sigh, and felt a lightness of spirit that had eluded her since the day she'd heard about her sister's death. "It will be okay, little mom. This time I'll make it all right."

Straightening again, she screwed up her courage and walked away to where Kurt was waiting.

"Have a look at Bill. I've taken a lot of photos, but after the way I was castigated in some of those rumors, I'd prefer not to be the only one who knows the truth now that Basie's dead."

She blinked in surprise. The hole on the middle of Bill's chest was hard to miss. Shocked, she stepped back. That could have been her or Kurt with a hole in them.

Misunderstanding, Kurt responded, "I know. I should have turned him over. Then the reason for their deaths would have been obvious. The bullet must have gone straight through into his pack. If Nichols finds the gun and can match it to the bullet, that will be all the proof you need of who killed them. I think it's stating the obvious to say that Bill died first."

Chelsea nodded, looking down at the man she had blamed for stealing her sister away from her. She knew he hadn't deserved this fate. He had been an innocent pawn in the game cousin Arlon was playing with all their lives, and now it was up to her to call checkmate.

She rolled her shoulders, but it didn't shift the weight, and it was a burden she couldn't transfer, not even onto Kurt's broad shoulders. She had already asked too much of him. Twice in the space of two months a member of the Tedman family had put his life at risk. A third time was *way* to much to expect of a man who had begun this adventure with her as a stranger.

A stranger who didn't want to know she loved him.

Chapter 15

Namche Bazaar

A week later Kurt rolled over in bed and pulled Chelsea closer, afraid to sleep in case he missed any part of their last night together. They were sharing a bed, but not a room. His room at the Peaks Hotel was one floor down.

Chelsea murmured against his neck. He felt a pinch as her sharp white teeth grazed the cord of his neck. She'd already put her mark on him. Some in places that would show, but what the hell, he could wear a turtleneck. And some in places no one but Chelsea would ever see.

They had hardly slept a wink, but already he could discern a faint gray strip where the edges of the curtains met. "Looks like I'll have to go soon."

She let out a strangled moan, muffled by his shoulder. "No! I don't want you to leave. The night's not over yet."

Her arms tugged him closer still, so close their heartbeats became indistinguishable from one another. She hooked one leg behind his, rubbing the softly curving flesh between her thighs against him, making little erotic mewls that drove him crazy until he drove into the damp cave filled with her warmth. This time he was determined to make it last.

Just one long, slow loving to keep the memory of Chelsea simmering in his heart when she returned to the States and he was living down in the antipodes, a whole wide continent and a deep ocean away.

Holding her, he rolled until she was on top. His shoulders were propped up in the mass of pillows on her bed.

She sat straight and proud like a princess. Her firm breasts were the most beautiful he'd ever seen, but he'd known that by instinct the first time they'd met.

Never in a million years had he imagined his hands holding the curve of her hips while her internal muscles squeezed and let go, squeezed and let go. "Oooh, Teddy bear, I'll give you anything you want as long as you don't stop that," he groaned.

She bent over him, her breasts level with his mouth, tempting him. He'd only to stretch out his tongue.

"You're lying, Kurt. If you love this so much, how can you let me go?"

He ignored the question and came up off the pillows instead, thrusting harder, deeper as she leaned back. His mouth followed one pink morsel, capturing it with a kiss. "You taste like heaven."

She took the thumb and forefinger of each hand and pinched the lobes of his ears. He didn't mind a bit and didn't stop filling his mouth with her, sucking the hard round tips against his tongue as he rocked his hips. He was in her to the hilt and it wasn't enough. He wanted more, wanted a lifetime, but it was impossible. This had to be the last time.

Kurt was panting as he ran his fingers down her spine till he found the spot that made her clench around him.

She squeezed him with her internal muscles, tighter, and tighter again.

Kurt felt the tension build with every thrust. Nothing could break his concentration, and he was intent on making Chelsea feel the same.

He thrust harder, lifting himself off the bed to fill her completely and then some. Kurt looked up into her face silvered by a Himalayan dawn, laced with fantasy. His fantasies.

He rolled over, fitting Chelsea under him, taking their lovemaking to the next level. Kurt plunged into her hot and fast they way she liked it. He felt her buck against him as he began to thrust. Her sighs and groans were music to his ears. He didn't care what Chelsea said about life without him being hell. If he died this moment it wouldn't worry him. He'd experienced heaven, and he was about to take Chelsea there with him again.

Chelsea was in an obstinate mood; this was her last chance to get through to Kurt. "You say I taste like heaven, but you're not addicted to the taste. You can't be if you're willing to go without it and me. And to me that sounds like hell."

Kurt held her close to his side. She was exhausted, but too frightened to close her eyes and miss one moment of the time they had left together.

"Hell for both of us, Teddy." His fingers trailed lazily down the curve of her hip as if he couldn't stop touching her, but it didn't prevent him from concluding, "I'll be miserable without you, but I have to protect your reputation."

Despair swamped her and she was feminine enough to hope it didn't show in her voice. "You could marry me. I said I love you—doesn't that matter?"

"I love you, too," he groaned. "But marrying me could be the worst decision you ever made in your life."

"But they can't say we colluded in Atlanta's and Bill's deaths now that we can prove Basie Serfontien was responsible. Once Paul passes on his evidence to the American authorities, we won't have to worry about that."

"Nothing is certain," he reminded her. "Certainty would mean your sister and Bill were still alive."

"Well, what about that report from Tedman foods. That proves the connection. Damn it, there's a photo of cousin Arlon shaking hands with Basie."

Chelsea's body had been sated with their lovemaking. It was the frustration of knowing she might never feel this way again that had her so uptight. "I knew the guy looked familiar. Who'd have thought he once worked for me? And if Paul Nichols had been doing his job properly he would have had Serfontien's phone bugged. He is just so behind the times."

"There speaks my little spy."

"All I do is translate."

"And that's why—" He broke off as she poked him with a finger and chuckled. "It's the sort of stuff that if you told me you'd have to kill me?"

She was leaving him no choice. Kurt would have to explain about Milo Jellic. Not until just before he left her bed, though. Kurt couldn't bear to see Chelsea turn away from him when she discovered he was the son of a man who had sold dope out the back of a cop car.

The sins of his father had been visited on him more than once in his adult life. He didn't expect this time to be any different. And even if Chelsea pretended, he couldn't let the paparazzi sharks turn her into their next victim. She would be fair game as soon as the news got out and they dug into his history.

The anonymity Chelsea had enjoyed in Paris before the accident wouldn't continue. Not now that she was so wealthy. Quite apart from Bill having no family, Chelsea would almost certainly inherit his fortune as well as her sister's, because the gunshot wound in his chest proved he died before his wife.

Chelsea had said she intended to leave her job when she got back. Going by the way she talked about Mac and her boss Jason Hart, Kurt knew they would be sorry to lose her, but it wasn't a job she could simply walk away from without being debriefed.

He wasn't so crazy in love with Chelsea that he couldn't see she had responsibilities to her organization as well as Tedman Foods.

She never needed to work again. Soon she would move on to even more exclusive circles, more high-toned than the rigorous one of undercover agents she already traveled in.

It was all too rich for his blood—almost as bad as Chelsea was for his equilibrium. He'd spent almost two months off balance just because she was near. Everything would get back to normal once they parted. All he had to keep remembering was that Chelsea would be much better off without him.

"Can you have someone bring my bags down from my room? Ms. Tedman, number three one two. I'll check out after breakfast."

When Chelsea had woken this morning, Kurt had been gone. Leaving the reception area, she polished her self-contained look as if she were a celebrity disguising her thoughts from the media Kurt was so worried about.

As if paparazzi were likely to hang around here. These heights were too close to heaven for the trash Kurt obsessed over.

The moment she saw him, her attempt dissolved and she began to beam. Surely a grin couldn't do much harm? "Would you like to share breakfast with me?"

Her smile wasn't returned, but he did say, "That sounds good. Let's just have something light out on the terrace."

"Lead the way," she replied. Had Kurt noticed how she had changed? Noticed the difference in her attitude from the last time they had sat on the terrace together? That she was no longer the wicked controlling madam she had been two months ago?

Kurt chose a table at the far end of the terrace, away from the comings and goings of guests through the foyer. "Croissants okay by you?" he asked as their server approached.

"Perfect." She swallowed a touch of nervousness, unable to remember the last time she'd felt so edgy. Maybe the first few times she'd taken a jump on her horse. Yes, that was it. She remembered a water jump that had scared the bejeebers out of her. She had been a teenager then. No wonder the feeling of restless butterflies in her stomach was so unfamiliar.

No, she was wrong. It was over a year ago when Mac had been out of touch for over a week and no one from IBIS knew if he was alive or dead. She remembered the glances cast her way by some of the others in the Paris office, as if there had been more between her and Mac than met the eye. Sure, she loved him, but as a dear friend, the only one she'd been able to talk to after she'd discovered Jacques's betrayal.

The terrace was quiet and their server efficient. In next to no time they had a pot of coffee, croissants and all the fixings on their table.

Chelsea might have learned to give up control, but she was still human, and knew when to pick her moments. She waited until Kurt had taken a large bite of buttery croissant, then lobbed her question. "You were going to tell me why marrying you could be the worst decision I ever made. I'm ready to listen."

Kurt took a deep breath and almost choked on flakes of pastry and black cherry conserve. "I might have known you wouldn't let me off the hook."

He washed his throat clear with a huge slug of coffee with cream, then refilled his cup as he waited for the caffeine surge, and took another drink of the almost black liquid. The color suited his mood. The last time he'd told a woman about Milo—a woman he'd thought he was in love with—she'd made an exit he could barely see for dust.

"When I was thirteen my father committed suicide—drove his car off the top of a cliff, and you know the kind of damage that can do."

"Oh, God, Kurt! How awful for you." Chelsea leaned across the table and took his hand in hers.

One touch and his fingers jolted as if zapped with a live wire. Had she noticed? He hoped not. All he wanted was to get this over with, not tie himself in knots by remembering how smooth her magnolia-blossom skin felt under his palm.

Like the magnolia planted next to the front gate of the house where he'd lived as a boy. It was only a hop, skip and jump from there to picturing the police car parked beside that tree, and from there to remembering how he'd raced up to it, glad that his father was home early.

Even when he'd backed off a step or two at the sight of their grave faces, he'd never guessed the officers had come to inform them of his father's death.

Chelsea hadn't noticed his withdrawal. "Thirteen is a bad age, filled with regrets. Only look what happened with Atlanta and me. Puberty has a lot to answer for."

"That wasn't the half of it. Next thing the family knew, reporters were hassling our grandmother, chivvying her for answers about my father's drug connections." That's when his hatred of the media had begun, when he'd discovered that the pen was truly mightier than the sword. He gulped down another swig of coffee, draining the cup. "Yeah, my father was a bent cop who'd been dealing in drugs.

"Grandma Glamuzina had always seemed old to me, but to my thirteen-going-on-fourteen-year-old eyes, she aged another century overnight. I hated that, hated seeing what their persistence did to her. After my dad died she was all we had. There were four of us boys, and my little sister, Jo. Each one of us has suffered in different ways from what our father did. For his sins."

"Is this what you think will hurt me? What your father did can't affect us now. It's in the past."

"Is it? When my eldest brother got engaged and her father found out about our family history, he did his best to break them up, and succeeded. Drago was very bitter. He lost his career as a wine maker because of my father. It doesn't go away. Every time another cop gets brought up by Internal Affairs, up it pops again from the newspaper archives. New Zealand may be small, but the media there have long memories. Do you want to be the subject of a tabloid rag?"

"I could stand the heat if I had you in the kitchen with me." She squeezed his fingers, and his grip tightened on hers. A reflex. You are a fool unto yourself, Jellic.

He choked back what he wanted to say to Chelsea, his Teddy bear, the woman he loved. Clinging to her fingers when what he really wanted was the lovemaking they'd shared in the night.

He wanted to hear her moan his name as she fell apart in his arms, but it would never happen again.

"What kind of man would it make me if I was willing to subject you to that kind of abuse?" He shook his head. "No way. I won't let that happen. Bad enough that going back home will open you and Tedman Foods up to public scrutiny without giving them more fuel to fire up their trashy tabloids."

He took his hand away from hers and wrapped it around what was left of his croissant. If he was eating he couldn't answer any more questions. "Besides, I've my family to think of, as well. My sister is not long married. My twin is working the Pacific Rim putting away drug barons and the like, trying to make up for all the harm he knows our father did. I'm sorry, Chelsea. My father has done too much damage to our family without me adding to it."

The croissant was gone in two bites, but he was saved by the concierge's arrival at their table. "Ms. Tedman, the porters have arrived to take your luggage to the helicopter."

Kurt pushed back his chair. "I'll organize that for you."

Chelsea stared at him from those wonderful gray eyes that could twist his heart, like now. "I'm sorry for everything, Teddy. I should never have let you fall in love with me," he murmured.

"I didn't need your help to fall for you. I think the mother goddess had a hand in it somewhere."

He stood. "You're dead right. It was probably just the high-flown setting. Once you're back in your own milieu your life will eventually get back to normal."

"Damn you, Kurt Jellic." Color flew into Chelsea's face and her eyes blazed. "Don't you dare try to dismiss my feelings." She looked around the terrace quickly as if mindful of the demand for secrecy he'd made. When she finished her remonstrance, her voice was low as if she was in pain. "Don't dare ever dismiss my love for you, Kurt. I can't, so why should you?"

The pain he'd caused her stabbed into him with every step that distanced him from Chelsea. He'd never told her it would be easy. He'd said only that there was no way out. His way or the highway—they both added up to him turning his back on the woman he loved.

The huge blades of the Alouette III helicopter circled— *whaup, whaup, whaup*—and Chelsea's heart kept time. She rubbed the back of her knuckles against her breastbone to ease the pain behind it. The soothing action didn't help. She wouldn't be soothed.

Kurt was shaking her hand in a casual gesture as they stood near the helicopter. The calluses she'd grown in the past couple of months matched his.

She matched him, damn it! Why couldn't he see that?

"I'm glad your friend Mac has come all this way to take you home. He looks like a good guy. He's the one you need now—he'll protect you and keep you out of harm's way until your cousin Arlon has been dealt with. I like him. You could do worse."

Was he deliberately trying to annoy her? She didn't notice other men. Her head, her heart, her eyes were filled with Kurt and she couldn't see past him. "I could do better."

"We've already gone into that, and you know this will be best for you…best for me." Now as he spoke his eyes went black, the pupils almost swallowing up the dark brown she loved. Like hers, his eyes were red and raw from the tumultuous night they had both spent.

"You can't lie worth a damn, Kurt Jellic. Not to me."

"Well, at least the money you spent on the helicopter wasn't wasted. It will get you where you want to go quicker than shank's mare. Not that all that walking doesn't look good on you."

What had happened to his demand that they keep away from everything personal? She wanted to say, *You look good on me,* but swallowed the edges of her rough humor deep down inside. That way she only hurt herself.

She hadn't told him that she wasn't being asked to pay for the helicopter. Or that it was one belonging to IBIS, tarted up in one of its many guises that no one could connect back to the bureau. She had already told him more about that side of her life than was allowed.

A sigh she had no control over shuddered through her. This had to be the hardest task he had ever set her. Climbing a mountain was nothing compared to leaving him, walking away from the man she loved without a hint of the emotions roiling inside her showing on her face.

She sucked air in hard through her nose and felt her nostrils flare. Did that give her away? Was that a loss of control? She looked at his stony features. Could he see what this cost her? Did he care?

When she found her voice it sounded as brittle as her control and likely to shatter as easily. "I'll transfer funds to Aoraki Expeditions as soon as I get home."

His eyes flashed, showing the first spark of real emotion since they had reached the helipad. "Look, I've been thinking about that. Have this one on me."

"No, damn it, no! Without you none of this would have been possible." She touched the chain at her neck. "Do you realize what this means—the jobs, the lives, towns even, you've helped save? This cost must be mine. Not yours. Go back to New Zealand, set up your lodge, try to be happy without me."

As the dam inside her cracked, she clamped her teeth into her bottom lip to stop the flood waiting to be let loose.

"That was a low blow, Teddy. I might feel content, but happiness isn't an emotion I've scheduled into my future plans. That doesn't mean I expect you to go around in sackcloth and ashes. All I ask is you don't let Bill's and Atlanta's deaths go to waste. That you build them a memorial that will outlive the monument I'll have built for them here."

She managed a smile. It was amazing how often she and Kurt thought along the same lines. "I'd thought of scholarships and maybe a climbing school where kids from the city can spend a little time learning to see more than skyscrapers—up here they have the originals. I thought we could give them a chance to care more for the beautiful world we all share. You know what I mean? Sometimes you have to see the reality to learn how to cherish it. I've learned all that up here in the Himalayas."

And more. She had learned how to cherish a man.

"Mac is waving to you. Looks like you need to leave." Kurt's mouth was as flat as his voice, his control absolute.

She cast a swift glance over her shoulder. Mac was indeed signaling for her to board the helicopter. "Yes, looks…like this is it," she whispered, her voice husky with the strain of the moment. But if he thought she would take her leave without a kiss he was wrong. No one could read anything into a goodbye kiss. It was what people did at airports.

Chelsea stretched up, hooked one arm around Kurt's neck and pressed her lips to his, pouring her heart into her kiss.

For a moment the world stood still as he relaxed into it. The next moment he was pushing her away. "Don't do this. You're killing me, Teddy bear."

"You haven't heard the last of me, Kurt Jellic, not by a long shot." She turned and ran for the helicopter. As soon as she was strapped in her seat with her headphones on, she looked out the window and saw Kurt walking away. With her heart in her throat, she made him a quiet promise. "I mean it. We'll meet again. I'm a fighter. You proved that by showing me I could reach the heights. This is not the end."

The helicopter rose. Out the window Kurt grew smaller and Mount Everest overshadowed Sagarmatha National Park. Before Mallory vanished in 1924 he had likened it to a prodigious white fang in the jaw of the world. And that was true. Being on the mountain had pierced her heart.

Beside her, Mac's voice came through her headphones. "Did you say something?"

"Just goodbye."

Till we meet again.

The sound of the departing helicopter was still hanging in the air like a frozen shower of sound when Kurt realized he'd made the worst mistake of his entire life. He'd let Chelsea go.

He turned to face the fading whir of blades until he could no longer pick out the black speck flying between two of the mountains.

After all his protestations that he was doing what was best for Chelsea, he'd been wrong. Though his reasons were as valid now as when he'd quoted them that morning, there was one exception, a big one.

Living in two separate hemispheres could never be what was best for them *both*.

If knowing he'd made a mistake was one side of the coin, working out a way to rectify his blunder was the other.

Sure, she loved him, but what did he have to offer her? Nothing but a half-built lodge in one of the most beautiful but least populated parts of New Zealand. He needed to finish the project. And he would, if he had to mortgage his soul to get it done.

It wasn't going to happen in a day, or even sixty, but then look at all the business Chelsea had to sort out. Surely he could have the lodge finished by the time she was free to join him?

Next problem—how to explain his about-face without looking a complete jerk.

It would take a certain amount of subtlety.

What the hell? He could do subtle.

Unlike his father, Kurt Jellic wasn't completely irredeemable.

He could learn from his mistakes.

Chapter 16

Aoraki, New Zealand
The following February

Kurt looked at the people seated around the great room of his soon-to-be-opening lodge. It felt like a hundred years since all his family had been in the same place at the same time. And how the family had expanded. Only he and Drago were still unattached. Jo had Rowan, Kel had Ngaire and little brother Franc had Maria.

Molly, his housekeeper, was handing out beer and wine to toast the success of his new venture. Her husband, Hemi, was in the kitchen preparing dinner. Once Molly had left the great room with its soaring windows that framed the view of Mount Aoraki, Kurt offered up a toast. "To Namche Bazaar Lodge."

Everyone concurred with his sentiment and drank up. "So

what do you think of the lodge now you've had the ten-cent tour?" he asked.

Drago answered first, and since he was the eldest brother, everyone else gave way. "I think you've made a good choice. Maybe I can stop worrying about you falling off the top of a mountain."

"I haven't retired completely. I'll still be doing a bit of guiding, but I also have another guide with local experience starting with the lodge soon."

Franc rubbed his hand on the arm of the love seat he and Maria were sharing. "This place is comfortable, and there is no denying everything about the place is first-class."

"I love it," chimed in Maria.

Kurt had heard Maria's story and couldn't believe she could look so relaxed after recently going through a harrowing kidnapping. And *good on* his brother for rescuing her.

Kurt felt a twinge of conscience. He hadn't handled his own love life as well as Franc had. Each and every day Chelsea was on his mind. He thought of her first thing each morning, and her name was on his lips every night as his head hit the pillow. He might be thirty-four years old, but there was still a Teddy bear he wanted to take to bed.

He smiled at his family, hoping none of them recognized that it pained his heart. "I can't take all the glory. I did have an interior decorator. I took her advice, for I wouldn't have a clue what goes together."

Damn, he could say that again. If he'd ever had a clue about life he would have kept Chelsea glued to his side.

But his youngest brother hadn't finished with him. "Mountain climbing must pay, Kurt. I bet it cost you a bomb to bring this place up to scratch."

Franc's question gave him the opening he'd been looking

for to mention Chelsea, even if obscurely. "I have a silent partner."

"The best kind to have," said Kel. Pulling Ngaire to him, he planted a kiss on her lips. "This is how to do it," he finished, fending off his wife's fainthearted slaps. Ngaire was a hapkido master and could have put her husband on the floor with a flick of her wrist.

While all the teasing was going on Kel looked from him to Rowan. Kurt knew what he was asking—had his sister's wealthy tycoon husband, Rowan McQuaid Stanhope subsidized him? He shook his head. He hadn't told a soul who his partner was, though he wished like hell he could. In his own small way he was still doing his best to protect Chelsea until the time was right.

"Okay, you lot, listen up," Jo announced. His sister made it hard to forget she was a detective sergeant. "Rowan and I have some news regarding our inquiries into Dad's death."

Everyone went quiet. Until a few months ago Kel would have walked out of the room the moment their father's name was mentioned, but marriage seemed to have mellowed him.

"We've found the woman Dad was having an affair with. He should have known better. Her ex-husband is a drug lord that Dad had put inside. Since his release from prison, this guy has developed one of the largest crime syndicates in New Zealand. I hate to say it, but we haven't been able to touch him. He has a hidey-hole on Great Barrier Island that is protected from all sides. And as with Dad's *murder,* he pays others to do his dirty work."

Jo tucked her long dark hair behind one ear and took her husband's hand. The look she cast Rowan's way said it all. Theirs was a love for the ages.

Refreshed from that glance, Jo went on. "His ex-wife

swears that her husband put out a contract on Milo Jellic from inside prison, and she knows for certain through another woman that Rocky Skelton was paid to plant dope in Dad's car and to start the rumor that ruined Dad's reputation."

God, it hurt that even Milo had had more guts than him. At least he'd gone after the woman he wanted even if it had cost him his life. Damn it, he wasn't going to sit around any longer for someone to give him the okay to have a life with Chelsea.

Subtle hadn't worked. He was going to have to go with caveman.

His skin prickled with the need to go and call Chelsea immediately. Better still, he could check the times of the flights out of Christchurch to Los Angeles and then to Philadelphia. He had Chelsea's address.

The excitement was almost more than he could contain. If everything went according to the plans he was developing in the back of his mind while the others were talking about Milo, there *could* be more in his future than running a lodge and guiding people up the Southern Alps. He *would* have someone to share it with.

Kurt crashed out of his dream. His little sister was waiting for an answer. "That's great news, Jo. You and Rowan have done a great job—"

"But I'm not finished," she interrupted him. "There's more news, and in a way it's even bigger. We have a half brother."

The great room was silent for a second after Jo dropped her bombshell, then the talk started. Everyone turned to Jo, demanding to know who he was. All except Kel, whose face had turned white under his usual tan. Kurt knew his brother's pain, felt it as if it were his own. That's how it was with twins bound as closely as they were. He was probably the only one who realized that Kel's need to make up for Milo's wrongs stemmed from the great love he'd had for their father.

Jo had the floor again. "Okay, okay, give me a break and I'll tell you all I know. It appears we were all pretty clueless about the life our father led away from us. The affair that got him killed must have started a few months after Mom died and gone on for years."

That brought out a few grumbles, which Jo cut dead. "I know. I felt the same when I first heard, but we have to remember Dad wasn't the god we thought of him as kids, or the villain they tried to turn him into. He was just a man, like most of you."

Kel answered for them all. "Nailed it in one, Jo, as usual. Just don't tell me it was the brat who lived next door to us."

"She had him adopted. Having no illusions about the man she'd married, she knew he would have the baby killed if he found out, just like he did Milo. It was a private adoption through a lawyer. She never knew the couple's names. The only thing she cared about was that they were American and would take the baby out of New Zealand. But she did say she thought the adoptive father was coming to the end of his term at the American embassy. And that is where we start."

"I'll do it."

Everyone looked at Kel. "Let's face it, I have more contacts in the States than anyone else through working for GDEA. Anyway—" he shrugged "—it's about time I lent a hand. Just tell me the year and I'll get onto it as soon as we get back to the agency."

After that it was a free-for-all as the talk went back and forth. He didn't know about Drago, but now that most of the others were married, he was starting to feel like a fifth wheel in his own family.

But as soon as everyone went to dress for the celebration dinner, he'd book his flight, then get on the phone to the U.S. and let Chelsea know when he'd be arriving. He hoped he would find her at home. It would be getting late on the East Coast—what if she'd gone out with someone?

Another man echoed through his tortured thoughts.

After she'd paid more money than he thought he knew what to do with into the Aoraki Expeditions account, he'd had his lawyer draw up a partnership agreement. He'd sent her the legal partnership papers, hoping she wouldn't send them back unsigned, but he hadn't received even a few personal lines scratched on paper.

That didn't mean he hadn't sent her progress reports on the lodge. He had. And finally he'd sent her a copy of a magazine carrying an advertisement for the lodge's opening.

He had to admit he'd hoped she'd show up, but now it looked as if he'd have to get down on his knees and beg. And he would do it. He'd also have to admit to her he'd been wrong, but what the hell—she knew he wasn't perfect, knew he'd been wrong before.

When Kel finished, Rowan carried on where he left off. "It's agreed, then—we leave the half-brother business to Kel. Here's what else Jo and I want to do, but since it concerns the whole family, we need your agreement. Through certain sources that Jo and I have acquired through working in the New Zealand police force, we want to put out the word that we'll pay a reward of fifty thousand dollars for information on the guy who killed your father. We know who he is, but we need proof."

Kurt said, "I'll chip in for that."

A rumble of assent went around the room.

But Rowan wasn't having any of it. "If you don't mind, I'd

like to cover the reward myself. This is part of my wedding present to Jo. I told her I'd help her prove Milo was framed. We just didn't realize it would lead to a search for a murderer. All I need is the family's agreement and I can present Jo with the rest of her bride's gift."

Chelsea turned her rental car into the driveway of Namche Bazaar Lodge. If anything could show her Kurt had a sentimental streak it was the name he had chosen for his—their—lodge.

The red gravel crunched under the tires on her slow ride up to the door as she surveyed all the work he'd had done. The place was nothing like the half-built farmhouse he'd described to her on those long nights in Nepal. His way of keeping his hands off her had been to tell her stories of Atlanta and Bill and what he was going to do one day back at Aoraki, New Zealand.

After she had paid the money into his bank account she had been pleasantly surprised to receive the partnership papers in the mail. And when the progress reports began to arrive she had smiled, knowing her wishes were going to come true. The magazine he had sent had clinched the deal. It had turned up in her mail just as she'd finalized the deal that would free her from Tedman Foods forever. They could keep her name, but they couldn't have her. She belonged with Kurt. She had taken the magazine to be his way of issuing an invitation. In a few minutes she would know if she had been correct.

Darn it, she hoped so. She had missed the big idiot who had thought the way to make her happy was to deprive her of the one thing she wanted most in this world.

The moment she'd stepped on the plane to New Zealand, she had felt an uplifting of her spirits as if the worst was behind her—cousin Arlon was in jail.

Her debriefing from IBIS had been harder than anything. She had made friends there, and if she knew Jason, he would still keep her under his watchful eye. That was only natural, considering the secrets she held. Secrets that could affect global security.

She looked at Mount Aoraki. If she had thought of it, she might have brought some barley flour to cast to the wind and juniper to burn. The mountains backing the lodge looked big enough for their own mother goddess, and maybe if Chelsea had asked nicely, she would have looked kindly on her.

But it was too late—she'd arrived and she would have to do it off her own bat, as usual. Though if she got her own way in this, maybe not for much longer.

Jo and Rowan had given them all plenty to talk about, and for a minute Kurt didn't notice Molly had entered the room. "Mr. Jellic," she said, and four pairs of eyes focused on her. She laughed and looked behind her. "I rather think that it's Mr. Kurt Jellic the lady's looking for."

Kurt was sitting with his back to the entrance to the great room, but he could tell from the smiles on the other faces that it would be worth his while turning around.

His heart thundered in his ears as he picked up a vibration from Kel. Who else knew whom he was pining for…?

"Chelsea." He leaped from his chair, feeling clumsy in his rush to her side. Without speaking he touched her, ran the back of his knuckles down her face. She was real. His mind went blank. All he could think to say was "I didn't think you'd got my messages."

"Of course I did. I love you, silly."

He cradled her face between his palms. She was more

beautiful than he remembered, and he had some wonderful memories of her.

"Welcome home, Teddy bear."

Her chin rose until her lips were a mere heartbeat away. He closed the distance in less time than that. Never had a woman tasted so good. He drank from her lips, thirsting for her the way a man needs water to survive in the desert, knowing that his life had been a wasteland without her to share it.

The catcalls from the gallery reminded him they weren't alone. "This will only take a minute. Some people never grow up."

He turned her around to face his family, proud to be able to introduce her to such a crowd of generous and handsome people. "Everyone, I'd like to introduce you to my silent partner, Chelsea Tedman." *Soon to be my wife.*

Chelsea made no protest when Kurt hurried her out of the room with his arm around her after the introductions were over. It had been rather overwhelming being surrounded by five large men, all of whom were taller than her five foot eleven.

He showed her into the wide hallway that led from the entrance. A few steps into the corridor she started to say, "I like your fam—"

She got no further. Kurt turned, backing her against the wall. The smiles he had shown the others were gone. His face was a mask of concentration.

The unwelcome thought that he didn't really want her there spiked painfully into her thoughts, leaving her with a nervous sense of failure. Fear took its place as he roughly grabbed her wrists, raising them high, higher than her head as he flattened her against the wall with the weight of his body.

Her qualms dissolved as if they had never been as his lips took hers in a devastating kiss of possession. She fell into it, threw herself headfirst into the torrent of emotion that poured from him.

She had felt hollow without him, but no more. Kurt filled the empty spaces inside her.

Certain now that she had done right by coming here, Chelsea flung her arms around him and gathered him close, as close as they could get without coupling right there in the hallway. His kisses filled her, filled all the nooks and crannies in her heart and mind with all that he was, and everything they could be together.

She had taken a gamble on love and won.

Breathless, she moaned as their lips drew apart, with Kurt's chest heaving as if they were back in thin air. He brought her arms back down to her sides as her head spun, searching for a lucid expression to convey the meaning of all the emotions she was experiencing. Kurt beat her to the punch with a basic line. "God, Teddy, I needed that."

"Me, too, though at first I was simply glad I didn't seem to have broken another of your rules. And delighted you didn't turn me away."

"No more rules. We go with the flow." His large hand cupped the side of her face and tilted it toward his. "Besides, how could I do that? We're equal partners."

He brushed her lips with his, and talk ceased till they came up for air again. "Just minutes before you arrived I'd made a decision to book a flight and call you to say when I would arrive. The last few months have been filled with contractors, builders, decorators, plumbers—you name it. They ran me off my feet wanting answers to this, that and the other, yet I've never felt more lonely or empty in my life."

"Boy, do I know that feeling. I've sprinted from one tense situation to another, but you were all that filled my mind. For a while I just held my breath hoping you wouldn't send the money back. And then the partnership papers arrived and the reports and I was able to breathe again." A sigh ripped through her that started at the soles of her feet as she willed herself to fill him in on the crucial events she blamed for keeping them apart. Although it was difficult to think while the heavy weight of his ardor pressed hard against her belly.

She wanted him. He wanted her.

But Chelsea also needed all the extraneous business dealt with, needed to clear the muddy waters so that none of it spilled over onto the important agenda of the day—she and Kurt making beautiful love. She began rattling off the facts. "I may have to go back to the U.S. to appear at cousin Arlon's trial. Actually, they might need both of us there, unless he does a deal with the prosecutor. Either way, I hope he's in jail a long time."

For such a long time she had felt lost and unhappy. Now Kurt just kissed the tip of her nose and made her smile as he told her, "That's music to my ears. Whatever you want or need to do, from now on we do it together. I couldn't stand another excruciating, long span of time like the last few months have been."

"Then you'll be pleased to learn Maddie got cousin Arlon good. I don't how she managed it, but she had the number of his Swiss bank account, so all the money he embezzled will eventually go back to Tedman Foods."

Chelsea poked a finger through a gap between the buttons of his shirt, just to touch him.

It wasn't enough—she had to get the telling over so she could get him out of his clothes. "And I've sold all my shares in the company. Father will be turning in his grave, but I decided I wanted a life, and if I had to come to New Zealand to find it, I would do whatever it took."

He looked down after she contrived to unfasten one shirt button and was starting on the next.

"I guess I should have known the misery wouldn't last forever. From the first day we met, I discovered you're a woman who knows what she wants and goes for it. I promised you a tour. What do you want to see first?"

Before she left the States she had made a vow never to keep anything from Kurt again, the way she had before. Honesty had a lot going for it.

"I want to see your bedroom."

"You read my thoughts." He put an arm around her shoulder, pulling her close to his side, and they walked down the hallway as though they were joined at the hip, looking into each other's eyes. "Mind if we stop by the kitchen on the way?"

Chelsea pursed her lips and blew him a kiss. "As long as it's in the same direction as your bedroom."

"It's right about here," he said as the corridor formed a T and they turned right. Molly was in the kitchen helping a man dressed in typical chef's clothes—checked trousers and white jacket. "Hey, Hemi and Molly, I'd like you to meet the other half of my team. This is Chelsea Tedman." He turned his head to murmur in her ear, "Soon to be Chelsea Jellic."

Her jaw dropped, but he just grinned and asked Hemi, "Would you like to open a bottle of that bubbly you have cooling for me? And I'll take two champagne flutes with it. That's to go."

What a turnup for the books. This was the first time she had been proposed to in a kitchen in front of an audience, albeit an unknowing one. The best thing about it was Kurt had done it off his own bat, with no prompting from her.

"Down to the end, last door on the left," Kurt said, following her holding two champagne flutes in the curve of his palm, while his right hand held a newly opened bottle with a faint alcoholic mist wafting from its neck.

"Did I mention I've started the ball rolling on the memorials to Atlanta and Bill? My lawyer is handling the details. I thought it was better left to a professional, though I've named Bill's old college for the scholarships." She stopped and turned in front of the door he had indicated. "I thought Colorado for the climbing school. Not Aspen—it's too trendy. But whatever they come up with, the final decision will be yours."

"We'll decide together. Now open the door."

The well-oiled hinges swung the door silently open. Chelsea stopped and stared, with Kurt right behind her. She felt the heat radiating from his body and ached for his hand to cup her breast as it had the night they first met at the tavern.

"What do you think? Does the master suite live up to your expectations?"

The blue-gray tones of the high-end soft furnishings blended gracefully, and the dark wood of a highboy added a touch of hard masculinity that stopped the soft colors overpowering the huge room. "It far outstrips any expectations I might have had. This room, the whole house, is beyond anything. I fell in love with a rough-looking mountaineer and ended up with a cultured man whose taste exceeds my own."

Kurt laughed and the glasses clinked in his big hand. "Teddy bear, I depended on an interior decorator to get it all right. I must admit she was worried that the colors I chose for this room were too cool. But now you're here I know I picked them to go with your eyes. And we both know that when you and I get together we produce pure sexual heat. Go on in now. Take a closer look."

In the large mirror above the huge bed, Chelsea noticed her refection glow pink. She wandered about the room touching things, admiring pictures as Kurt poured them both wine. "I'll have your luggage brought through later. You're not going to need any clothes for a while."

"Promises, promises." Chelsea quirked a grin at him as she turned away from the large French windows that opened onto a secluded sheltered loggia. The far view was of the snow-capped mountains, the point of Aoraki standing high above the rest. "I can see you chose this room for the view."

He handed her a champagne flute filled with pale gold liquid starred with bubbles. "That, too, but mainly because this is the largest room, and after years of living in a tent most of the time, I wanted room to spread."

She took a sip of wine. The bubbles tickled her nose and she gurgled, "I hope you have left me some wardrobe space. I don't travel light."

He took the tall glass flute from her hand and set it down on the nightstand. "I remember. Don't worry. Everything in the master suite is perfect now. All it needed was you."

She reached for his shirt and pulled the edges apart, too impatient to fiddle with fastenings. The buttons popped, the material ripped—very satisfying sounds, for they laid his chest bare to her heated gaze. But she closed her eyes as her palms encountered the lean muscles that were all she remembered. She sighed in appreciation. "Mmm, I want you naked."

"I'll race you," he said, shrugging out of the remains of his shirt.

It was bright daylight outside, a far cry from the poorly lit shelters they had made love in before. Even in the Peaks Hotel the lighting had been dim, but now she faced him flaws and all with the mountains behind her. That hadn't changed.

Kurt swept her off her feet, an arm under her knees. When she was with him she never felt too tall or ungainly. Together they made a perfect couple.

As he laid her on the soft comforter she looked into his eyes, saw them black with passion—for her, for the moments ahead—and said, "Yes."

"Yes what?"

"Yes, I'll marry you."

He came down onto the bed beside her and began tracing the shape of her breast. "You'll need to take me in hand, Teddy. Only five minutes since I proposed and already I've taken your answer for granted. It's just not good enough, for I love you more than life itself. More than the mountains." He sighed as his mouth latched on to her breast. His breath was hot against her skin as he suckled her, and the sensation proved her memories weren't false, weren't just products of her lonely imagination.

She clasped the back of his neck, holding him closer as heat spiraled inside her. While she was able, she huskily whispered a few words. "Not to worry. I'll make sure you'll never be able to take me for granted again."

She clung to him as the sensual heat they produced sky-rocketed out of control. "I love you, Kurt," she told the only man who had had the courage to take her to the top of the world.

* * * * *

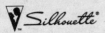

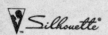

If you enjoyed what you just read,
then we've got an offer you can't resist!

Take 2 bestselling love stories FREE!

Plus get a FREE surprise gift!

Receive a **FREE copy of** Maggie Shayne's **THICKER THAN WATER** when you purchase **BLUE TWILIGHT.**

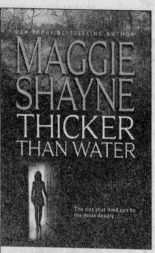

To receive your FREE copy of THICKER THAN WATER, written by bestselling author Maggie Shayne, send us 1 proof of purchase from Maggie Shayne's March 2005 title BLUE TWILIGHT.

For full details, look inside BLUE TWILIGHT.

COMING IN APRIL 2005
From

INTIMATE MOMENTS™

Blue Jeans and a Badge

by award-winning
author

NINA
BRUHNS

Bounty hunter
Luce Montgomery
has been searching for
something all her life.
Just what, she doesn't
know. But she's pretty
sure it's not love. When
a job in New Mexico
leads her to cross paths
with sexy chief of police
Philip O'Donnaugh,
the sizzling attraction
between them might
cause Luce to change
her mind—and lose
her heart....

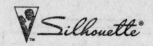
Silhouette®

COMING NEXT MONTH

#1357 SWEPT AWAY—Karen Templeton
The Men of Mayes County

Oklahoma farmer Sam Franzier and Carly Stewart weren't likely
to get along: he was a single father of six, and she wasn't one for
children. But when the two unexpectedly became neighbors, Carly
found herself charmed by his kids and falling for this handsome family
man. Problem was, love simply wasn't in Sam's plans—or was it?

#1358 RECONCILABLE DIFFERENCES—Ana Leigh
Bishop's Heroes

When Tricia Manning and Dave Cassidy were accused of murdering her
husband, they did all they could to clear their names. Working closely,
the passion from their past began to flare. But Dave wasn't willing to
risk his heart and Tricia was afraid to trust another man. Could a twist
of fate reconcile their differences?

#1359 MIDNIGHT HERO—Diana Duncan
Forever in a Day

As time ticked down to an explosive detonation, SWAT team agent
Conall O'Rourke and bookstore manager Bailey Chambers worked to
save innocent hostages and themselves. The siege occurred just hours
after Bailey had broken Con's heart, and he was determined to get her
back. This ordeal would either cement their bond or end their love—
and possibly their lives.

#1360 COLE DEMPSEY'S BACK IN TOWN—
Suzanne McMinn

Now a successful lawyer, Cole Dempsey was back in town and there
would be hell to pay. Years ago his father had been accused of a crime
he didn't commit and Cole was out to clear his name—even if it meant
involving long-lost love Bryn Louvel. Cole and Bryn were determined
to fight the demons of the past while emerging secrets threatened their
future.

#1361 BLUE JEANS AND A BADGE—Nina Bruhns

Bounty hunter Luce Montgomery and chief of police Philip
O'Donnaugh were on the prowl for a fugitive. As the stakes rose, so did
their mutual attraction. Philip was desperate to break through the wall
between them but Luce was still reeling from revelations about her past
that even blue jeans and a badge might not cure....

#1362 TO LOVE, HONOR AND DEFEND—Beth Cornelison

Someone was after attorney Libby Hopkins and she would do anything
for extra protection. So when firefighter Cal Walters proposed a
marriage of convenience to help him win custody of his daughter, she
agreed. Close quarters caused old feelings to resurface but Libby had
always put her career first. Could Cal show Libby how to honor, defend
and love?